Don Pendleton's **Mack**
Bolan®

Conflict Zone

A GOLD EAGLE BOOK FROM
W⊕RLDWIDE®

TORONTO • NEW YORK • LONDON
AMSTERDAM • PARIS • SYDNEY • HAMBURG
STOCKHOLM • ATHENS • TOKYO • MILAN
MADRID • WARSAW • BUDAPEST • AUCKLAND

Recycling programs
for this product may
not exist in your area.

First edition June 2010

ISBN-13: 978-0-373-61537-7

Special thanks and acknowledgment to
Mike Newton for his contribution to this work.

CONFLICT ZONE

Pure good soon grows insipid, wants variety and spirit. Pain is a bitter-sweet, which never surfeits. Love turns, with a little indulgence, to indifference or disgust; hatred alone is immortal.

> —William Hazlitt
> "On the Pleasure
> of Hating" in
> *The Plain Speaker*
> (1826)

I can't stop hate. No one in history has come close, so far. But I can interrupt atrocities, beginning now.

> —Mack Bolan
> "The Executioner"

For Corporal Jason Dunham, USMC
April 14, 2004
God Keep

PROLOGUE

Esosa Village, Delta State, Nigeria

David Uzochi had been fortunate. He'd left home an hour before dawn to hunt, and he had been rewarded with a herd of topi when his ancient Timex wristwatch told him it was 8:13 a.m.

With game in sight, it came down to his skill with the equally ancient .303-caliber Lee-Enfield bolt-action rifle he carried, its nine-pound weight as familiar to Uzochi as the curve of his wife's hip or breast.

He'd nearly smiled, thinking how pleased Enyinnaya would be when he brought home the meat, but he had caught himself in time, before the twitch of his lip or glint of sunlight on his white teeth could betray him to the grazing topi.

His first shot had been the only one he needed. As the other topi dashed away frantically to save themselves, Uzochi had been swift to clean his kill. There was no time to waste, when flies appeared to find a wound almost before the skin was broken, and the brutal sun began corrupting flesh before the last heartbeat had time to fade away.

The four-mile walk back to Esosa was a good deal shorter than his outward journey, since he was no longer seeking game, and he wouldn't rest once along the way, despite the forty-something kilograms of flesh and bone draping his left shoulder. Uzochi drew a kind of buoyancy from his success, doubly thankful that he had meat enough to share with some of his neighbors.

The sound of the explosion made him break stride, pausing long enough to lock on its apparent point of origin.

The pipeline. What else could it be?

He cursed the Itsekiri bastards who were almost certainly responsible. Their war against pipelines and the pumping fields meant less than nothing to Uzochi, but he understood the Itsekiris' hatred for his people, the Ijaw. And if this raid had brought them near Esosa…

Any doubt was banished from Uzochi's mind when he saw the first black plume of smoke against the clear sky. The pipeline passed within a thousand yards of his village, and how could any Itsekiri cutthroat neglect such a target when it was presented?

Uzochi began to run, jogging at first, until he stabilized the topi's deadweight to his new pace, then accelerating. He couldn't sprint with the topi across his shoulders, and he never once considered dropping it.

Whoever managed to survive the raid would still need food.

Tears blurred his vision as he ran, thinking of Enyinnaya in the Itsekiris' hands. Perhaps she'd seen or heard them coming and had fled in time.

A distant crackling sound of gunfire, now.

The sudden pain he felt was like a knife blade being plunged into his heart. It didn't slow him, rather the reverse, but in his wounded heart David Uzochi knew he was too late.

Too late to save the only woman he had ever loved.

Too late to save the child growing inside her.

But, perhaps, not too late for revenge.

If he'd forgotten where the village lay, Uzochi could have found it by the smoke. When he was still a half mile distant, he could smell the smoke and something else. A stench of burning flesh that killed his appetite and made his stomach twist inside him.

It was over by the time he reached Esosa. Twenty minutes since he'd heard the last gunshots, and by the time he stood in front of the smoking ruins of his home, even the dust raised by retreating murderers had settled back to earth.

Uzochi didn't need the dust, though. He could track his enemies as he tracked game, with patience that assured him of a kill.

He would begin as soon as he had dug a grave for Enyinnaya and their unborn child. As soon as he had cooked a flank steak from the topi over glowing coals that once had been his home.

He needed strength for the pursuit.

Strength, and the ancient Lee-Enfield.

It meant his death to track the Itsekiri butchers, but he wouldn't die alone.

CHAPTER ONE

Bight of Benin, Gulf of Guinea

They had flown out of Benin, from one of those airstrips where money talked and no one looked closely at the customers or cargo. In such places, it was better to forget the face and name of anyone you met—assuming any names were given—and rehearse the standard lines in case police came later, asking questions.

Which plane? What men? Why would white men come to me?

"One minute to the beach," the pilot said. His voice was tinny through the earphones Mack Bolan wore.

The comment called for no response, and Bolan offered none. He focused on the blue-green water far below him and the coastline of Nigeria approaching rapidly. He saw the sprawling delta of the Niger River, which had lent its name both to the country and to Delta State.

His destination, more or less.

"Still time to cancel this," Jack Grimaldi said from the pilot's seat. He spoke with no conviction, knowing from experience that Bolan wouldn't cancel anything, but giving him the option anyway.

"We're good," Bolan replied, still focused on the world beyond and several thousand feet below his windowpane.

From takeoff, at the airstrip west of Cotonou, they'd flown directly out to sea. The Bight—or Bay—of Benin was part of the larger Gulf of Guinea, itself a part of the Atlantic Ocean that created the "bulge" of northwestern Africa. Without surveyor's tools, no one could say exactly where the Bight became the Gulf, and Bolan didn't count himself among the very few who cared.

His focus lay inland, within Nigeria, the eastern next-door neighbor of Benin. His mission called for blood and thunder, striking fast and hard. There'd been no question of his flying into Lagos like an ordinary tourist, catching a puddle-jumper into Warri and securing a guide who'd lead him to the doorstep of an armed guerrilla camp, located forty miles or so northwest of the bustling oil city.

No question at all.

Aside from the inherent risk of getting burned or blown before he'd cleared Murtala Muhammed International Airport in Lagos, Bolan would have been traveling naked, without so much as a penknife at hand. Add weapons-shopping to his list of chores, and he'd likely find himself in a room without windows or exits, chatting with agents of Nigeria's State Security Service.

No, thank you, very much.

Which brought him to the HALO drop.

It stood for High Altitude, Low Opening, the latter part a reference to Bolan's parachute. HALO jumps, coupled with HAHO—high-opening—drops, were known in the trade as military free falls, each designed in its way to deliver paratroopers on target with minimal notice to enemies waiting below.

In HALO drops, the jumper normally bailed out above twenty thousand feet, beyond the range of surface-to-air missiles, and plummeted at terminal velocity—the speed where gravity's pull canceled out drag's resistance—then popped the chute somewhere below radar range. For purposes of stealth, metal gear was minimized, or masked with cloth in the case of weapons. Survival meant the jumper would breathe bottled oxygen until touchdown. In HAHO jumps, a GPS tracker would guide the jumper toward his target while he was airborne.

"Four minutes to step-off," Grimaldi informed him.

With a quick "Roger that" through his stalk microphone, Bolan rose and moved toward the side door of the Beechcraft KingAir 350.

It was closed. Bolan donned his oxygen mask, then waited for Grimaldi to do likewise before he opened the door. They were cruising some eight thousand feet below the plane's service ceiling of 35,000, posing a threat of hypoxia that reduced a human being's span of useful consciousness to an average range of five to twelve minutes. Beyond that deadline lay dizziness, blurred vision and euphoria that wouldn't fade until the body—or the aircraft—slammed headlong into Mother Earth.

When Grimaldi was masked and breathing easily, Bolan unlatched the aircraft's door and slid it to his left, until it locked open. A sudden rush of wind threatened to suck him from the plane, but he hung on, biding his time.

He was dressed for the drop in an insulated polypropylene knit jumpsuit, which he'd shed and bury at the LZ. Beneath it, he wore jungle camouflage. Over the suit, competing with his parachute harness, Bolan wore combat suspenders and webbing laden with ammo pouches, canteens, cutting tools and a folding shovel. His primary weapon, a Steyr AUG assault rifle, was strapped muzzle-down to his left side, thereby avoiding the Beretta 93-R selective-fire pistol holstered on his right hip. To accommodate two parachutes—the main and reserve chutes, hedging his bets—Bolan's light pack hung low, spanking him with every step.

"Two minutes," Grimaldi said.

Bolan checked his wrist-mounted GPS unit, which resembled an oversize watch. It would direct him to his target, one way or another, but he had to do his part. That meant making the most of his free fall, steering his chute after he opened it, and finally avoiding any trouble on the ground until he'd found his mark.

Easy to say. Not always easy to accomplish.

At the thirty-second mark, Bolan removed his commo headpiece, leaving it to dangle by its curly cord somewhere behind him. He was ready in the open doorway, leaning forward for the push-off, when the clock ran down. He counted off the numbers in his head, hit zero in a rush and stepped into space.

Where he was literally blown away.

EIGHT SECONDS FELT like forever while tumbling head over heels in free fall. It took that long for Bolan to regain his bearings and stabilize his body—by which time he had plummeted 250 feet toward impact with the ground.

He checked his GPS unit again, peering through goggles worn to shield his eyes from being wind-blasted and withered in their sockets. Noting that he'd drifted something like a mile off target since he'd left the Beechcraft, he corrected, dipped his left shoulder and fought the wind that nearly slapped him through another barrel roll.

Lateral slippage brought him back on target, hurtling diagonally through space on a northwesterly course. Bolan couldn't turn to check the Beechcraft's progress, but he knew Grimaldi would be heading back to sea, reversing his direction in a wide loop over the Gulf of Guinea before returning to the airstrip in Benin, minus one passenger.

The airfield's solitary watchman wouldn't notice—or at least, he wouldn't care. He had been paid half his fee up front, and would receive the rest when the Stony Man pilot was safely on the deck, with no police to hector him with questions. Whether he had dumped Bolan at sea or flown him to the Kasbah, it meant less than nothing to the Beninese.

Twenty seconds in and he had dropped another 384 feet, while covering perhaps four hundred yards in linear distance. His target lay five miles and change in front of him, concealed by treetops, but he didn't plan to cover all that distance in the air.

What goes up had to go down.

Bolan couldn't have said exactly when he reached terminal velocity, but the altimeter clipped to his parachute harness kept him apprised of his distance from impact with terra firma.

Eleven minutes after leaping from the Beechcraft, Bolan yanked the rip cord to deploy his parachute. He'd packed the latest ATPS canopy—Advanced Tactical Parachute System, in Army lingo—a cruciform chute designed to cut his rate of descent by some thirty percent. Which meant, in concrete terms, he'd only be dropping at twenty feet per second, with a twenty-five-percent reduction in potential injury.

Assuming that it worked.

The first snap nearly caught him by surprise, as always, with the harness biting at his crotch and armpits. At a thousand feet and dropping, he was well below the radar that would track Grimaldi's plane through its peculiar U-turn, first inland, then back to sea again.

And what would any watchers make of *that*, even

without a Bolan sighting on their monitors? Knowing the aircraft hadn't landed, would they then assume that it had dropped cargo or personnel, and send a squad of soldiers to investigate?

Perhaps.

But if they went to search the point where the Stony Man pilot had turned, they would be missing Bolan by some ten or fifteen miles.

With any luck, it just might be enough.

He worked the steering lines, enjoying the sensation as he swooped across the sky, with Africa's landscape scrolling beneath his feet. Each second brought it closer, but he wasn't simply falling down. Each heartbeat also carried Bolan northward, closer to his target and the goal of his assignment, swiftly gaining ground.

Four hundred feet above the ground, the treetops didn't look like velvet anymore. Their limbs and trunks were clearly solid objects that could flay the skin from Bolan's body, crush his bones, drive shattered ribs into his heart and lungs. Or, he might escape injury while fouling his chute on the upper branches of a looming giant, dangling a hundred feet or more above the jungle floor.

Best to avoid the trees entirely, if he could, and drop into a clearing when he found one. *If* he found one.

While Bolan looked for an LZ, he also watched for people on the ground below him. Beating radar scanners with his HALO drop didn't mean he was free and clear, if someone saw him falling from the sky and passed word on to the army or MOPOL, the mobile police branch of Nigeria's national police force.

Bolan wouldn't fire on police—a self-imposed restriction he'd adopted at the onset of his one-man war against the Mafia a lifetime earlier—and he hadn't dropped in from the blue to play tag in the jungle with a troop of soldiers who'd be pleased to shoot first and ask questions later, if at all.

Better by far if he was left alone to go about his business unobstructed.

Bolan saw a clearing up ahead, two hundred yards and closing. He adjusted his direction and descent accordingly, hung on and watched the mossy earth come up to meet him in a rush.

GRIMALDI DIDN'T like the plan, but, hey, what else was new? Each time he ferried Bolan to another drop zone, he experienced the fear that this might be their last time out together, that he'd never see the warrior's solemn face again.

And that he'd be to blame.

Not in the sense of taking out his oldest living friend, but rather serving Bolan up to those who would annihilate him without thinking twice. A kind of Meals on Wings for cannibals.

That was ridiculous, of course. Grimaldi knew it with the portion of his mind that processed rational, sequential thoughts. But *knowing* and *believing* were sometimes very different things.

Granted, he could have begged off, passed the job to someone else, but what would that accomplish? Nothing beyond handing Bolan to a stranger who would get him to the slaughterhouse on time, without a fare-thee-well. At least Grimaldi understood what had been asked of Bolan, every time his friend took on another mission that could be his last.

The morbid turn of thought left the ace pilot disgusted with himself. He tried to shake it off, whistled a snatch of something tuneless for a moment, then gave up on that and watched the Gulf of Guinea passing underneath him. Were the people in the boats craning their necks, tracking his engine sounds and following his progress overhead? Was one of them, perhaps, a watcher who had seen the Beech-craft earlier, reported it to other watchers on dry land, and now logged his return?

It was a possibility, of course, but there was nothing he could do about it. Radar would have marked his plane's arrival in Nigerian airspace and tracked him to the inland point where he had turned. The natural assumption would be that he'd dropped something or someone; the mystery only began there.

Or, at least, so he was hoping.

Nigeria imported *and* exported drugs. According to reports Grimaldi had seen from the Nigerian Drug Law Enforcement Agency, Colombian cocaine and heroin from Afghanistan came in via South Africa, while home-grown marijuana was exported by the ton. Police, as usual, bagged ten percent or more of the illicit cargoes flowing back and forth across their borders, when they weren't hired to protect the shipments.

So, they might think he had dropped a load of drugs.

And then what?

It was sixty-forty that they'd order someone to investigate the theoretical drop zone, which meant relaying orders from headquarters to some outpost in the field. Maybe the brass in Lagos would reach out to their subordinates in Warri, who in turn would form a squad to roll out, have a look around, then report on what they found.

Which should be nothing.

If they went looking for drugs, they'd check the area where Grimaldi had turned his plane, then backtrack for a while along his flight path, coming or going, to see if they'd missed anything. There were no drugs to find, so they'd go home empty-handed and pissed off at wasting their time.

But if they *weren't* looking for drugs…

He knew the search might be conducted differently if the Nigerians went looking for intruders. Whether they were educated on HALO techniques or not, they had to know that men manipulating parachutes could travel farther than a bale of cargo dropping from the sky, and that the men, once having landed, wouldn't wait around for searchers to locate them.

It would be a different game, then, with a different cast of players. MOPOL still might be involved, but it was also possible that Bolan could be up against the State Security Service, the Defense Intelligence Agency or the competing National Intelligence Agency. The SSS was Nigeria's FBI, in effect, widely accused of domestic political repression, while the NIA was equivalent to America's CIA, and the DIA handled military intelligence.

In the worst-case scenario, Grimaldi supposed that all three agencies might decide to investigate his drop-in, with MOPOL agents thrown in for variety. And how many hunters could Bolan evade before his luck ran out?

Grimaldi's long experience with Bolan, starting as a kidnap "victim" and continuing thereafter as a friend and willing ally, had taught him not to underestimate the Executioner's abilities. No matter what the odds arrayed against him, the Sarge had always managed to emerge victorious.

So far.

But he was only human, after all.

One hell of a human, for sure, but still human.

Grimaldi trusted Bolan to succeed, no matter the task he was assigned. But if he fell along the way, revenge was guaranteed.

The pilot swore it on his soul, whatever that was worth.

He didn't know jackshit about Nigeria, beyond the obvious. It was a state in Africa, beset by poverty—yet oil rich—disease and chaos verging on the point of civil war, where he would stand out like a sore white thumb. But the official language was English, because of former colonial rule, so he wouldn't be stranded completely.

And if Bolan didn't make it out, Grimaldi would be going on a little hunting trip.

An African safari, right.

He owed the big guy that, at least.

And Jack Grimaldi always paid his debts.

TOUCHDOWN WAS better than Bolan had any right to expect after stepping out of an airplane and plummeting more than 24,000 feet to Earth. He bent his knees, tucked and rolled as they'd taught him at Green Beret jump school back in the old days, and came up with only a few minor bruises to show for the leap.

Only bruises so far.

Step two was covering his tracks and getting out of there before some hypothetical pursuer caught his scent and turned his drop into a suicide mission.

Bolan took it step by step, with all due haste. He shed the parachute harness first thing, along with his combat webbing and weapons. Next, he stripped off the jumpsuit that had saved him from frostbite while soaring, but which now felt like a baked potato's foil wrapper underneath the Nigerian sun. That done, he donned the combat rigging once again and went to work.

Fourth step, reel in the parachute and all its lines, compacting same into the smallest bundle he could reasonably manage. That done, he unsheathed his folding shovel and began to dig.

It didn't have to be a deep grave, necessarily. Just deep enough to hide his jumpsuit, helmet, bottled oxygen and mask, the chute and rigging. If some kind of nylon-eating scavenger he'd never heard of came along and dug it up that night, so be it. Bolan would be long gone by that time, his mission either a success or a resounding, fatal failure.

More than depth, he would require concealment for the burial, in case someone came sniffing after him within the next few hours. To that end, he dug his dump pit in the shadow of a looming mahogany some thirty paces from the clearing where he'd landed, and spent precious time replanting ferns he had disturbed during the excavation when he'd finished.

It wasn't perfect—nothing man-made ever was—but it would do.

He had a four-mile hike ahead of him, through forest that had so far managed to escape the logger's ax and chainsaw. As he understood it from background research, Nigeria, once in the heart of West Africa's rain forest belt, had lost ninety-five percent of its native tree cover and now imported seventy-five percent of the lumber used in domestic construction. Some conservationists believed that there would be no forests left in the country by 2020, a decade and change down the road toward Doomsday.

That kind of slash-and-burn planning was seen throughout Africa, in agriculture, mineral prospecting, environmental protection, disease control—you name it. The native peoples once ruled and exploited by cruel foreign masters now seemed hell-bent on turning their ancestral homeland into a vision of post-apocalyptic hell, sacrificing Mother Nature on the twin altars of profit and national pride.

Of course, the foreigners were still involved, and if they didn't always have traditional white faces, they were every bit as rapacious as Belgium's old King Leopold or Germany's Kaiser Wilhelm. Africa still had treasures to steal or buy cheaply, and Nigeria's main claim to fame was petroleum.

Which brought Bolan's mind back front and center to

his mission as he slogged through a forest whose upper canopy steamed, while its floor lay in warm, muggy shade.

The oil rush was on in Nigeria, had been for years now, and like any mineral boom, it spawned winners and losers. The haves and have-nots. In Nigeria's case, the have-nots—or rather, some of them—had taken up arms to demand a piece of the action. Barring concessions that pleased them, they aimed to make life untenable for the haves.

Which led to Bolan traveling halfway around the world, sleeping on planes and later jumping out of one to drop from more than four miles high and land on hostile ground where he'd be hunted by both sides, if either one detected him.

All for a young woman he'd never met or heard of previously, whom he'd never really get to know, and whom he'd never see again if he pulled off the job at hand and saved her life.

The really weird part, from a "normal" individual's perspective, was that none of it seemed strange to Bolan. Hell, it wasn't even new. The maps and faces changed, of course, but it was what Mack Bolan did.

Well, *some* of what he did.

The rest of it was killing, plain but often far from simple. He'd received the Executioner nickname the hard way, earning it. A few had nearly rivaled Bolan's record as a sniper when he wore his country's uniform.

As for the rest, forget it.

If there was another fighting man or woman who could match his body count since Bolan had retired from military service to pursue a one-man war, it ranked among the best-kept secrets of all time.

He had a job to do, now, in Nigeria. Helping a total stranger out of trouble.

And there would be blood.

CHAPTER TWO

Stony Man Farm, Virginia

Thirty-three hours prior to touchdown in Nigeria, Bolan had cruised along Skyline Drive in Virginia's Blue Ridge Mountains, watching the marvels of nature scroll past his windows. As always, he knew that the drive was only the start of another long journey.

His destination that morning wasn't the end.

It was a launching pad.

He blanked that out and took the Blue Ridge drive for what it was: a small slice of serenity within a life comprising primarily tension, violent action and occasional side trips into Bizarro Land.

Bolan enjoyed the drive, the trees and ferns flanking the two-lane blacktop, and the chance of seeing deer or other wildlife while en route. He'd never been a hunter in the "sporting" sense, and while he'd never thought of carrying a placard for the other side, it pleased him to see animals alive and well, wearing the skins or feathers they were born with.

When you'd dropped the hammer on enough men, he supposed, the "game" of killing lost its dubious appeal.

But stalking human predators, well, that was Bolan's job. And it would never end, as long as he survived.

So be it. He had made a choice, in full knowledge that there could be no turning back, no change of mind or heart once the decision was translated into action. Bolan was the Executioner, and always would be.

War without end. Amen.

Which didn't mean he couldn't stop and smell the roses when he had the opportunity. What was he fighting for, if not the chance to lead a better and more peaceful life?

Of course, he fought for others. Sacrificed his future, in effect. There'd be no wife and kiddies, no white picket fence, no PTA meetings or Christmas parties at the nine-to-five office. No pension or gold watch when he'd put in his time.

Just death.

And he'd already had a preview of his own, stage-managed in Manhattan by the same folks who had built the installation that lay five or six miles down the scenic route.

Mack Bolan was no more.

Long live the Executioner.

BOLAN CLEARED security without a hitch. He passed a tractor harrowing one of the fields on his left as he drove toward the main house. Stony Man was a working farm, which paid some of the bills and supported its cover, since aerial photos would show cultivated fields and farmhands pursuing their normal duties.

Those photos wouldn't reveal that the workers were extremely motivated cops and members of America's elite military teams—Navy SEALs, Special Forces, Army Rangers, Marine Corps Force Recon—who spent duty rotations at Stony Man under a lifetime oath of secrecy. All armed. All dangerous.

There were risks involved in spying on Stony Man Farm. Each aircraft passing overhead was monitored on radar and by other means. If one appeared too nosy, there were means for dealing with the problem.

They included Stinger ground-to-air missiles and a dowdy-looking single-wide mobile home planted in the middle of the Farm's airstrip. If friendly aircraft were expected, a tractor pulled the mobile home aside to permit landing. If intruders tried to land uninvited, the trailer not only blocked the runway, but could drop its walls on hinges to reveal quad-mounted TM-134 miniguns, each six-barreled weapon capable of firing four thousand 7.62 mm rounds per second.

Fifty yards out from the farmhouse, Bolan recognized Hal Brognola and Barbara Price waiting for him on the wide front porch. A couple of young shirtless warriors in blue jeans and work boots were painting the upper story of the house, a procedure that Bolan had never observed before. He caught Price glancing his way and couldn't help smiling.

The home team waited for him where they stood. Bolan climbed the three porch steps and shook their hands in turn. Price's greeting was professional, giving no hint of all the times they'd shared a bed in his upstairs quarters at the Farm, when he was passing through.

"Good trip?" Brognola asked, as always.

"Uneventful," Bolan answered.

"That's the best kind. Join us in the War Room?"

Bolan nodded, then followed Brognola and Price inside.

The War Room occupied roughly one-quarter of the farmhouse's basement level. It was basically a high-tech conference room, with all the audiovisual bells and whistles, but Brognola had always called it the War Room, since discussions held around its meeting table always ended with an order to destroy some target that duly constituted authorities found themselves unable to touch by legitimate means.

Sooner or later, it came down to war.

Bolan supposed that somewhere in the Farm's computer database there was a tally of the lives that had been terminated based on orders issued in that room. Bolan had never made a point of keeping score, and didn't plan on starting now, but sometimes he got curious.

The Farm wasn't his sole preserve. It issued orders to the fighting men of Able Team and Phoenix Force, as well, while dabbling here and there in God knew what covert attempts by other agencies to hold the savages at bay. Sometimes—most times—it worked, but only in the short-term. In the long war of Good versus Evil, whoever laid down the ground rules, there was no final victory, no irredeemable defeat.

There was only the struggle.

And it was about to resume.

Aaron Kurtzman—"the Bear" to his friends—was waiting when they reached the War Room, seated in the motorized wheelchair that was his chief mode of conveyance since a bullet in the back had left him paralyzed from the waist down. That had occurred during a raid on Stony Man, initiated by a traitor in the upper levels of the CIA, and it accounted for the ultrastrict security that cloaked the Farm today.

"I won't ask you about your trip," Kurtzman said, smiling as he put the crunch on Bolan's hand.

Brognola humphed at that, making the others smile, then said, "Consistency's a virtue."

"Absolutely," Price told him as she took her usual seat. "No one would ever doubt your virtue, Hal."

"In my day, civilized discourse required amenities,"

Brognola said. "But hey, screw it. Let's get to work, shall we?"

"Sounds good," Bolan replied, smiling.

"What do you know about Nigeria?" Brognola asked.

"It's in West Africa," Bolan said. "Ruled by France, then Britain, until independence in the early sixties. Trouble with Biafra in the same decade. There's oil, and everybody wants it. Drugs, coming and going. Tribal conflict verging on a civil war at times, and throw in some religious upheaval. Advance-fee frauds that go around the world through e-mail. Bribes are the order of the day, never mind corruption. That's it, in a nutshell."

"You've hit all the basics," the big Fed acknowledged. "Are you up to speed on MEND?"

"Guerrillas. Terrorists. The acronym escapes me at the moment," Bolan said.

"You're still well ahead of the norm," Brognola said. "It's the Movement for Emancipation of the Niger Delta, waging armed resistance against the federal government and foreign oil companies. You've heard of Marion King Hubbert?"

"No," Bolan replied. "Can't say I have."

"No sweat. He died in 1989," the big Fed stated. "A geophysicist with Shell Oil, out of Houston, best known for his theories on capacity of oil and natural gas reserves. It boils down to what they call Hubbert Peak Theory."

"Which is?" Bolan coaxed.

"Bare bones, the idea that Earth and every part of it have finite petro-gas reserves. Extraction supposedly follows a bell curve, increasing until pumping hits the 'Hubbert peak,' and then declining after that."

"Sounds right," Bolan replied. "They aren't making any more dinosaurs."

"So true," Brognola said. "Anyway, the word from

so-called experts at State is that MEND wants to create an 'artificial Hubbert peak,' whatever the hell that means. I don't claim to understand it, but one of MEND's spokesmen—a character calling himself Major-General Godswill Tammo—says the group plans to seize total control of the oil reserves in Delta State."

"How are they doing so far?" Bolan asked.

"They haven't captured any fields or pumping stations, but it's not for lack of trying," Brognola replied. "Their main deal, at the moment, is attacking pipelines, storage tanks, whatever they can reach. Also, they're big on snatching CEOs and members of their families, whenever they can find an opening. Which brings us to the job at hand."

Bolan sat quietly, waiting.

"Bear, if you please," the big Fed prompted.

A screen behind Brognola came to life, displaying a candid photo of a ruddy-faced, balding corporate type wearing a tailored suit that Bolan knew was expensive.

"Jared Ross," Brognola said by way of introduction. "He's an executive V.P. in charge of production for K-Tech Petroleum, based in Warri. That's a Delta State oil town, with roughly one-fifth of the state's four-point-seven million people. Most of the foreign oil companies working in Nigeria have their headquarters in Warri, operating refineries at Ekpan, more or less next door."

Bolan made the connection, saying, "He's been kidnapped?"

"Not exactly. First, some background on the local tribes. They're mainly Itsekiri and Ijaw, with Ijaw outnumbering the Itsekiri something like nine million to four hundred and fifty thousand. Anyway, for centuries they seemed to get along okay, but back in 1997 some genius in Lagos created an Ijaw government council, then put its headquarters in the heart of Itsekiri turf, in Warri. Maybe the result was intentional. Who knows? Long story short, when the smoke cleared, hundreds were dead and half a dozen petro installations had been occupied by rebels, cutting back production until soldiers took them out. MEND got its start from there, and in addition to the oil issue, you now have tribal warfare going full-blast in a region where they once had peace."

Kurtzman spoke up, saying, "Beware the Feds who say, 'We're here to help.'"

"Which would be us, in this case," Brognola replied. "Except the government in Lagos doesn't know it, and we weren't invited."

"What's the angle?" Bolan asked.

"You nearly had it when you asked if Jared Ross was kidnapped. It's his daughter," Brognola elaborated as another photo filled the screen.

Bolan saw a young woman in her late teens, maybe early twenties, smiling for the camera. She was blond and blue-eyed, fresh-faced, living the American dream. Bolan hoped it hadn't turned into a dead-end nightmare.

"How long ago?" he asked.

"Last week," Brognola said. "Six days and counting, now."

"Do they have proof of life?"

"Seems so. The ransom note was flexible. MEND will accept a hundred million dollars for her safe return, or K-Tech's pull-out from Nigeria."

"That's optimistic," Bolan said.

"It's fantasy. And Daddy doesn't trust the local law to get her back. At least, not in one piece and breathing."

So that's where I come in, Bolan thought.

"I've got a CD file with all the players covered," Brognola informed him, "if you want to look it over on your own."

"Sounds good," Bolan replied. "When would I have to leave?"

He already knew the answer, nodding as Brognola frowned and said, "They should've had us on it from day one. Let's say ASAP."

ALONE IN THE second-floor bedroom he used when at the Farm, Bolan read through Brognola's files on his laptop. He started with background on Jared and Mandy Ross, found nothing unique or remarkable on either, and moved on to meet his opposition.

MEND, as Brognola had noted, was the source of most guerrilla violence in Delta State, but pinning down its leadership was problematic. An anonymous online article from *The Economist,* published in September 2008, described MEND as a group that "portrays itself as political organisation that wants a greater share of Nigeria's oil revenues to go to the impoverished region that sits atop the oil. In fact, it is more of an umbrella organisation for several armed groups, which it sometimes pays in cash or guns to launch attacks." It's so-called war against pollution, Bolan saw, consisted in large part of dynamiting pipelines, each of which then fouled the area with another flood of oil. And more often than not hundreds of villagers perished while collecting the free oil, engulfed in flames from inevitable explosions.

According to the files Brognola had provided, two men seemed to dominate the hostile tribal factions that were presently at war in Delta State. Ekon Afolabi led the Itsekiri militants, a thirty-six-year-old man who'd been in trouble with the law since he was old enough to steal. Somewhere along the way, he had discovered ethnic pride and politics. Depending on the point of view, he'd either learned to fake the former, or was using it to make himself the Next Big Thing within his sphere of influence.

The candid shots of Afolabi showed a wiry man of

average height, with close-cropped hair, a wild goatee and dark skin. In addition to tribal markings, his scrabble to the top, or thereabouts, had left him scarred in ways that would be useful for identifying his cadaver, but which didn't seem to slow him in any kind of violent confrontation.

Afolabi's second in command was Taiwo Babatunde, a hulk who nearly dwarfed his boss at six foot three and some three hundred pounds, but from his photos and the file Bolan surmised that Babatunde lacked the wits required to plot a palace coup, much less to pull it off and run the tribal army on his own. Call him the boss man's strong right arm, a blunt tool that would flatten Afolabi's opposition on demand.

And likely have a great time doing it.

The file named Afolabi's soldiers as prime suspects in a dozen oil field raids, at least that many pipeline bombings and the murder of a newscaster from Delta Rainbow Television Warri who had criticized MEND for its violence. Communiqués demanding ransom for the safe return of Mandy Ross, while carefully anonymous, had been dissected by the FBI's profiling team at Quantico, who claimed that certain trademark phrases ID'd Afolabi as their author.

Bolan hoped the Feds were right.

The Ijaw tribal opposition's leader was Agu Ajani, turning twenty-nine next week, if he survived that long. He was another bad guy from the get-go, and while anyone could blame it on his childhood—orphaned at age four, warehoused by the state, then written off the first time he went AWOL, living hand-to-mouth among eight million strangers on the streets of Lagos—Bolan only cared about Ajani's actions in the here and now.

By all accounts, he was a ruthless killer with a clear sadistic streak, one of the sort who'd rather leave his enemies shorthanded, courtesy of a machete or meat cleaver, than to kill them outright. Which was not to say he hadn't put his share of bodies in the ground. Official sources credited his Ijaw faction with a thousand kills and counting in the ethnic war that ravaged Delta State.

In photos, Ajani didn't look the part. He favored floral-patterned shirts, the tourist kind, with short sleeves showing off his slender arms. A missing pinky finger on his left hand told the story of a near-miss in a knife fight, but he'd won that scrap and every one thereafter.

Up to now.

If Ekon Afolabi's number two was a behemoth, Ajani's was a smaller version of himself, some thirty pounds lighter and three or four inches shorter, with a bland face that belied his rap sheet. Daren Jumoke was a suspect in half a dozen murders *before* he turned political and started killing in the name of his people. Jumoke's "civilian" victims had been women, who were also raped. Bolan guessed that his juvenile record, if such things existed where he was going, would reveal a violent bully with a hyperactive sex drive and a deaf ear when it came to females saying no.

Killing Jumoke, Bolan thought, would be a public service. As it was, his gang apparently had no connection to the Ross kidnapping—but that didn't mean he couldn't find a way to use them in a pinch, maybe as cannon fodder to distract his Itsekiri opposition.

Bolan was starting to read about his native contact in Warri, one Obinna Umaru, when a muffled rapping on his door distracted him. He answered it and smiled at finding Barbara Price on his threshold.

"Finished your homework yet?" she asked.

"Almost."

"I don't want to distract you."

"I could use a break," he said, and stood aside.

She brushed against him, passing, and it sent a tingle racing through his body, as if he had touched a bare low-voltage wire.

"So, Africa again," she said. "Your shots all up-to-date? Dengue fever? Yellow fever? Typhoid?"

"My rabies shot is out of date," he told her.

"Don't let anybody bite you, then."

"I'll make a note. Coffee?"

"It keeps me up all night," she said, and smiled. "You have a few cups, though."

"Will I be needing it?" he asked.

"Homework. You said it wasn't finished."

It was Bolan's turn to smile. "Now that I think of it, I've barely started."

"It's best to be thorough."

"I hear you." Still smiling, he said, "Maybe I ought to take a shower first. To freshen up and clear my head."

"Sounds good," she said, hands rising to the buttons of her blouse. "I have to tell you, I've been feeling dirty all day long."

CHAPTER THREE

Delta State, Nigeria

Bolan smelled the Itsekiri camp before he saw it. Supper cooking and open latrines, gasoline and diesel fuel, gun oil and unwashed bodies.

The unmistakable odors of men at war.

He had to watch for lookouts, as well as snares and booby traps. MEND's rebels knew that they were hunted by the state, and by their tribal adversaries. They'd be foolish not to post guards on the camp's perimeter, but Bolan wouldn't know how thorough they had been until he tested the defenses for himself.

Beginning now.

There'd be no cameras or other electronic gear, of course. He would've heard a generator running by the time he closed the gap to half a mile, and there was nothing on the wind but human voices and the clanking, clattering that no large group of humans in the wild seemed able to avoid. So much the better for his own quiet approach, if he could spot the posted guards and take them down without a fuss.

He found the first one watering the ferns, his rifle

propped against a nearby tree, well out of splatter range. The guy was actually humming to himself, eyes closed and head thrown back, enjoying one of nature's little pleasures.

It was easy, then, when Bolan stepped up close behind him, clapped a hand over his mouth and gave his head a twist, driving the black blade of his Ka-Bar fighting knife into the lookout's throat. One thrust dealt with the vocal cords, the right carotid artery and jugular, ensuring silence even as it robbed the brain of vital oxygen and sent the guard's life-blood spouting in a geyser that would only stop when there was no more left for atricles and ventricles to pump.

Which took about two minutes.

Bolan didn't wait around to watch. He left the dead-man-gasping where he lay, scooped up his battle-worn Kalashnikov, and moved on through the forest shadows, looking for his next target.

Not victim, since—in Bolan's mind at least—human predators invited mayhem with their daily actions, through their very lifestyle. He had no time for philosophical discussions with the folks who claimed that "every life has value" or that "everyone deserves a second chance."

Some lives, based on objective evidence, were worse than useless. They spread pain and misery every day that they continued. Most had scorned a thousand chances to reform and find a place within the millieu known as civilized society. They had not merely *failed,* but rather had defiantly refused to play the game by any rules except their own.

And when they couldn't be controlled, when the prisons couldn't hold them, when they set themselves above humanity and any common decency, they earned a visit from the Executioner.

He couldn't reach them all, of course—only the worst of those who came to his attention, who were physically accessible and whose predation took priority over the other millions of corrupt, sadistic scum who flourished all around the globe.

Right here, right now, he had a job to do.

The second guard wasn't exactly napping, but he had allowed his mind to wander, maybe thinking of his next trip into Warri, all the sex and liquor he'd enjoy when his commanders let him off his leash. A party to remember when they shipped him off to raid another oilfield, blow another pipeline, blitz another Ijaw village to the ground.

The pipe dream ended with a subtle sound behind him, not alarming, but enough to make the young man turn, one eyebrow raised, to check it out. Both eyebrows vaulted toward his hairline as a strong hand clutched his throat and slammed him back against the nearest tree before the Ka-Bar's blade ripped through his diaphragm to find his heart.

Two down. How many left?

Bolan moved on, seeking more targets—and the one life he had come to save.

THERE WAS A POINT where even fear became mundane, when human flesh and senses had to let go of panic or collapse. No conscious choice determined when the mind and soul had had enough. No individual could say with any certainty what his or her limit was, and resolve to fear no more.

But on her seventh morning of captivity, when Mandy Ross awoke from fitful sleep, she realized that somehow she was less afraid than she had been on waking yesterday. She had survived another night intact, and misty daylight lancing through the forest shadows didn't bring the sense of waking terror that had been her only real emotion for the past six days.

Of course, she was afraid, convinced the worst still lay ahead of her, but there was nothing she could do about it. It was all out of her hands.

For instance, Mandy's captors hadn't raped her yet, although she recognized the looks they gave her, and she didn't need a crash course in whatever dialect they spoke to understand what some of them were saying when they flashed grins in her direction.

It was coming, she supposed. And so was death.

The leader of her kidnappers had made that crystal-clear. If K-Tech Petroleum didn't meet their demands, she would be killed. Not merely shot or stabbed, mind you, but hacked up into pieces while alive, the odd bits mailed off to her father and to K-Tech's various directors as an object lesson in obedience.

The problem, simply stated, was that while her father was a wealthy man, he didn't have a hundred million dollars or the prospects for obtaining it by any means before the deadline imposed by her captors ran out. And even though he was in charge of K-Tech's operations in Nigeria, he obviously couldn't grant the kidnappers' alternative demand, for a company pull-out. Even if he lost his mind and tried to order an evacuation of all K-Tech workers from the country, he'd be countermanded by his bosses in a heartbeat, either fired or placed on leave until he had regained his senses.

Nope.

The way it looked to Mandy Ross, she was as good as dead.

The thing, now, was to face her death as bravely as she could—or maybe hasten it along herself, before the goons who'd snatched her took it in their pointy little heads to stage an orgy with her as the guest of dishonor.

They hadn't left her much in terms of weapons, but she'd thought about the problem long and hard over the past few days, as it became more and more obvious that she would never leave the rebel camp alive.

She had no blades or cutting tools of any kind, no rope or any other kind of ligature with which to hang herself, no toxic substances that she could swallow in a pinch. Childhood experience had taught her that you couldn't suffocate yourself by force of will alone, holding your breath. At some point, you passed out and started breathing automatically, as nature reasserted its control.

But she had teeth, and with some effort she supposed that she could reach the same veins in her wrists that other suicides accessed with knives and razors. It would hurt like hell, but only for a little while. When her only other option was to wait around until she was gang-raped, then fileted alive, well, anyone who thought that was a choice needed to have his or her head examined.

The only question, now, was how long she should wait.

How much time did she have?

To hell with it, she thought. There's no time like the present. Get it done.

NIGHT FELL HARD in a tropical country. There was no dusk to speak of, no romantic twilight. Having screened most of the sun from ground level, casting massive shadows all day long, the great trees played their final trick at sundown, producing the illusion of a switch thrown by a giant to put out the lights.

Bolan had witnessed the effect on four continents and knew what to expect. He'd almost reached the campground clearing when he lost daylight, and only needed moments for his night eyes to adjust.

Three guards lay dead behind him, in the forest, which cleared roughly one-quarter of the camp's perimeter. He hoped it would be all he needed, but he didn't have an exit strategy so far, and wouldn't until he had found out where the MEND terrorists were confining Mandy Ross. From there, once she was extricated from whichever hut or tent they kept her in, he could decide on how to flee.

A narrow unpaved road allowed the rebels access to the world beyond their forest hideout, passable for Jeeps, dirt bikes and—if it didn't rain too hard—the ancient army cargo truck that stood out in the compound's motor pool. Bolan had no idea where following that track might lead him, and he filed it as a last resort, without trying to guess.

He had considered that he might find Mandy Ross already dead or hurt so badly that she couldn't travel. Even with real soldiers, passions sometimes flared out of control, resulting in atrocities. If that turned out to be the case, Bolan could switch from rescue to revenge mode in a heartbeat. And whatever he might see inside the camp, he'd keep to himself, most definitely never sharing with the victim's family.

How much could one endure and still go on?

It all depended on the person, both their outward strength and inner fortitude. Some persevered while others crumbled and surrendered, let themselves be swept away. He had no take on Mandy Ross, as yet—except that nothing in her affluent and privileged life would have prepared her for her present circumstance.

Scanning the camp with practiced eyes, he noted points of interest: the command post, the motor pool, a commo tent with a pole-mounted satellite dish for some kind of battery-powered commo setup. The men slept in puptents or out in the open, but one other hut caught his eye.

The only one with a sentry outside it.

If that wasn't the camp's one-room jail, then what was it?

Bolan was determined to find out.

He had begun to move in that direction, following the tree line still, using the shadows, when he saw one of the MEND gunners heading for the guarded hut. He was five-nine or -ten, wiry and muscular, bearing a metal plate of food, wearing a pistol on his right hip and a sheathed machete on the left. Bolan watched him dismiss the guard after some muffled talk that almost sounded like an argument.

The guard left, and the plate-bearer entered the hut. Before he closed the door, Bolan had time to glimpse the startled face of Mandy Ross.

"WHAT DO YOU want?" Mandy Ross asked.

"I've brought your supper," the grinning gunman said.

"I'm not hungry," she replied, and almost giggled, thinking, I'll just nibble on my wrists tonight, if you don't mind.

"You must keep up your strength," the intruder said, still smiling.

She recognized him as an officer, second or third in charge of things around the camp. His name was James Something-or-other, which would have surprised her if she hadn't spent the two weeks prior to her abduction meeting Africans with Anglo given names who were her father's business colleagues. As it was, she focused on her captor's face and words without distractions.

"Strength for what?" she asked him. "Are we marching somewhere?"

"Marching? No." He laughed at that. "But after being kept so long in this place, you must need some exercise."

She saw where he was headed, his dark eyes sliding up and down her body like a physical caress, and tried to head him off.

"I'm fine."

"Indeed, you are," James Something instantly agreed.

"Thanks for the food," she said. "If you don't mind, I'll eat my monkey meat alone."

"Tonight is lizard, I believe," he said. "Perhaps you need something to stimulate your appetite."

"No, thanks, all the same."

"But I insist."

Still keeping up the smile, James looked around her tiny cell, as if expecting that it would have sprouted decorations other than the folding cot that was its only furniture. She guessed that he was looking for someplace to set the plate. At last, he turned back toward the door and placed it on the hut's dirt floor.

"Perhaps you'll want it afterward," he said.

"You're making a mistake," Mandy reminded him. "Your boss laid down the hands-off rule."

James shrugged. "What he does not know, will not hurt him. It will be our little secret."

"Oh, you think so?"

"I can guarantee it," James replied, resting his left hand on the hilt of his machete. "Even if I must remove your tongue."

"He'd never notice that, I guess." She fairly sneered at him.

"Accidents happen. Possibly, you tried to run away and I was forced to shoot you."

"So, you like them dead? Sounds just about your speed."

James shrugged. "I strive for flexibility."

"You'll have it, when Azuka pulls your spine out through your ass."

James blinked at mention of his master's name, but never lost his mocking smile.

"I do not fear him," he replied.

"So it's true, then," Mandy said.

"Excuse me?"

"You're not just another ugly face. You're stupid, too."

That wiped his smile off, finally. James sprang at her, swinging an open hand, but Mandy ducked and back-pedaled to the farthest corner of her tiny hut.

"Where will you run?" he asked her. "I can chase you all night long."

"I'm betting that's the *only* thing you'd manage all night long." She spat at him.

"I'll teach you some respect!" James snarled, advancing toward her in a half crouch, primed to spring.

"Or I'll teach you to sing soprano," Mandy threatened.

"I enjoy a challenge."

"Start with something simple, like that body odor," she replied.

His smile had turned into a snarl, teeth bared and clenched. She could almost hear James growling like an animal as he crept forward.

"You will beg for death before I'm finished with you, American!"

"So, skip the foreplay," she replied, "and shoot me. It's the only way you're getting what you want."

"We'll see." He almost giggled with excitement.

James was so intently focused on his target that he had to have missed the sound of the hut door opening and closing. Mandy felt despair wash over her, until she saw a soldier standing on the threshold, watching her.

His voice was pure America as he told James, "Okay, let's see it now."

AZUKA BANKOLE WAS tired. It seemed that he was always tired these days. Patrols and skirmishes, the oilfield raids and guarding hostages—they all took time and energy. Though he had just turned thirty-one last month, Bankole felt as if he was already getting old.

The ganja helped, of course.

Prime smoke, imported from Edo State, Delta's next-door neighbor to the north, where everyone agreed the best plants in Nigeria—perhaps in all of Africa—were grown.

The government agencies tried to eradicate cannabis farming, but nothing thus far had succeeded.

Based on what he knew of history and human nature, Bankole believed nothing ever would.

And that was fine with him.

He had a fat joint rolled and ready, already between his lips—a match in hand—when he heard someone just outside the open door of his command post. First, it was a nervous shuffling of feet, then clearing of the throat. At last, the interloper worked up nerve enough to knock.

"What is it now?" Bankole asked.

A shadow fell across the threshold. Looking up, Bankole recognized Omo Kehinde. He took modest pride in knowing all his men by name, although in truth, there were a number of them he'd be happy to forget.

"Captain?" Kehinde made a question of it, as if trying to confirm Bankole's identity.

"Yes, it's me," Bankole answered, feeling irritated now. "What do you want?"

"I am supposed to guard the prisoner," Kehinde said.

"So?"

"My time to guard the prisoner is now."

"Then go and do it. Why tell me?"

"Captain, Lieutenant Okereke ordered me to leave my post," Kehinde said, standing with eyes downcast. "I had no choice but to—"

"Obey. I understand."

Bankole understood too well, in fact. He'd given strict orders that no one was to touch the hostage without his express permission, which hadn't been granted. Knowing that James Okereke had a certain way with women, Bankole had taken him aside, in private, to repeat the order personally. The lieutenant had smiled, nodded and said he understood.

Of course he understood, Bankole thought. But now, the first time that my back is turned…

"I'll deal with this," Bankole told his nervous soldier. "You have done your duty and should fear no punishment."

"Yes, Captain. Thank you, Captain."

With regret, Bankole dropped the ganja joint into a pocket of his sweat-stained shirt, stood and took a second to confirm that he hadn't removed his gun belt. There was no need to inspect the holstered pistol on his hip, since it was always loaded, with a live round in the chamber.

It was time to teach his men an object lesson.

Okereke, never the best lieutenant in the world, would make a fine example for the rest.

And what would happen if he had damaged the hostage, against Bankole's orders? What would Ekon Afolabi say—or do—when he found out? Punishing Okereke first might help Bankole's case. If it didn't, well, there was nothing he could do about it now.

Spurred by a sudden sense of urgency, he brushed past Kehinde and out of the CP not quite double-timing, but leaving no doubt that he was a man in a hurry, with places to go and people to see.

Or to kill.

No one tried to intercept or to pester him with questions as he crossed the compound, striding toward the hut that held his one and only prisoner. Bankole felt his anger building with each step he took, its heat evaporating the fatigue that plagued him.

He should thank James Okereke for the swift shot of adrenaline, before his own swift shot ended the skulking bastard's worthless life.

BOLAN'S BERETTA COUGHED once through its sound suppressor, and dropped the rapist in his tracks. The dead man shivered and then lay still, blood drooling from the keyhole in his forehead.

Bolan recognized the stunned young woman from her photos, but he still went for the confirmation. "Mandy Ross?"

"Uh-huh. And you are?"

"Taking you away from here, if that's all right."

"I thought you'd never ask."

"It's getting dark outside," he said, "but anyone who's looking won't have any problem seeing us. Say nothing. Follow where I lead, no questions and no deviations. If we make it to the tree line unobserved, we've got a fighting chance."

"And if we don't?"

He shrugged. "We still fight, but it may not go so well."

"Okay," she said. "It beats waiting for them to come dismember me. Let's do it."

Bolan stooped and drew the dead man's pistol from its holster. It was a Polish MAG-95 in 9 mm Parabellum, with a full magazine and a round already in the chamber. He handed the weapon to Mandy and asked, "Have you ever fired a pistol?"

"A couple of times, at the country club range."

"This is easy," he told her. "The trigger's double-action. All you have to do is aim and squeeze—but not unless I say so or you see someone I've missed sneaking around behind us. Got it?"

"Yes."

"You should have sixteen shots," Bolan went on, rolling the dead man onto his back and plucking two more magazines from pouches on his belt. "With these, it's forty-six. Reload by—"

"I know this part," Mandy interrupted him. "You push a button—this one?—and the clip falls out."

"That's it. Ready to leave now?"

"Yes, please."

Bolan cracked the door and scanned the slice of compound he could see without emerging, then stepped clear with Mandy on his heels. No one was watching that he noticed, and the shadowed tree line beckoned to him, forty yards or less from where he stood.

Without another word, he moved in that direction, walking with a purpose, trusting Mandy to keep up with him. She had the world's best motivation to avoid falling behind: survival.

They were halfway to the outskirts of the camp before a harsh voice bellowed an alarm behind them. Bolan half turned, saw a soldier sprinting toward them with his pistol drawn, rousing the camp with shouted warnings. Almost instantly sentries appeared on Bolan's left, racing to cut off his retreat into the forest.

"Change of plans," he snapped at Mandy. "Follow me!"

She did as instructed, running after Bolan as he turned and raced toward the line of vehicles that formed the compound's motor pool. A shot rang out behind them, followed instantly by half a dozen more.

Before Bolan could turn and counter that incoming fire, the same harsh voice commanded, "Not the woman! She must not be harmed!"

Which gave Bolan an edge, of sorts. He might be fair game for the rebels, but that didn't mean he had to take it lying down.

Turning, he raked the compound with a long burst from his Steyr AUG. Mandy was firing at the same time, yelping as the first shot stung her palm and ears, then getting used to it.

Bolan saw one of their opponents drop, and then another. When a third fell and the rest scattered for cover, he called to Mandy, "Hurry up! We're going for a ride."

Most military vehicles had simple starter mechanisms, since ignition keys were quickly lost or broken in adverse conditions. Bolan chose a Jeep at random, slid behind the wheel and gunned its engine into snarling life while Mandy scrambled for the shotgun seat.

"Hang on!" he said, and floored the gas pedal, aiming the Jeep's nose at the nearest gunmen, barreling through the middle of the camp to reach the only access road beyond.

CHAPTER FOUR

In a rush of panic, Azuka Bankole forgot his own orders and those he'd received from his commander. He tracked the speeding Jeep with his pistol, rapid-firing round after round toward its tires, then the driver, praying for a lucky shot to stop the fleeing vehicle.

Around him, every soldier with a weapon followed his example, laying down a storm of fire that somehow failed to halt the Jeep. How was it possible?

His parents might have said that forest demons were responsible. Bankole had abandoned superstition as a child—or thought he had, at least—and reckoned careless shooting was responsible. He had been taught to squeeze a trigger, not to jerk it, but the lessons learned while practicing on lifeless stationary targets were too easily forgotten in the heat of combat.

Bankole's pistol slide locked open on a smoking chamber, and he dropped the empty magazine, groping for a replacement from his gun belt. By the time he found it, the Jeep was out of sight, vanished into the dark maw of the forest road that granted access to the camp for vehicles.

Behind it lay chaos.

The Jeep had flattened several of Bankole's soldiers, and at least two of their tents. From one, a man's pained voice called out for help. Others, still fit and frantic, had begun to chase the Jeep on foot, firing into the night.

Bankole strained his throat calling them back, knowing that every second wasted gave his enemy a greater lead. As his guerrillas rallied to him, Bankole was on the move, leading them to the motor pool.

"Go after them!" he shouted. "The woman must not get away!"

Whatever happened in the next half hour could decide Bankole's fate. If he allowed the hostage to escape, he had no doubt that Ekon Afolabi would demand his life in payment for that failure. If his soldiers killed the woman, trying to recapture her, his fate might be the same—but he could offer the defense of having told his men she had to be caught alive.

Bankole's only other option was to send his men in pursuit, then flee alone in some other direction and try to escape Afolabi's long reach. The prospect was attractive, for perhaps two seconds, then his mind snapped back to harsh reality.

What did he know of life outside of Delta State, much less outside Nigeria? He would be lost beyond the relatively small and violent world where he had grown into a savage semblance of manhood.

Bankole could run, but he couldn't hide.

The only realistic choice, then, was to stay and fight; take apparent defeat and turn it into something that would pass for triumph.

Two Jeeps and three dirt bikes were already in hot pursuit of the escaping hostage and her rescuer, whoever he might be. Bankole leaped into the final Jeep, hammered the dashboard starter button with his fist and revved the engine, hesitating only for a moment while three soldiers filled the empty seats.

"Remember that we need the girl alive," he said before he gunned the Jeep and followed those who'd gone before.

But *did* they, really?

Granted, he had orders to protect her, but he hadn't counted on a bold escape. Bankole knew there was a good chance that his men would wound or kill the hostage, either accidentally or for the hell of it. And what would happen to Bankole then?

A sudden inspiration made him smile.

If anything went wrong, it was the white man's fault for meddling where he didn't belong. Who was to say that *he* didn't kill the woman himself? If he was dead, then he couldn't dispute Bankole's version of events.

Perfect, Bankole thought, plunging down the tunnel of the forest road, his headlights burning through the night.

THE JEEP BOLAN HAD chosen was a rattletrap, but it could move. He drove with the accelerator nearly floored, knowing that he was finished if an antelope or some other creature charged out in front of him. He couldn't stop short at his present speed, and anything he struck would likely wind up in his lap or Mandy's.

She was swiveled in her seat, up on one knee and watching their trail for any sign of a pursuit. It wasn't long in coming.

"Dirt bikes," she informed him half a heartbeat after Bolan saw the first headlight reflected in his trembling, sagging mirror. Two more joined the chase almost immediately, followed farther back by the first Jeep to join the chase.

"Is this as fast as we can go?" she asked, then squealed as their Jeep hit a pothole, nearly pitching her out of her seat.

"Sit down and hang on!" Bolan snapped. "We're lucky to have wheels at all, but it isn't a racer."

"So sorry," she said. "But I don't feel like going back into my cage."

"That won't happen," he told her with more confidence than he felt.

Three bikes could mean six shooters, but he doubted they were riding double. Three or four men to a Jeep, however many were behind him on the narrow road. Wherever he was forced to stop and fight, Bolan knew he'd be outnumbered.

Situation normal.

"You've got me at a disadvantage," Mandy said a moment later. "What's your name?"

"Matt Cooper," he replied, using the name on his passport.

"I guess my father sent you?"

"Not exactly," Bolan said, checking the mirror.

Three Jeeps were back there now. The growling dirt bikes had already cut his lead by half.

"What's that mean?" Mandy asked.

Bolan shot her a sidelong glance and said, "We'll talk about it later, if there's time."

"You mean, if we're alive?"

"Well, if we're not, there won't be much to say."

She laughed at that, a brittle sound, cut off almost before it left her lips.

"Want me to shoot the bikers?" she inquired.

"Can you?"

She half turned in her seat again, raising the pistol taken from her would-be rapist.

"Let's find out," she said.

She spaced her shots, took time to aim, their vehicle leaving the sharp reports behind. After her fourth shot, Mandy yelped, "I got one!"

Bolan's rearview mirror proved it, as the second dirt bike back in line veered to the right and plunged into the forest. Bolan couldn't tell if she had hit the driver, his machine, or simply cracked his nerve with a near-miss, but she had taken out one of their enemies, in any case.

"Good work," he told her.

"I'm not finished yet. I owe these pricks for—"

Bolan saw the muzzle-flashes in his mirror, ducked instinctively and heard one of the bullets from the lead Jeep strike the rear of his.

"Get down!" he warned.

Mandy obeyed, but only to a point. She peered around the backrest of her seat and raised her weapon for another shot. When she'd fired two without apparent hits, she answered, "What the hell. I'd rather die out here than go back in a box and wait to see what happens next."

He couldn't fault her logic or her nerve, but Bolan didn't want to see her killed by stubborn anger. Mandy squeezed off three more rounds, then gave a little squawk and dropped back in her seat.

"Damn it! I'm shot!" she said.

"Show me," Bolan demanded.

Mandy held her right arm out to him, showed him where blood spotted the sleeve.

"Call it a graze," said Bolan. "Next time, it could be between your eyes."

"They aren't that good," she said.

"They don't have to be good, just lucky," he replied.

The hunters wouldn't need real skill until he stopped to fight on foot. And how long he could keep the Jeep on the road was anybody's guess.

THE GRAZE ON Mandy's arm burned furiously, but she recognized at once that she had suffered no great injury. Untended in the wilds of Africa, the wound might fester, maybe kill her with gangrene, but that took time.

And Mandy Ross knew time was running out.

She'd *maybe* hit one of the bikers, and she'd keep on trying for the others, but it was ridiculous to think that she could stop them all.

Still, she'd been truthful with the mysterious Matt Cooper. She would rather be shot in the forest than dragged back to camp, raped and tortured to death. If living wasn't one of Mandy's options, she would choose the quickest exit she could find.

It suddenly occurred to her that she could turn the borrowed pistol on herself, right here, right now, and end the whole ordeal. But while she might have done so in her prison cell, short moments earlier, the suicide solution didn't appeal to her now.

Not yet.

Cooper was some kind of hellacious soldier, it appeared, and while there was a chance that he could reunite her safely with her family, Mandy would help in any way she could.

With that in mind, she craned around the stiff back of her seat again and triggered two quick shots at their pursuers. One bike swerved, but didn't spill, and she supposed the sound she thought might be a bullet striking the lead Jeep had been illusory.

If she had hit the speeding vehicle, she didn't slow it down.

More flashes from the Jeep now, and a lethal swarm of hornets hurtled past her, one drilling the Jeep's windshield between her seat and Cooper's.

Too damned close.

Gritting her teeth, she peered around the seat and fired again.

AZUKA BANKOLE CURSED bitterly, swerving his Jeep from left to right on the forest roadway, trying to keep an eye on the action ahead. He knew that shots were being fired, and he had passed the wreckage of one dirt bike without stopping, but he couldn't get a fix on what was happening.

And in his haste to join the hunt, he had neglected to pick up a two-way radio before he left the camp. It was a clumsy error, but made little real-world difference, since none of his men in the other Jeeps had radios, either.

So far, only those in the lead vehicle had traded gunfire with the fleeing hostage and her savior. Firing from the second Jeep in line would put the forward troops at risk, while firing from Bankole's, at the back of the procession, would be worse than useless.

Flooring the accelerator, feeling every bump and dip along the way as sharp blows to his spine and neck, Bankole gained ground steadily, until his grille was no more than eight or nine feet from the tailgate of the vehicle in front of him. At that speed, if the second Jeep stopped suddenly, collision was inevitable.

But he didn't care.

If possible, he would have swept the other Jeeps and dirt bikes off the road, giving himself free access to the enemy. His men were good enough at fighting in most circumstances, better still when raiding unarmed villages, but they weren't trained soldiers in any true sense of the word.

They would do their best, but was it good enough?

He had rushed out of the camp with nothing but his pistol, and its magazine was empty. Swallowing embarrassment, he shot an elbow toward the man beside him, ordering, "Reload my gun!"

"What, sir?"

"My pistol. Put in a fresh magazine!"

The soldier nearly blanched at that, but did as he was told, reaching across the space between them, past Bankole's elbow and the gearshift, to remove his pistol from its holster. He extracted the spent magazine, then found himself with both hands full until he slipped the empty into his breast pocket.

"Sir?"

"Yes? What?" Bankole snapped, eyes on the narrow road.

"The other magazine, sir?"

"On my belt, for God's sake!"

"Yes, sir."

Fairly trembling, the soldier leaned closer, snaking an arm beneath Bankole's, reaching for the ammo pouches on the left front of his pistol belt. The way he cringed and grimaced, he could have been mistaken for a creeping pervert in a porno theater, risking his life for an illicit hand-job.

"Hurry up, damn you!" Bankole gritted.

"Yes, sir!"

At last the job was done, the gun reloaded, safely holstered, while the nervous soldier wiped his sweaty face with a discolored handkerchief. Bankole almost had to laugh at that, but there was no room in his world for levity this night.

More gunshots echoed down the road, stinging his ears as he sped through the rippling sound waves, but the fugitives were still in motion, still retreating at top speed.

Could no one stop them now?

Enraged, he shouted at the troops who could not hear him. "Aim, you bastards! Make those bullets count!"

A BLOWOUT ALWAYS came as a surprise. On city streets, at thirty miles per hour, it was nerve-racking. At sixty-something on a freeway, it could kill you. Same thing in an unfamiliar forest, when you were being chased by twenty thugs with guns.

The blowout *didn't* kill Bolan or Mandy Ross, but when

a bullet ripped through the Jeep's left rear tire, Bolan knew they were in for bad trouble.

"Hang on!" he warned, fighting the wheel to keep the vehicle upright and moving for at least a little while longer. They couldn't travel far, dragging the Jeep's tail in the mud and cutting furrows with a rusty rim, but just a few more yards...

"When I stop," he said, "bail out my side into the woods."

"You're stopping?"

"Either that, or slow to a crawl and let them kill us where we sit."

"So stop already. Jeez!"

Bolan slammed on his brakes and cranked the steering wheel hard-left, nosing the Jeep into a gap between two looming trees. Another second saw him out and seeking cover, slipping the Steyr AUG off its taut shoulder sling. Mandy Ross followed Bolan, then passed him and knelt by a tree of her own, gun in hand.

There was no time to talk about strategy, optimal targets or anything else. Headlights blazed in his eyes, wobbling this way and that as the bikers reacted and tried to avoid the ambush, framed in light from the Jeeps at their back.

They were just shy of good enough. One guy laid down his bike, rolling clear in the dirt, while the other veered off to his right—Bolan's left—and plowed into a tree.

The Executioner fired at the closer one first, semiauto, one round through the chest as he lurched to his feet and then tumbled back down in a sprawl. If he wasn't dead, he was well on the way.

Number two had been dazed when his bike rammed the tree, but he came up with pistol in hand and got off two quick rounds in the heartbeat of life he had left. Bolan's second shot punched the guy's left eye through the back of his head. The soldier was dead on his feet, reeling through one more short step before he collapsed, leaving Bolan three Jeeps and all hands aboard to contend with.

High beams washed over the scene, bleaching tree trunks and ferns, forcing Bolan to squint. He lost sight of Mandy for a moment, then her pistol was banging away at the enemy. Two, three, four shots in a row, echoing through the woods.

And had she scored?

The lead Jeep swerved from Mandy's barking gun and ran over the second biker Bolan had put down, pinning his corpse beneath one of its tires. The occupants sprang clear, using their vehicle for cover as the others arrived. If any of them had been hit by Mandy's fire, it didn't show.

IT COULD HAVE BEEN a standoff, then, but Bolan didn't plan to hang around to trade shots with the MEND gunners until sunrise. He'd already beamed a silent signal from a small transmitter on his combat harness to a satellite miles overhead, from which it would rebound to a receiver Jack Grimaldi carried with him.

The scrambled signal came down to a single word.

Ready.

Meaning that Bolan had succeeded in retrieving Mandy Ross, and they were on their way to rendezvous with the Stony Man pilot, to be airlifted from a selected hilltop to the K-Tech Petroleum complex in Warri.

There'd been no way to explain that they were being chased by gunmen bent on killing them, that it might slow them or that Grimaldi might wind up waiting in vain for passengers who never showed.

"Ready" meant Grimaldi would be airborne by now

and on his way. Another loop over the Gulf of Guinea, then the run toward shore beneath radar. To find…what?

The ace pilot could wait a little while, but not forever. If they meant to catch that ride, they had to move.

Bolan palmed a frag grenade, yanked the pin and pitched the bomb overhand, across the road and into the trees where his enemies clustered. He hadn't warned Mandy, and the blast brought a little squeal from her lips, but she recovered and had her piece ready when two of the MEND gunners lurched from cover.

Bolan took the taller of them with a head shot, and was swinging toward the second when he heard Mandy's pistol popping again, four shots in rapid fire. At least one found its target, spinning him and punching him back toward the trees with an odd little hop before falling facedown.

Bolan left him to Mandy, in case the guy got up again, but she'd already shifted to fire at the other guerrillas concealed in the tree line. Two more shots, and Bolan saw her pistol's slide lock open on an empty chamber.

That would leave her with one magazine of fifteen rounds, assuming it was fully loaded when he'd pulled it from the dead man's ammo pouch. He couldn't help her if she burned through that too quickly, but with any kind of luck, their problem might've been resolved by then.

To which end, Bolan lobbed another frag grenade a few yards to the left of where his first had landed, waiting for the smoky flash and cries of pain. Before the echoes faded, he was up and moving, charging across the road on a diagonal tack, falling upon his enemies while they were still dazed and disoriented.

Hoping Mandy wouldn't shoot him by mistake.

A couple of the gunmen saw him coming, but they couldn't manage a response in time to save themselves. He stitched them both with 3-round bursts of 5.56 mm manglers, sweeping on to spray the other four still on their feet. Then he switched to semiauto, dealing mercy rounds to those who had been gutted by the shrapnel from his two grenades.

And silence, finally, along the forest road.

Until Mandy called, "Cooper? Are you all right?"

"We're clear," he told her, easing from the shadows, back into her line of sight. "Nobody left on this side."

"Jesus." She had a vaguely dazed expression on her face as she emerged from the tree line, pistol dangling, asking him, "Are they all dead?"

"They are," he told her. "And we're running late."

"For what?"

"Our lift back to your father."

"Daddy? Really?"

"I didn't go through all of this to tell you lies," Bolan said.

"The Jeep's wrecked," she reminded him.

"We've got more wheels to choose from," he replied. "You feel like two, or four."

"Whatever's fastest."

"Two it is," he said, slinging his rifle as he moved toward the nearest dirt bike.

GRIMALDI BROUGHT a chopper for his second run into Nigeria. There'd be no room to land a plane, and paperwork had been completed—forged, of course, but still impressive—on the whirlybird.

It was a Bell 206L LongRanger, seating seven, powered by an Allison 250-C20B turboshaft engine. Its 430-mile range was adequate, since he'd be refueling in Warri, and its cruising speed of 139 miles per hour would put him over the LZ in two hours and change, if he met no opposition along the way.

And if he did, well, he was done.

The Bell wasn't a gunship, and it wouldn't outrun military aircraft if the Nigerian air force happened to spot him, despite his running underneath their radar. At last count, they had six Mil Mi-24 helicopters on tap, assuming they didn't send one of their fifteen Chengdu F-7 jet fighters to blast him out of the sky with rockets or twin 30 mm cannons.

Either way, he'd be dead, leaving Bolan and his damsel stranded. Which was simply unacceptable.

Pickups were always worse than drops. This time, he'd actually have to set down on the ground while Bolan and the girl scrambled aboard. If they had company, the best that the ace pilot could do to help was wave the Springfield .45 he carried in a shoulder rig and tell them what he thought about their ancestors.

But leaving without Bolan and his charge wasn't an option. Never had been, never would be.

Only if Grimaldi reached the arranged LZ and saw them dead, beyond the slightest shadow of a doubt, would he return alone the way he'd come. And what would happen then?

A sat-phone message to the Farm, for starters, bearing news that everyone on-site had dreaded from the day they first broke ground.

And after that?

Grimaldi didn't want to think about what Brognola would do, how he'd react. Whether retaliation would be ordered, or the whole thing would be written off as fubar from the jump.

Who would they even target, in retaliation for eliminating Bolan? Could they pin it on an individual or group of heavies beyond question? Would the scorched-earth treatment help to ease their suffering?

Grimaldi couldn't answer that, but if it happened, he intended to be part of the first wave.

And then all thoughts of loss and grief were banished as he saw Bolan astride a dirt bike, on the chosen hilltop, with a young blonde just dismounting. Leave it to the big guy to pick up a stylish date.

Smiling, Grimaldi took the chopper down.

CHAPTER FIVE

Effurun, Delta State

Ekon Afolabi often stroked his sparse, red-tinged goatee when he was in a thoughtful mood. This day, pacing his office like a caged animal, he yanked the wiry hairs as if attempting to uproot them.

"Say it again, Taiwo. How many dead?"

"Fifteen, at least," Babatunde replied. His voice rumbled out of his massive body as if he were speaking from deep in a pit.

"And then, the woman gone, of course."

"I need to speak with Bankole," Afolabi said.

"He's one of those who died, Ekon."

"Lucky for him. Who is still alive, then?"

"From the camp?"

"I don't mean from the Lagos red-light district. Think, Taiwo!"

"Sorry." The huge man looked as if he meant it. "There were thirty-five or forty men in camp. Subtract fifteen, you have—"

"For God's sake, don't start doing math," Afolabi

snapped. "Question all of them. They must remember something more about this shambles than a 'big white man.' Did he say anything? If so, was there an accent to his voice? Did he leave anything behind, aside from bodies? Can we find out who he was and where he came from?"

"I will ask them, Ekon."

"No. Send Pius to do it. I can't spare you here, with this shit going on."

The lie was intended to soothe his lieutenant's feelings, in case he worked out for himself that Pius was smarter, more adept at drawing the truth out of people without using brute force as a first resort. Pius would obtain the information Afolabi wanted and report it without stumbling over any bits, forgetting what was most important in the lot.

And once he had that information, *then* Afolabi could unleash Babatunde to do what he did best.

"It could have been the girl's father," Babatunde said, as if talking to himself.

"Too soft," Afolabi replied. "The only way he could kill fifteen men is by stealing their savings online and letting them starve."

"I mean, he could have hired someone," Babatunde explained.

Afolabi paused in the midst of his pacing and beard-tugging, just long enough to close his eyes and offer up a silent prayer for strength. He had no special god in mind, nor any hope of a response, but it relaxed him all the same.

"You may be onto something, Taiwo," Afolabi granted, having reached the same conclusion within seconds of discovering that Mandy Ross had been rescued. "We must look into that."

"It will be done," his chief lieutenant promised.

"I'll leave you to it, then," the MEND warlord replied dismissively.

As Babatunde lumbered from his office, Afolabi turned his mind to what had to follow in his campaign against K-Tech Petroleum. There was no question of receiving any ransom, now that Mandy Ross was free. He took for granted that there would be no chance to recapture her. The men in charge of K-Tech's corporate security would see to that, most likely flying her back to the States as soon as she was cleared for travel by a battery of high-priced doctors.

Afolabi had no fear of being charged with her abduction. First, State Security would have to catch him. Then they'd have to prove he was responsible for the kidnapping, which should be impossible. He'd never met the hostage, hadn't spoken to a soul from K-Tech Petroleum about the ransom and hadn't touched any of the letters sent demanding payment. Some of those whom Mandy Ross *had* seen were dead now, and the rest would soon be scattered to MEND's outposts in the hinterlands of Delta State.

But being free and clear of charges didn't satisfy him. Failing payment of the ransom he'd demanded, Afolabi craved revenge for the humiliation he had suffered at the hands of the anonymous "big white man."

Jared Ross might be beyond his reach, at least for now, but Afolabi wasn't giving up. He would find someone he could punish.

And his vengeance would be terrible.

Warri, Delta State

A LIMOUSINE WAS waiting when the Bell LongRanger settled gently down onto its helipad inside the K-Tech Petroleum compound. Bolan had thought of dropping Mandy Ross at Warri's airport, but he'd opted for her dad's home base in deference to its superior security.

"You've never met my father?" Mandy asked.

"We move in different circles," Bolan said.

"Well, sure, I guess so. But I thought, since you were hired to come and get me—"

"Wrong word," he interrupted. "I was asked to help you, if I could. There's no payday."

She fairly gaped at him. "You're kidding, right? You did all this for nothing?"

"Don't sell yourself short," Bolan said, and left it at that.

"Thanks, I think. But—"

"No buts," Bolan cut in. "We're square. Hit the deck."

Reluctantly she turned away from him, released her safety harness and climbed down onto the tarmac. By the time she'd turned to face the limo, men were piling out of it. The first half dozen were security, ex-soldiers by the look of them, with weapons bulging underneath their jackets. Mandy's father was the last out of the car, appearing older in the flesh than in the photographs Bolan had seen, but that was understandable.

Having your only child abducted by a gang of murderers could do that, adding gray hairs overnight—and worse, in some cases. All things considered, Jared Ross seemed to be bearing up all right. His face lit up at the sight of Mandy, and relief was leaving wet tracks on his cheeks as she ran into his embrace.

"You want to do the handshake bit?" Grimaldi asked him from the pilot's seat.

"I'll skip it," Bolan said. "The deal was that we get to use the helipad as needed, with no questions asked. They've also got a spare room waiting, when you're ready. Carte blanche at the cafeteria."

"Be still my heart," Grimaldi said, half smirking. "I'd say Daddy got himself a bargain."

"Someone else has got his markers," Bolan said. "We're just the go-to guys."

"As usual," Grimaldi answered. "Wouldn't it be nice to get an oil well for a Christmas present? Maybe just a little one?"

"And change tax brackets?" Bolan said. "No thanks."

In fact, he hadn't filed a tax return since he had died officially, back in Manhattan, several years ago. He also had no income, in the normal sense, but managed to collect enough in passing for his simple needs.

It was remarkable how generous a loan shark or a drug dealer could be when you negotiated in their native language: pure brute force.

Bolan watched Mandy Ross vanish into the limousine and wished her well. Her father lingered on the pavement for another moment, meeting Bolan's gaze through the LongRanger's tinted Plexiglas, and raised one hand in some kind of peculiar half salute before he turned away. Bolan sat still until the stretch had pulled away before unbuckling his safety rig.

"What now?" Grimaldi asked.

"You hit that cafeteria, or catch some shut-eye," Bolan said. "I need to see a man downtown."

"I don't mind riding shotgun," Grimaldi remarked.

"I wouldn't want to spook him," Bolan answered. "He's expecting one white face, not two."

"I kind of hoped that we were finished."

"We are," Bolan said. "I've got some solo work to do. Putting some frosting on the cake."

"Why do I get the feeling someone will be choking on it?" Grimaldi asked.

"Well, you've seen me cook before."

"Okay. But if the kitchen gets too hot…"

"You'll be among the first to know," Bolan replied.

Besides the borrowed wheels, he had a chance of clothes waiting, to trade-off with his sweaty, battle-stained fatigues. There should be time enough for him to shower, change and stow his hardware in the drab sedan K-Tech had furnished him, before he had to meet his contact.

As to what would happen after that, well, it was anybody's guess.

"THERE WAS SOME difficulty overnight, I understand," Huang Li Chan said. His voice was soft, but no one well acquainted with him would mistake it for a casual or friendly observation.

"Yes, sir," Lao Choy Teoh replied.

The two men sat with Chan's large desk between them, in his office on the top floor of a building owned by China National Petroleum, in downtown Warri. A glass of twenty-year-old Irish whiskey rested on the desk in front of Chan. None had been offered to his visitor.

"You may explain," Chan said.

As CNP's top man in Nigeria, Chan had no need to browbeat his subordinates. They recognized, to the last man and woman, his authority within the firm, and in the country. No Chinese except Beijing's ambassador in Lagos had authority to countermand Chan's orders. Anyone who tried was likely to be slated for a quick flight home and some "reeducation" on the precedence of duty to the state.

"Apparently the kidnapping of Jared Ross's daughter has been unexpectedly resolved," Teoh replied.

"How so?"

Chan had received his own report of the event, but he desired both confirmation from his chief lieutenant and more detailed explanation of the incident.

"Our friends at MEND report a raid against the camp where she was held. Some of their personnel were killed, the woman was extracted and pursuit proved fruitless. They are furious and crave retaliation, but confusion handicaps them at the moment."

"There is more?" Chan asked.

"Yes, sir. A helicopter bearing unknown passengers landed at K-Tech Petroleum's compound a few hours after the raid. It wasn't a corporate aircraft, yet it remains."

"And you find that significant?"

"The timing is…suggestive, sir. Of course, we don't know who the helicopter brought to visit Ross."

"You've run the registration number?"

The International Civil Aviation Organization, an agency of the United Nations, issued alphanumeric code numbers to aircraft for use in flight plans and maintained the standards for aircraft registration—"tail numbers" in common parlance—including the code numbers that identify an airplane or helicopter's country of registration. The ICAO's nearest regional office, serving West and Central Africa, was a short phone call away, in Dakar, Senegal.

"I have, sir," Teoh confirmed. "The 'J5' prefix indicates official registration in Guinea Bissau."

"What brings it here, then?" Chan wondered out loud.

"I'm afraid we don't know, sir."

"But can we find out? That's the question, eh, Lao?"

"As you say, sir."

Subservience had its limits. Although he enjoyed wielding power, beyond any question, Chan sometimes wished for aides who displayed more initiative than simple fawning obeisance.

"We once had eyes inside K-Tech Petroleum," Chan said.

"She was dismissed, as you recall, sir. Their security discovered her communications with our private operative."

"Yes, a nasty business."

"Thankfully resolved," Teoh added, "by her suicide."

If such it was. Chan had been raised from infancy to trust the state and to deny religion in all forms, but he wasn't inclined to question a convenient miracle. And if someone in his employ had helped the burned spy to decide that her life was intolerable, how was Chan to know?

"Make every effort to identify the latest visitors," he ordered. "Maintain tight surveillance on the K-Tech grounds and staff. Inform me instantly of any new and unfamiliar faces on the scene."

"Yes, sir."

"And while you see to that," Chan said, "I will attempt to pacify our Itsekiri friends."

THE WARRI headquarters for Uroil—with its home office in Yekaterinburg, on the eastern slope of the Ural Mountains—stood a mere two thousand yards from the office building owned by China National Petroleum. Its drab gray walls and modest logo gave nothing away to passersby.

"Bad news for the Chinese today, I take it," Arkady Eltsin said. "And their underlings, too."

"Unfortunately, not so bad for the Americans," Valentin Sidorov replied.

As an agent of Russia's Foreign Intelligence Service—known as the SVR—Sidorov answered first to Moscow, but his present orders placed him at Uroil's and Arkady Eltsin's disposal. Eltsin understood that his command of Sidorov had limits, and he hadn't tested them.

Not yet.

"The Ross girl," Eltsin said, nodding. "Who was it, do you think? The CIA?"

"I doubt it," Sidorov replied. "The quality of personnel available to them is scandalous, these days. So much of what they used to do is handled now by private military companies, it's doubtful they could manage any kind of paramilitary operation. Or that they would risk it, in the present climate."

Eltsin knew what that meant, as would anyone who'd watched the great United States in recent years. After declaring "war on terror," Washington had botched the liberation of two nations from Islamic dictators, had let bin Laden slip away despite repeated vows to punish those responsible for 9/11 and had alienated most of its long-time allies in the process. The CIA, while given carte blanche to abduct and abuse suspected terrorists in the guise of "extraordinary rendition," was kept on an increasingly short leash in other spheres.

"Remember Cuba?" Eltsin asked, then snorted. "No, of course you don't. You weren't born yet, for God's sake!"

"I'm familiar with the history," Sidorov replied.

"I was going to say that Langley couldn't manage a new Bay of Pigs nowadays, but forget it. Who do you suspect?"

"No one yet. Without more information, I'd only be guessing."

"So guess," Eltsin urged. "We're all friends here, supposedly. Let your hair down for a change."

That was funny, considering Sidorov's buzz cut that left his scalp shining through stubble, but Eltsin refrained from laughing at his own bon mot.

"All right, if you insist. One of the private firms, most likely. There were nineteen in America, at last count, half a dozen in the U.K., and at least one each from Australia, Japan, Norway and South Africa. Take your pick from Raytheon, Gray Talon, Omega or any of the rest."

"That doesn't exactly narrow it down," Eltsin chided.

"How can I? If the individuals responsible could be identified…"

"It would accomplish nothing, I suppose, to ask our Ijaw comrades?"

"I'm told the girl was rescued by a white man," Sidorov

replied. "The Ijaw would not hire one, even if they could afford the going rate for such an operation. And why would they wish to help K-Tech Petroleum?"

"To vex the Itsekiri, I should think," Eltsin replied.

Sidorov frowned, considered it and shook his head.

"No. They might raid the camp themselves and steal the girl, then ask for ransom on their own behalf. But as it is, they hate white foreigners as much as Afolabi's people do."

"They don't hate *us*," Eltsin reminded him.

"You think not? Dam the flow of money to their war chest, and find out how loyal they are to Mother Russia."

"You're a cynic, Valentin."

"A realistic judge of human nature," Sidorov said, correcting him.

"You think they're human, then? I'm not so sure," Eltsin said.

"They'll surprise you, one day, when you least expect it," Sidorov replied. "It won't be pretty."

"Perhaps, when we have pumped their country dry," Eltsin returned. "Not as long as they're in love with money and have something left to sell."

"I'll reach out to Ajani and Jumoke," Sidorov told Eltsin. "There's a chance that we can stir the pot a bit, after this incident."

"And see what floats up to the top," Eltsin replied. "Vodka, before you go?"

"WHY AREN'T YOU coming with me?" Mandy Ross demanded, staring down her father with a measure of intensity he'd thought impossible for one so pampered.

"Hon," he said, "we've been all over this. You know the answer. This is where I work. I have to be here."

"No, you don't!" Mandy insisted. "Let somebody else come in and man the shooting gallery. Somebody—"

"Younger?" he anticipated her, half smiling.

"Older," she replied. "Someone who's finished living anyway, and doesn't have a family. Someone who won't mind being shot or blown to pieces by a pack of murderers."

"I can't just cut and run," Ross said.

"Oh, wait—I know this one. Because it isn't manly, right? I've got a news flash for you, Dad. Even Dirty Harry knew when to quit. A man should know his limitations."

That made him bristle. "Are you saying I've reached mine?"

"That's right!" she said. "For this place, here and now, I am. There's nothing in this country worth your life. The money doesn't matter."

"You say that because you've always had it," he replied.

"I've always had you, too. Ask me which one I'd rather do without."

"Mandy, this trouble should be settled soon."

"Oh, sure. And it's been going on how long, now? Since the sixties? We learn history at Vassar, Dad. I've learned that nothing ever changes for the better here."

"It may surprise you."

"With your funeral?"

Ross felt his irritation slipping over into anger.

"That's enough!" he snapped. "You're on the jet in one hour and out of here, even if Clint has to hog-tie you. Got it?"

"Right, then." He couldn't tell if her eyes were glassy with anger or brimming with tears. "Will you at least send Cooper with me?"

"Who?"

"Matt Cooper. Jesus, Dad! The man who saved my life? Does any of this ring a bell?"

"Sorry," he said. "We weren't exactly introduced."

"Whatever. Can he drive me to the airport?"

"Sorry, no. He's gone already," Ross told her, fudging

it, unsure if that was literally true or not. "His job's not done, apparently."

"Apparently? As if you didn't know."

"He doesn't work for me, Princess."

"I see. He does a good deed every day, and this time he just happened to select Nigeria. Makes perfect sense."

"He was referred to us, all right? By whom, I couldn't say. That kind of thing is need-to-know, and it appears I don't."

"I swear, Dad, sometimes—"

"If you plan on packing anything, you need to start right now," he warned. "One hour till your flight. Tick, tock."

She turned and fairly stormed out of the office, which was bad, in terms of parent-child relations, but a bonus if it got her moving without any further argument. When she was gone, he buzzed Clint Hamer in.

"All ready, boss?" asked K-Tech's top security consultant in Nigeria.

"We're getting there. You know the drill, right?"

"Absolutely. Straight out to the airport, wait until she's airborne, then straight back."

"And anyone who tries to stop you on the way—"

"Will wish he hadn't, while he's bleeding out," Hamer replied.

"Sounds fair to me," Jared Ross said.

BOLAN HAD half expected that the loaner car would be a classic from Detroit, but K-Tech had surprised him. He supposed it stood to reason, after all. When they were pumping oil from five continents, why would the corporate brass care whose engine burned the fuel and spewed its waste into the atmosphere?

So, he was looking at a reasonably new and clean Toyota Yaris, four doors and a hatchback, in some kind of silver-gray shade that he thought should be unobtrusive in traffic. It wouldn't be the fastest car on the road, or much good for ramming, but Bolan wasn't planning to enter a NASCAR event.

He needed wheels for pure mobility, and possibly to help him stay alive. If the loaner should be damaged in the process, he'd find some way to replace it.

That was life.

Grimaldi, having taken his advice, wasn't around when Bolan stored most of his hardware in the trunk. A baggy shirt, unbuttoned and untucked, hid the Beretta 93-R in a fast-draw shoulder rig, with spare mags pouched under his right arm. And just to be on the safe side, he held back a couple of Russian-made RGO-78 frag grenades—the "defensive" model, with ball bearings packed around eighty-five grams of TNT, with an effective killing radius of twenty yards.

Bolan was hoping that he wouldn't need the pistol or grenades for his preliminary meeting with Obinna Umaru, but he knew that banking on a free ride was the quickest way to wind up lying in a gutter or a shallow grave. He would hope for the best, and prepare for the worst.

He had a map of Warri and an hour to kill before their scheduled meeting at a marketplace on the city's north side. Bolan decided to spend the time touring his new battleground, and checking for tails in the process.

But first, he wanted to check out the car.

No matter where you went, on every continent, auto theft was a problem. Millions of company cars came with LoJack technology or its equivalent, GPS systems that let the home office keep track of all wheels on the road, for whatever reason. Bolan had no reason to believe that Jared Ross would shadow him, but it was best for all concerned—and Bolan, in particular—if his movements in Warri went unobserved.

Once he was safely off the K-Tech lot, Bolan found a place to park and went to work. He used a simple scanner, the size of a cigarette pack, tuned to the standard LoJack frequency of 173.075 megahertz and found the transceiver hidden underneath the padded liner in the trunk. He took it out, pitched it into a nearby vacant lot strewed with rubbish, and then performed a second scan of the Toyota, running through assorted other frequencies that might betray a second homing device.

His ride was clean.

Now all he had to do was to pass the time until his rendezvous, ensuring that he wasn't followed from the K-Tech property by either friend or foe.

For in the present situation, either one could get him killed.

CHAPTER SIX

Obinna Umaru was worried. He was early for his meeting with the stranger from America, and while he had taken every precaution en route from his home, he still couldn't escape a sense that he was being watched.

Perhaps, at last, he was becoming truly paranoid.

It would be no surprise, considering the secret life he had selected for himself. At twenty-three, Umaru supplemented his moderate income from computer data analysis with covert paychecks from Nigeria's National Intelligence Agency, the State Security Service, the National Drug Law Enforcement Agency—and yes, the American CIA.

That last addition to his list of moonlighting engagements had given Umaru pause, forced him to consider that he might somehow be a traitor to his homeland, but he had finally decided that the rate of crime and terrorism in Nigeria had grown beyond all reason. Anything that he could do to make a difference would be worthwhile, even if it meant working with a group of foreigners.

And if he made some money in the process, why, so be it.

Umaru wasn't an idealist, nor was he deluded. He understood that the CIA worked first for American interests, and only thereafter considered the needs of other nations. But Yankee interests were generally served by suppressing violent crime, and Umaru had cause to believe that America's competitors for oil and other natural resources in Nigeria—specifically, the Russians and Chinese—each played a role in the perpetuation of endemic mayhem nationwide.

So he would serve whoever served his country best, within the limits of his understanding and ability.

And he would try not to be murdered in the process.

To that end, Umaru had armed himself with a folding knife and a black-market pistol. It was a Chinese QSZ-92 semiautomatic, exported for foreign sale as the NP-42. Chambered in 9 mm, it weighed 1.7 pounds with its 15-round magazine loaded, and the double-action trigger allowed Umaru to draw and fire without first cocking the hammer.

Umaru had practiced with the pistol until he felt confident that he could draw and hit a man-size target, provided, of course, that the target stood still and didn't return fire. As for living men with guns, trying to kill him, well, Umaru hoped that he would never have to test himself.

The marketplace was crowded, the perfect place to lose yourself. But by the same token, it made spotting a tail more difficult. Each time Umaru glanced around, he found a different pair of eyes appearing to examine him. Was one of them a spy, sent to observe him, or was he a victim of his own imagination?

Even though he took precautions to avoid surveillance every day, Umaru realized that he could have betrayed himself a thousand times since he became a paid informant of the state. Aside from being seen with one or another of his handlers, there was a chance of leaks from any of the agencies he served. Worse yet, some of the groups were bitter rivals. If one learned that he was talking to the competition, even in a common cause, might he be sacrificed as punishment?

It was conceivable, but in the absence of compelling evidence, Umaru chose to be a cautious optimist. And, in his cautious mode, he chose to triple-check the warning signs of possible surveillance.

Was he seeing the same faces on his trail, day after day? Had there been any indication that his flat was penetrated, searched by experts? Had his car been tampered with, as far as he could tell?

When he had answered all those questions in the negative, Umaru should have felt relieved. But he didn't. The nagging sense of someone staring at him, breathing down his neck, simply wouldn't evaporate.

Another test, then.

Picking up his pace, he chose a shop at random, turned in off the sidewalk, ducked inside and found a hiding place among the racks of hanging clothes. A salesclerk watched him but didn't seem terribly surprised, as if such actions were routine.

If no one followed him within the next few moments, would it prove—

A slender man with stubble on his sunken cheeks entered the shop, jaundiced eyes sweeping the place without appearing to notice the merchandise. Seeming angry, he turned to the clerk.

"A man came in here," he declared. "Did you see—"

The clerk's eyes had already betrayed Umaru. His pursuer was turning when Umaru struck, lunging out of the racks with his pistol drawn, slamming its butt hard against the man's nose. He went down with a grunt, crimson spurting, while Umaru broke toward the street.

And realized his grave mistake just as he reached the

sidewalk, with a sudden stirring in the crush of bodies to his left.

He should have used the back door.

Too late to make amends, he turned and ran.

KELSEY DANJUMA knew something was wrong when the target came barreling out of the small shop where Sani Fulani had trailed him. He broke to the west, running hard through the crowd and—could that be a gun in his hand?

"He's running!" Danjuma snapped into a tiny microphone clipped onto his lapel. A squawk of recognition issued from the single earpiece as he added, "May be armed. I'll check on Sani."

That required only a moment as Danjuma rushed across the road and barged into the shop. Fulani was struggling to rise from the floor, flinging blood from his scalp with each shake of his head, while the salesclerk circled around him and yelled complaints.

"What happened?" Danjuma asked his point man, as if the answer wasn't obvious.

"He hid and jumped me," Fulani said with a bitter curse. "A lucky punch."

Danjuma leaned in close and rasped, "Lucky for you that I don't kill you here and now."

He turned and left the shop without waiting to see if Fulani would collect himself and follow. Danjuma's target was in flight, might be escaping even now, and there'd be hell to pay if that happened.

The job had sounded simple when he got his orders. Take a team of men and follow a man called Obinna Umaru, suspected of working against MEND's best interests. See where he went and who he spoke to. Try to find out if he was connected to some public agency.

And if proof positive was found—kill him.

In fact, Danjuma had planned to liquidate Umaru, no matter what he learned about the man. If his superiors had doubts about this stranger, that was tantamount to a death sentence in Danjuma's mind. One more Nigerian wouldn't be missed, particularly not in Warri, where the price of human life had hit rock bottom years ago.

Danjuma could no longer see Umaru as he left the shop, but voices in his ear told him the runner was continuing along a westward path across the marketplace. That meant he was running away from his car, and would have to turn back if he planned to collect the Volkswagen.

"Aliko!"

It required a moment for Aliko Ndebe to answer. His "Yes, I hear you" sounded breathless from running.

"Get back to his car and stay there," Danjuma said, "in case we lose him."

"But—"

"No buts! Do it now!"

"Yes. Okay."

Danjuma didn't doubt that he would be obeyed, no matter how reluctantly. His word was law on missions where he called the shots, and anyone who challenged him was marked for sudden death. He'd only had to pull the trigger once, to make that lesson stick.

The voices of his other soldiers, five in all, allowed Danjuma to follow the runner's progress without seeing him, tracking Umaru on a mental map of the large market-place. Danjuma issued orders that should send his men to intercept the fleeing target. If they failed…

Sani Fulani overtook him in the crush, holding one hand against his head to stanch the flow of blood. His other hand was underneath his floppy shirt, clutching the pistol tucked into his belt.

"I want that bastard!" Fulani growled. "He's mine!"

"No one cares what you want," Danjuma said. "Mind your manners and remember who's in charge here, or the shooting starts with you."

Fulani shot a glare at him, then ducked his head and muttered, "As you say."

"Now, follow me, before he gets away."

Danjuma knew that his masters suspected Umaru of some betrayal, but beyond that, he knew no details. Surely the subject's behavior was clear evidence of his guilt—but what guilt? Did it even matter?

Umaru, by his own actions, condemned himself. Danjuma knew that he wouldn't be criticized for acting swiftly and decisively to make the problem go away.

But he would have to catch Umaru first.

And even God couldn't protect him from the wrath of Ekon Afolabi if he let the runner get away.

DRIVING IN WARRI was a pain, but no more so than any other crowded African city Bolan had been called upon to navigate during his travels. In a foreign country, you adapted to the local customs, tried your best to fit in with the locals, and if that meant driving like a maniac whose doctor has proclaimed that he has fifteen minutes left to live, so be it.

Bolan had no idea what laws applied to drivers and pedestrians in Warri, or Nigeria at large, but social Darwinism seemed to be the rule most commonly observed. Survival of the fittest—or the fastest—kept cars swerving while their horns blared, leaving those on foot to duck and dodge as if their lives depended on it.

Which, it seemed, they actually did.

Bolan was now in the spirit of the game, not quite enjoying it, but merging with the rush of northbound traffic that would take him to his destination. He was ahead of schedule, knowing that he'd have to find a parking lot with some kind of security in place, before he left the loaner to explore the marketplace on foot.

Whatever happened after that would happen in its own good time.

Working with locals had advantages and drawbacks. Bolan trusted Hal Brognola to vet his contacts, but he knew that there was only so much Stony Man could learn about a stranger living half a world away. They took referrals, checked out anything that could be checked, and left the rest to Bolan's instincts. So far, he'd been lucky—luckier, in fact, than some of those who'd signed on to assist him in his foreign wars—but that could change at any time.

No startling revelation there.

He'd judge Umaru as he judged anyone else—by his appearance and demeanor, by his words and conduct. If there came a time when Bolan thought Umaru had betrayed him or was planning to, he'd take the necessary steps to cancel out that threat.

According to his map of Warri, Bolan had three-quarters of a mile to go before he reached the marketplace. His brain was registering landmarks, even as he watched the motorists, pedestrians, goats and stray dogs that made urban driving an adventure best pursued by those with nerves of steel. At Bolan's present speed, he ought to reach his goal within the next five minutes max.

Which meant that it was time to start looking for a parking lot.

He wanted something fenced or otherwise contained, with watchmen on the premises, where he could leave the car and keep the keys. Assuming that his options would be limited, he started looking early, allowing time to walk the final distance, if it came to that.

There was nothing on the south side of his destination,

so Bolan kept driving, circling the huge marketplace. The crowd was dense, but Bolan knew that he was bound to generate a fair amount of curiosity once he had plunged into that crush on foot.

He made a mental note to find some other way of meeting local contacts in the future, if and when he worked in regions where his race might be an issue. White faces were a common sight in Warri, granted, but the locals mainly saw them going in and out of downtown offices, hotels and government facilities. Outside that sphere of influence, they were as rare as the proverbial hen's teeth.

A tall sign for a public parking lot caught Bolan's eye, and he was cruising toward it when a gunshot echoed through the marketplace. He had been driving with his windows shut, the A/C on, but now he cracked a window on the shotgun side and waited.

There! More shots from somewhere to his right.

And coming closer, by their sound.

Instinctively his hand found the Beretta slung beneath his left armpit, prepared to fire in self-defense whether the danger was related to his current job or not, but something stopped him short of drawing it.

A running man.

More to the point, a running man he recognized from photos he had viewed at Stony Man.

Obinna Umaru, running for his life.

UMARU WASN'T SURE where he was going, only that if he stood still too long and tried to catch his breath, he would stop breathing altogether. He'd lost count of how many armed strangers were chasing him now, but the first gunshot told him they had no great interest in taking him alive.

After his confrontation with the unknown gunman in the shop, Umaru had concealed his pistol once again, trying his best to pass unnoticed through the market crowd. It did no good, however, and he quickly realized that several men were tracking him.

But for how long?

Umaru had been doubly careful about tails, going to meet the stranger he knew only as Matt Cooper. That, and white skin, were all Umaru had to help him recognize his contact, and it now appeared that someone was ahead of him.

If he hadn't been followed to the market, it could only mean that someone with foreknowledge of his meeting had betrayed him. That thought frightened Umaru almost as much as the men with guns, who seemed intent on killing him right then and there.

Because, if he eluded them, who could he trust?

Which of the several agencies he served had sprung a deadly leak? If he was known as an informer, how long would it be until a bullet to the head obliterated consciousness forever? If he escaped the marketplace, could he go home?

Not likely. But he had to face his problems one by one, in order of priority.

The first shot, he supposed now, might have been a signal from one hunter to the others, but the next two clearly had been meant for him. Umaru thought they came from different directions, based on the spray of blood from two wounded bystanders, and the way their bodies fell to left and right.

Umaru ducked his head and ran once more, drawing his pistol as he fled. There was no hope of being inconspicuous under the present circumstances. He could run, and sell his life as dearly as he could if there was no way out.

With one round in the QSZ-92's chamber, he could fire sixteen shots without reloading. Umaru knew it was important to keep track of such things in a combat situation, but his brain threatened to vapor-lock at any moment, leaving him bereft of common sense.

He ducked and dodged around the market stalls, jostling strangers on all sides, receiving shoves and curses in return for his rudeness. But fewer blocked his path once they had seen Umaru's gun and heard the others firing at him from the crowd. At least it seemed that he would have a relatively clear path to his own death, when it came.

Most likely, sometime in the next few moments.

Out of nowhere, some part of his agitated mind wondered what would become of Cooper, the intruding stranger, once he had been slain. Would the white man arrange some other contact? Would he continue on alone?

Or was he even still alive?

Had the men who stalked Umaru now procured his name and whereabouts from Cooper? Perhaps under torture? Having netted and killed the big fish, were they cleaning up small-fry?

Umaru couldn't rule it out, but in the last analysis it made no difference. Whoever meant to harm him, for whatever reason, it would all be academic if they killed him on the spot. Dead men had no worries, unless they believed in Hell.

Umaru, for his part, didn't believe.

He thought that daily life, for many of his fellow countrymen, was worse than anything a god or demon could devise as punishment for so-called sins.

Umaru jettisoned all speculation from his mind as he discovered that he was about to lose his cover. Fleeing, he had cut across the southwest corner of the marketplace and would emerge from it entirely sometime in the next few seconds.

Or should he turn back and chart another course, running in circles, using strangers whom he passed as human shields, until he had a clear shot at his enemies? Would that prolong his life? And was it worth the cost to others?

While no great humanitarian in his own eyes, Umaru didn't fancy wallowing in someone else's blood to save himself.

Unless, of course, it was the blood of enemies.

He reached the border of the marketplace, ducking another gunshot, and was on the verge of stepping into traffic when a car stopped short in front of him, blocking his path.

Its driver told him, "I'm Cooper. Could you use a lift?"

"No, thank you," Umaru said. "But I badly need a ride."

KELSEY DANJUMA cursed, watching his target run around a silver-gray Toyota and get in on the passenger's side. The car sped off, bearing the man he was supposed to kill, leaving Danjuma no recourse beyond a hasty parting shot that missed its mark.

He spun in a demented circle where he stood, shouting into his tiny microphone, making a spectacle for those who simply saw a stranger, gun in hand, enraged and talking to himself.

"Cars! We need cars *now!* The bastard's off on wheels!"

Amos Buhari's voice crackled inside one ear, saying, "I'm in the car. Where are you!"

"West side of the market! Hurry!"

"On my way."

Sani Fulani arrived then, panting from his run, the right side of his face a scabrous mass of drying blood. He seemed to be on the verge of chastising Danjuma, then thought better of it and settled for cursing the strangers around him.

Feeling his own anger reach and pass its boiling point, Danjuma snarled into his microphone, "Amos! Where are you?"

"Here," the voice inside his ear said as a car screeched

to a halt in front of him. Buhari had another soldier with him, in the backseat, leaving room for Danjuma up front and Fulani in back.

"After them!" Danjuma barked.

"Where are they?" his driver demanded.

"Goddamn it! That way" He stabbed a finger toward the spot where Umaru had vanished in traffic. "A silver Toyota! Get after them."

Buhari did as he was told, accelerating in pursuit of a vehicle he hadn't glimpsed and couldn't see now. As they shot forward, Danjuma was back on the air, directing his scattered soldiers to find their cars and fall in behind him as soon as they could.

"Umaru drives an old Honda," Buhari said, keeping his eyes fixed on the road and dodging traffic like a pro. "It's sitting where he left it when he reached the market."

"So we're after someone else," Danjuma answered. "Someone who was waiting for him."

"Ah. The man he was supposed to meet?"

"I didn't see the bloody shitter, did I?"

"How should I know?"

"I just *told* you. Now— Wait! That's it!"

He pointed to a gray or silver car, running a block ahead of them. It seemed right, but—

"You said Toyota," Buhari reminded him. "That's a Datsun."

"Shit! They all look alike!"

"So, do we give up now?"

Danjuma turned on him. "And tell Ekon what? That we lost him?"

"It's true," Buhari said.

Fulani, behind them, was cursing a blue streak until Danjuma spun and snapped at him, "Shut up and clean your face! You look like death warmed up."

"It won't be *my* death when—"

"Won't it?" Danjuma raged, thrusting his pistol toward Fulani. "I say shut your mouth, and you're still talking. Why not kill you?"

"Kelsey, I apologize," Fulani said. Not really meaning it, but frightened now, at last.

As he should be, Danjuma thought. As we should all be, if we can't find Umaru and whoever took him away.

"Silver Toyota," Amos Buhari said, as if answering a prayer. "Looks like a Yaris four-door."

"I don't know the model," Danjuma said. "Catch up to it, and we'll see if it's Umaru."

More tense moments passed as they drew closer to the silver car, gaining despite the traffic all around them. Now Danjuma saw two silhouettes in the Toyota. Likely men, based on their size and shape, but still no faces visible.

"Closer!"

"I'm trying," Buhari said.

"Don't try. Do it!"

He ignored the driver's muttered curse to check in with his other soldiers. They were following in two cars now, but well behind Danjuma's vehicle and out of sight. He issued terse directions, craning forward in his seat as Buhari passed one intervening car and then another.

Almost there.

CHAPTER SEVEN

"I get the lift thing," Bolan told his passenger. "An elevator, right?"

"You are correct," the winded runner said, turning to stare behind them, toward the marketplace.

"And you, I hope, are Obinna Umaru."

"If I'm not," Umaru said, forcing a smile, "then you have made a great mistake."

"I didn't plan on starting out this way," Bolan said.

"Nor did I. I may have lost my car back there," Umaru said.

"Meaning they've burned you? In which case, you also can't go home."

Instead of cursing, Umaru expelled a weary sigh and slumped into his seat—but half turned sideways, facing Bolan at the steering wheel, and glancing frequently back toward their rear.

"I took precautions," he insisted. "Two full hours getting to the market, and I saw no one behind me, anywhere."

"Which either means they're good at what they do, or else they knew where you were going."

"That has worried me," Umaru said. "If I have been

betrayed, my life is finished here. And yours, as well, before you've even gotten started."

"Put a hold on the depression, will you?" Bolan said. "They haven't caught us yet. And if they do, they may be in for a surprise."

Umaru looked back once again and stiffened. "They are coming, Mr. Cooper," he declared.

"Try 'Matt' for size," Bolan replied as he confirmed the speeding chase car in his rearview mirror. "Are you packing?"

Umaru blinked at him, confused, then answered, "Ah. You're asking if I have a weapon?"

"Right."

"Yes, I do."

Umaru drew a semiauto pistol from beneath his baggy shirt, but kept it pointed at the floorboard, with his index finger well outside the trigger guard. It was a hopeful sign, suggesting competence.

"Chinese," Bolan observed. "You see a lot of that, I guess, these days."

"Chinese, Russian, American, Korean, British—take your pick," Umaru said. "We're blessed with many weapons in Nigeria."

"I take it that you've handled some before."

"When I was younger," Umaru said, "I spent two years in the army."

"See much action?" Bolan asked.

"More than I cared to. But I don't swoon at the sight of blood."

"That's good to know, because you may be seeing some."

"I hope it's not my own," Umaru said, forcing a nervous little laugh that came out sounding like a cough.

Bolan gunned the Toyota, abandoning the final remnants of restraint in driving, but the chase car kept advancing. It had more under the hood than Bolan's ride, and the still-faceless strangers inside it were hell-bent on bagging Umaru.

On bagging *both* of them, now.

Bolan had made a snap decision at the market, based in equal parts on mercy and self-interest. If the odds had gone against him, he might now be saddled with a stranger, stalked by gunmen for some reason totally divorced from Bolan's mission. As it was, he'd found the right man unexpectedly, but now he'd likely have to fight to keep him.

And to stay alive himself, assuming that he couldn't lose the tail they had acquired.

"We've got two choices," Bolan told Umaru. "We can keep running like this and hope we shake them, or we need a place to stand and fight, without civilians in the way."

"There are too many of them," Umaru said.

"I count four, unless they've got some dwarfs in the backseat."

"At the market, there were more. I'm sure of it."

"Maybe the hasty exit left some of them stranded. Anyway, we play the hand we're dealt. So, if I can't ditch them, where are we going?"

Even with his map of Warri and his brief sightseeing tour, Bolan didn't know the city as a local would. He couldn't guess which neighborhoods were relatively posh and which were urban combat zones. He didn't know which streets were mobbed by shoppers in the daytime, versus those that only came to life at night.

And if he tried to pick a killing ground by guesswork— or was forced to fight on unfamiliar ground, before he was prepared—the death toll could extend to innocents.

"Please lose them, if you can," Umaru said. "But failing that, I know a place."

"WHERE DOES the damned fool think he's going?" Kelsey Danjuma demanded.

Amos Buhari, still speeding to catch the Toyota, replied, "I don't know."

"What?"

"I said—"

"I heard you, Amos. How would you know where he's going?"

"You asked—"

"I was talking to myself, for God's sake!"

"How am I to know that, Kelsey?"

"Will you catch the car, for God's sake, and stop playing games with me?"

Buhari didn't answer, which saved Danjuma from the risky task of pistol-whipping him as they sped through city traffic.

Anyway, he couldn't blame Amos, since he *had* voiced the stupid rhetorical question. Obinna Umaru's escape had unhinged him, but Danjuma was determined to assert control and salvage what he could from the chaotic situation.

Starting now.

They were gaining on Umaru and his unknown rescuer, despite the other vehicles that shared the street, in spite of suicidal jaywalkers and cyclists. In a few more moments— if Buhari closed the gap a little more and they weren't distracted by police—Danjuma would be close enough to risk a pistol shot.

It would be risky, in such traffic, but Danjuma cared nothing for innocent bystanders. They were simply obstacles to be dodged or eliminated, whichever method was the most convenient for himself. It wouldn't be the first time he had killed or wounded strangers while attempting to eliminate an enemy.

Nor would it be the last.

And they were almost close enough.

Danjuma's weapon was a Walther P-5 pistol, like the ones issued to officers and noncoms in the Nigerian army. In fact, it had been stolen from a military shipment eighteen months ago, by MEND members from the Itsekiri tribe. Its magazine held only eight 9 mm rounds, but half a dozen spares resided in Danjuma's pockets.

He could spare a few shots now to stop his enemies and finish them once and for all.

Closer.

When only one vehicle blocked his shot, Danjuma cranked down his window and felt the rush of hot air in his face. Clutching the Walther in his right hand, he was ready when Buhari made his move, swerving around the final obstacle and racing forward, giving him the shot.

Danjuma took it, leaning from his open window as he quickly aimed and fired.

UMARU SAW the muzzle-flash and flinched from it instinctively, embarrassing himself. Matt Cooper registered the shot but didn't seem to notice Umaru's reaction, busy as he was negotiating traffic and watching his rearview mirror.

"Shall I try to shoot them?" Umaru asked.

"Not yet," Bolan answered. "Point me toward that place you know, in case we have to stop and take them out."

Not stop and fight, Umaru noticed, wondering if Cooper truly had such confidence in his ability to triumph when outnumbered four-to-one. That thought was barely formed when he corrected it, acknowledging his own role in whatever happened next, and scaling back the odds.

They *might* survive a fight at two-to-one, but he was worried that the other unknown gunmen who had stalked him through the marketplace might join in the pursuit, catch up in time to weight the odds more heavily against Umaru and the grim American.

A second gunshot echoed from the chase car, and this time the bullet found its mark. Umaru heard it strike the rear of the Toyota and cursed himself as he recoiled once more.

"It's natural," Bolan advised him, still without a side-long glance. "The day you give up ducking bullets, you're as good as dead."

"They've marked your car," Umaru said unnecessarily.

"Not mine," Bolan replied. "It's out on loan."

"Still, if it's seen by the police—"

"Let's think about survival first, before the body shop. Ready to tell me where we're going?"

"Yes, of course. I'm sorry."

"Wasting time," Bolan said.

"Right."

Umaru sketched their route as calmly and succinctly as he could, while flinching at the sounds of gunfire from behind them. One shot ricocheted from the Toyota's window trim, while two more missed the car and frightened other drivers into swerving out of Bolan's way.

"Left at the next light," Umaru said, smothering an urge to point that might betray them, if the shooter in the chase car saw his gesture.

"Left it is," Bolan affirmed, but seemed to wait until the final instant before cranking on the steering wheel.

Centrifugal force shoved Umaru against the passenger's door, bracing his free hand against the dashboard while tires squealed. He turned in time to see the chase car make the turn, falling a little farther back, but still not lost.

"Three blocks, then turn right," he advised Bolan.

"Got it. And what's our destination?"

"In America, it would be called the red-light district. There are brothels, taverns, other things. Rarely patrolled by the police in daylight."

"Not much action at the moment, then?" Bolan asked.

"I expect that most of those who work there are asleep. The real action won't start until—"

Another car came out of nowhere, charging from a side street to sideswipe Bolan's Toyota. He seemed to glimpse it just before the hit, adjusting to absorb the shock, but it still slowed them. They nearly missed their right-hand turn, and in that moment Obinna Umaru thought that he might die.

He knew immediately that the hit wasn't an accident. Umaru saw the other driver's scowling face, and while he didn't recognize it, any fool could see the rage and malice that distorted it.

The hostile reinforcements had arrived.

"Hang on!" Bolan said as he took them through the turn, still banging fenders with the crash car, plainly hoping it would crash.

Umaru did his part. Thrusting his pistol through his open window, he fired twice into the snarling face and saw it instantly awash with blood.

"HE'S SHOT Rashidi!"

Even as he blurted the obvious, Amos Buhari fought to make the coming right-hand turn at speed. It meant swerving around the car Rashidi Ibru had been driving seconds earlier, when he collided with the fugitive Toyota, then apparently received a bullet for his trouble.

As they made the squealing turn, Kelsey Danjuma saw his other soldiers in the stalled car grappling to expel Ibru from the driver's seat. Perhaps they could rejoin the chase and help Danjuma win it. If they failed, at least they'd have a chance to flee on foot before police arrived.

"Don't stop!" he warned Buhari, just in case fleeting concern for clumsy comrades might have swayed him, but Danjuma's driver showed no signs of slowing. In fact, he was accelerating once again, regaining ground lost during the distraction.

"Still not crippled," Buhari said as he sped after the silver-gray Toyota. "Try shooting the tires!"

"Just catch them, will you? I know when and where to shoot."

Except he wasn't doing very well, so far. He'd wasted half a dozen of his first eight rounds, with only two hits on the target vehicle, and neither one of them significant. And while he *had* fired at the tires, Danjuma knew the only one he might have hit would be a spare tire in the trunk.

Disgusted with himself and those assigned to serve him on this bungled hunt, Danjuma fought an urge to scream and empty his weapon in rapid-fire, knowing the shots would be wasted.

And after all that had happened, after he had seen Ibru killed or gravely wounded, Danjuma knew that he wasn't simply pursuing a target.

Not anymore.

He was locked in a struggle where death lay in wait for one side or the other—and maybe for both.

That prospect made Danjuma agitated, but it didn't frighten him, per se. He was a fatalist, believing that all people lived on borrowed time, and while some timid souls strove constantly to hoard their dwindling days, Danjuma avidly pursued Life, clutched it by the throat and squeezed it dry.

If it was time for Death to clutch his throat, in turn, so be it. He would charge and fight until the bitter end.

"I think they're heading for Ughelli," Buhari said, naming the Warri suburb that Danjuma often visited at night.

"They're early for the floor shows," he remarked, wondering exactly what his quarry had in mind.

"But not the street show," Buhari said, grinning fiercely now. "The traffic will be light and we can—"

"Drive, don't talk!" Danjuma snapped. "There's time enough to gloat when we are standing in his blood."

He fired another shot at the Toyota, just for emphasis, and cursed his shaky aim as it went wild.

"WE'RE ALMOST there," Umaru said.

Watching the chase car rush to close with him, Bolan replied, "And where is there, again?"

"Ughelli, which I spoke of," Umaru said. "Only three or four more blocks."

A bullet struck the car's rear window and shattered it. Backseat awash in pebbled safety glass, sitting with shoulders hunched, Bolan managed to squeeze a few more miles per hour out of the Toyota, but he couldn't shake the hunters now.

They were too close, intoxicated by the scent of blood.

Another block, and with the chase car nearly on his bumper, Bolan glimpsed the other back in action, racing to catch up. He'd seen Umaru shoot the driver, reckoned that the guy was either dead or comatose by now, but his companions had recovered from their shock and were back in the game.

Call it seven-to-one, at a glance, and Bolan knew he couldn't let the chase cars box him in. Whatever move he made, it had to be on his terms.

And he had to make it soon.

"Hang on. Be ready," he advised Umaru, giving his companion all of two whole seconds to prepare himself, without explaining what he had in mind.

Which was an old-fashioned bootlegger's turn, requiring split-second coordination of the brake and the accelerator, firm hands on the wheel and a machine that wouldn't roll too easily. The net result was a tire-torturing 180-degree reversal, leaving Bolan and Umaru facing back the way they'd come, with two cars full of gunmen hurtling to meet them.

Umaru didn't ask what was required of him once the Toyota came to rest. Bolan palmed his Beretta left-handed, triggering 3-round bursts at the lead car, while Umaru fired right-handed toward the crash car from their recent close encounter.

Bolan saw his rounds strike home, stitching a spiderweb pattern across the first vehicle's windshield before it imploded, filling the startled driver's lap with broken glass and blood gushing out of a throat wound. When the wheelman raised his hands, a vain attempt to stanch the flow, he gave up trying to control his car but kept his foot on the accelerator.

Bolan winced at the near-miss, but fired another three rounds at the other vehicle in passing, taking out the driver's rear window. He saw someone slump behind it, but the car was there and gone too quickly for him to confirm a second kill.

To his right, the other speeding car had veered off course, as well, but it was spitting bullets as it passed, stitching Umaru's side of the Toyota with a deadly rain. Umaru ducked, then spun toward Bolan.

"Are we going now?" he asked.

Bolan already had his door open and one foot on the pavement as he answered, "We aren't finished yet."

KELSEY DANJUMA grappled with the corpse slumped in the driver's seat, seizing the wheel and stabbing at the brake pedal with his left foot in time to stop the car before it jumped the curb and slammed into the drab facade of a tavern that hadn't yet opened for business. In the process, Amos Buhari slumped into him, drenching Danjuma with warm, sticky blood.

It was hardly a new sensation, fresh blood on his hands, but Danjuma recoiled nonetheless, half lurching from his seat to strike the dashboard with his side, before the car came finally to rest, its engine stalling out.

Danjuma tumbled from the vehicle, saw Sani Fulani already out of the backseat and moving, firing his pistol. Their fourth man, young Friday Achebe, was trying to exit the car, but his hands had lost most of their cunning. They fumbled at the door latch, set below his shattered window, while Achebe tried to blink away the blood veil covering his face.

A scalp wound, more than likely, but it could be something worse. In any case, Danjuma had no time to waste on first-aid treatment or consoling wounded soldiers. Any moment now could be his last, and he didn't intend to die or flee before he'd finished off his enemies.

But where were they?

A bullet sizzled past Danjuma's face, missing his ear by half an inch or less and sending him to ground. Hiding behind and half under the car, he searched for targets but his field of vision was restricted. Any sort of movement to his right was screened from view, unless an enemy drew close enough for Danjuma to glimpse his feet. On the left, he was still half exposed and aware some unseen shooter could probably take him.

Danjuma was startled, therefore, when Achebe finally mastered his door latch and slumped from the car, down on one knee at first, breathing hard with a wet rasp behind it, then finally lurching upright. Achebe had to have drawn or found his gun at the same time, because he fired two shots across the street, toward some target Danjuma couldn't see.

And that target returned fire. Three rapid shots, one of which struck the car with a clang, while at least one hit Friday Achebe. Danjuma saw his soldier's legs slip out from under him, dropping him first into a seated posture with his back against the car. From there, he toppled over to his left and lay unmoving on the pavement.

More shots now, their echoes rattling back and forth across the street, keeping the local denizens indoors until the storm of trouble passed. Danjuma knew Ughelli's rowdy district fairly well, but he had never seen it dead like this before, at any time of day or night.

And he would soon be dead, as well, unless he took some action to defend himself.

His hunt had turned into a small pitched battle, and Danjuma feared that he was on the losing end. Two of his men were definitely down and out. As for the rest, he'd lost sight of Fulani and could only guess which of the barking guns were still in friendly hands.

Get up and do something! a small voice in his head demanded.

Cursing viciously, Kelsey Danjuma leaped upright and raised his pistol, scanning for a target, any target. All he prayed for was a chance to shoot.

Someone to kill.

BOLAN WAS MOVING when Umaru finished off the wounded man beside the first chase car. Another gunman, standing in the middle of the street, tracked Bolan with his pistol, always firing just a crucial pace behind him, cursing every miss.

A recessed doorway on his right gave Bolan shelter long enough to catch his breath and let the shooter waste a few rounds on the drab facade of the tavern where Bolan took cover. Anger had gotten the best of his would-be killer, but that didn't mean the guy couldn't get lucky and take Bolan down.

It was time to be done with him.

Bolan went low and outside, belly-down on the pavement while taking his shot—three for one, with the 93-R's selective fire system. Two of the slugs nailed his target for sure, traveling at 1,900 feet per second, striking with 560 foot-pounds of destructive energy.

It was too much for human flesh and bone to bear. The shooter vaulted backward, arms outflung as if he hoped to fly, but gravity exerted its control. He hit the pavement with a sound like someone's bag of laundry touching down and moved no more.

That still left at least two shooters. One of them chose that moment to pop up behind the first chase car and charge into the open, firing as he came. He pegged a shot at Bolan, then swung back to bring Umaru under fire.

Bolan squeezed off a burst that cut the gunner's left leg out from under him, but even through that shock and pain, his adversary didn't fall. Though slumped and kneeling, he turned back toward Bolan, steadying his weapon in a tight two-handed grip.

And that was when Umaru shot him from across the street, either a lucky shot or skill beyond what Bolan had expected from a guy whose former military training likely emphasized long guns and tedious close-order drills.

Umaru's bullet struck the kneeling shooter in the head and finished him, although the dead man didn't drop immediately. For a second, Bolan suspected that his hips were locked somehow. It was the kind of crazy thing you saw sometimes, in combat or the aftermath of fatal accidents. Bodies could come to rest in odd positions, some apparently defying physics, but this shooter's corpse surrendered after two or three heartbeats, and he collapsed.

How many left?

Another moment, crouching in the open, told him there

were none. They'd managed to survive it, unlike their opponents. Now, all that they had to do was get away before police arrived.

And start the whole damned thing again, from scratch.

CHAPTER EIGHT

Lao Choy Teoh sat facing Ekon Afolabi in a small spare office situated on the third floor of CNP's building in downtown Warri. Afolabi had removed the floppy hat that he had worn to shield his upper face upon arrival, but he left the fake beard plastered to his chin. Each time he spoke, the mustache quivered in a way that made Lao want to laugh.

Instead he had poured tea, serving the guest himself, and made no protest when the Itsekiri warlord wedged a plug of tobacco into his cheek, adding a bulge that made the wiry stage beard even more hilarious.

"We've been apprised of your most recent difficulties," Lao told Afolabi. "My employer has requested that I ask if we can help in any way."

"The girl was stolen back from us," Afolabi said, cutting to the chase with no pretense that they had met to speak of legitimate business. "Many of my men were killed."

All caught on tape for future reference, if it was ever necessary for the men in charge of CNP to find new allies in Nigeria and help displace the old.

Not that their first instinct would be to place Afolabi on

trial for his crimes. Court cases only granted fools and maniacs a chance to speak, when silence was best for all concerned.

"You think that K-Tech did this?" Lao inquired.

"Who else? A white man comes to save the white girl. It is obvious."

Lao shrugged. "Americans employed by Jared Ross are not the only white men in Nigeria," he said.

"Who, then?"

Another shrug would be too much, Lao thought. Such things preoccupied his mind when he was dealing with a shaky ally who might one day be his mortal enemy if anything went wrong between them.

"Certainly, you *may* be right," Lao said. "It's logical, I grant you. But suppose that someone else wished to embarrass you—and MEND, of course. Who might it be?"

Confused and wary, Afolabi gave his beard a thoughtful tug, remembering too late that it wasn't his own. Now part of it was dangling from the right side of his jaw, the wobbling effect increased. Lao bit his tongue as Afolabi tried to mash the flap of fake hair back in place.

"I don't know," Afolabi said at last.

"Consider that it might be someone allied with your enemies, the Ijaw. Someone who's aware of CNP's quiet support of MEND."

Quiet was understating it by half. The whole connection between MEND and CNP was strictly covert, known only to Lao, to Huang Li Chan and, presumably, some of the company's controllers in Beijing.

"You mean, the Russians?" Afolabi asked.

Now it was time to shrug again.

"I can't be sure, of course," Lao said. "But might it not make sense to them? Their SVR, in fact, is no more than the KGB renamed to make it palatable in the West. Its tactics haven't changed, and they have much experience in Africa."

"Russians," Afolabi said, starting to consider it. "But—"

"They support the Ijaw, as we know, hoping to gain petroleum concessions for themselves. MEND is an obstacle to that pursuit. Whatever harms the Itsekiri—and, by inference, your foreign friends—should please Uroil and Moscow."

"When you put it that way—"

Lao decided not to oversell it. "I could be mistaken," he replied with a self-deprecating smile. "I'm only human, after all. Perhaps the woman's father *did* effect her rescue, using mercenaries."

"One man only," Afolabi said, correcting him.

"Which makes it all the more embarrassing. Such men exist, of course. Most of them work for private military companies today, since army pay is pitiful. But…"

"What?"

"Oh, never mind. A fantasy, perhaps."

"Tell me!"

Lao frowned, making a show of his reluctance to proceed.

"If you insist," he said. "I simply wondered if the Russians and Americans might be collaborating somehow. We've heard much about their spirit of cooperation since the Soviet Union collapsed. American capital floods the former socialist republics."

"Is it not the same in China?" Afolabi asked, squinting one eye in an attempt to make himself look clever.

"With a crucial difference," Lao said. "Beijing surrenders nothing, merely profits from the West's eternal greed. Americans don't infest our banks and corporations. *We* are using *them,* while Moscow grovels in its poverty, pleading for table scraps."

"You've given me a lot to think about," Afolabi said.

"May I give you nothing more?" Lao asked.

"There is a matter of expenses, and the payments due to widows."

Lao removed a satchel from beneath the desk he occupied and handed it to Afolabi. It was weighted down with cash.

"A little something for the cause," Lao said. "If we can help in any other way—"

"I'll be in touch," Afolabi said. "Certainly, if you hear anything that might identify the men responsible for our embarrassment…"

"You'll be the first to know," Lao said.

"WE NEED NEW WHEELS," Bolan said as they cruised the darkened streets of Warri. He kept hoping that they wouldn't meet police along the way and have to talk about the bullet holes that decorated the Toyota.

"It is best to take one from the parking lot of a hotel," Umaru told him, "or a shopping center. We can switch the license plates."

"You've done this kind of thing before?" Bolan asked, smiling.

"Call it misspent youth," Umaru answered with his own brief smile.

"You did all right, back there, for someone out of practice," Bolan said.

Umaru didn't answer for a moment, then he said, "Five years ago, I killed two men. I was a soldier then, of course. Guerrillas had kidnapped workers from a Shell refinery in Yenagoa and were holding them for ransom. It's the same old story. I was in the troop assigned to liberate the hostages."

"You did your duty, then," Bolan said.

"Yes." Another silent moment passed before Umaru said, "I still recall the first boy's face. He meant to kill me, but when I shot him he looked…surprised."

"It's always a surprise at some level, to be on the receiving end."

"I think he was about sixteen years old. Of course, I can't be sure."

"He made a choice. Unless you'd rather that he left you in the dirt and walked away, there's nothing you should second-guess."

"It's not that I feel guilty," Umaru said. "I was certainly relieved to be alive. But that felt wrong, somehow."

Bolan heard that, and he supposed that he could still recall the first face that he'd studied through a sniper scope, if he set his mind to it. But what was the point?

Life went on.

At least, for the living.

And right now, the living needed new wheels.

He let Umaru point him toward a shopping center on the west side of Warri, where physical security was lax and closed-circuit cameras were nonexistent. Bolan didn't relish ripping off some innocent civilian's ride, but neither was he keen on going back to Jared Ross and turning in one shot-up loaner for another. Most particularly not when Ross had stuck him with a LoJack monitor the first time.

It had been a funny kind of thank-you for his daughter's life, and while Bolan had no reason to believe the oilman wanted him dead, neither did he plan to cultivate any kind of ongoing relationship. He'd liberated Mandy Ross as a favor for Hal Brognola, not her father—and as a way into the chaotic mess that was modern Nigeria. Now, well inside, with the pot simmering, any further ties to K-Tech would be deadweight strung around his neck.

And Bolan needed that like a hole in the head.

"There is the shopping center," Umaru said. "You call it a mall, I think?"

"Tonight," Bolan replied, "I call it our used-car lot. Let's go shopping."

VALENTIN SIDOROV liked to think that Russians rivaled any other race for subtlety, including the Chinese. For that reason, he had declined to meet Agu Ajani and his well-armed entourage at Uroil's offices in Warri. The idea of having Ijaw gunmen on the premises, cleaned up or not, had simply made him cringe.

But meet they must. And so Sidorov found himself walking alone through one of Warri's rougher neighborhoods, the only white face on the street, with nothing but the weight of a GSh-18 semiautomatic pistol slung beneath his arm to comfort him.

For this occasion, Sidorov had loaded the pistol with Russian 7N31 +P+ armor-piercing 9 mm rounds, just in case he was required to fire at vehicles, through walls, whatever stood in his way. Eighteen in the magazine, one up the spout and two spare clips in pouches readily accessible from almost any pose a living body could attain. If all else failed, and one of his enemies was still breathing after fifty-five shots, Sidorov also carried an ivory-handled switchblade for last-ditch emergencies.

But he hoped none of that would be needed as he approached the address he'd received from Ajani's second in command an hour earlier. Tarnished brass numerals marked a door that had faded from crimson to a washed-out pink over time from exposure to merciless sunlight. The coded knock struck Sidorov as vaguely childish, but it worked.

Daren Jumoke, the lately politicized rapist, stood on the threshold, looked Sidorov up and down and asked him, "Are you armed?"

"Are you?" the Russian countered.

"I require your weapons," Jumoke said.

Turning from the open doorway, Sidorov advised him, "Tell your master not to waste my time again."

Before he'd taken three steps, the Nigerian called after him, "Wait! It's a standard matter of security."

Sidorov paused and turned to face him.

"Your attitude's insulting," he replied. "And if you think I've paid you so much money in the past two years, hoping I'd get the chance to kill your boss man in this seedy shithole, you're delusional."

Jumoke glared at him, but shrugged it off a moment later, stepped aside and beckoned Sidorov to enter.

They found Agu Ajani seated at a table in a side room, flanked by men with automatic rifles held at port arms, index fingers well inside the trigger guards. Sidorov found that he couldn't resist another dig against Jumoke, telling him, "I see why you were worried."

"Worried about what?" Ajani asked his number two.

"It's nothing," Jumoke said. "Just a Russian joke."

"Perhaps we can get down to business, then," Ajani said.

"My thoughts exactly," Sidorov replied as he took the table's only vacant chair, leaving Jumoke standing. "It appears your rivals from the Itsekiri tribe have suffered an embarrassing setback."

Ajani frowned. "Who should I thank for that?" he asked.

"I'll happily take credit for it," the Russian said. "But in fact, my people had no part in the delivery of Ekon Afolabi's hostage. Moscow may cooperate with the Americans on paper, but I don't share that attitude on operations in the field."

"So, the Americans retrieved their oilman's daughter?"

Sidorov shrugged. "I'm more concerned with what comes next. As you should be."

"And what comes next for us?" Ajani asked.

"An opportunity presents itself," Sidorov said, "to put more pressure on our common enemies, when they can least afford it. I, for one, would hate to waste that chance."

"I DON'T TRUST the Chinese," Taiwo Babatunde said.

"You trust no one," Ekon Afolabi said.

"Not true!" his giant second in command replied. "I've always trusted you."

"And I appreciate it," Afolabi said, hoping that he wasn't required to use that trust as an offensive weapon of betrayal sometime in the not so distant future.

"The Chinese, though…"

"They are generous," Afolabi said.

"For a reason," Babatunde replied. "They want our oil, and anything else they can grab while they're at it."

"It's not *our* oil yet," Afolabi reminded him. "Making demands and achieving our goals are two different things."

"I know that!"

"We lost our leverage on Jared Ross last night," Afolabi said. "He is mocking us today, most likely celebrating with champagne. Until we make him weep, he won't respect us."

"Well, his daughter's gone," Babatunde replied. "One of our people at Osubi saw the K-Tech jet take off. She's well out of Nigeria by now, and safely on her way back home."

"Striking a child isn't the only way to break a man. What does he love more than his family?"

"I don't know, Ekon."

"Money," Afolabi stated simply. "Profit. Since our demand for ransom failed, we need to seek another course of action."

"Yes," Babatunde said. He didn't suggest one.

"Well?"

"Um…"

Afolabi somehow managed not to roll his eyes while interrupting. "Would it not be fitting," he inquired, "for us to chastise K-Tech Petroleum? Have we no rights to the wealth of our own homeland?"

Babatunde beamed at that, saying, "We do! We should! They must be punished!"

"Excellent. You are my strong right arm, as always, Taiwo."

Praise always infused Babatunde with childlike pleasure, and it cost Afolabi nothing. And, in this case, he was merely speaking honestly. Despite his mental deficits, Babatunde had helped place Afolabi where he was today— in the top ranks of MEND, with his influence felt statewide. Together, they still might accomplish great things.

And if the time came when Afolabi had to choose between his own ambition and his second in command's survival, he would mourn the need to bid his friend goodbye forever. He would make the giant's death as quick and merciful as possible.

"We should begin a new campaign at once," Afolabi said, shrugging off the maudlin moment. "And it must be clear that we hold foreigners responsible for every drop of oil extracted from our nation. For every naira taken from our pockets, banked on foreign soil."

Granted, the naira—Nigeria's base unit of currency— was worth less than a U.S. penny at the moment, but Afolabi believed in fighting for principals.

Especially if they could make him rich.

"Another pipeline bombing, perhaps?" Babatunde surmised.

"Perhaps a little something more dramatic," Afolabi said. "Why not a whole refinery? K-Tech's, of course. I daresay *that* will capture their attention and convince them that we are not to be trifled with."

"An excellent idea, Ekon."

"Is it? I hope so. Shall we bring the plan to life?"

These little moments were among the best, planning new action in an atmosphere of righteous hope. And if the plans succeeded, that was better still.

As they began to plan the largest raid they'd ever launched, Afolabi momentarily allowed himself to hope that this time they might win.

THE TROUBLE with drawing up hit lists in cities like Warri was the abundance of targets. Where to start? Which should be the grand finale? And how many stops should he make in between?

Bolan had suffered similar problems during his one-man war against the American Mafia, while waging his urban campaigns in New York and Chicago, Detroit and L.A. The Mob had owned so much, employed so many fronts and bought so many "public servants," that a blitz demanded personal restraint.

Bolan needed to keep his eye on the ball.

Umaru made two lists, writing in square block capitals, blue ballpoint pen, inside a notebook they'd found in the car. The new ride was a Honda Civic sedan, four years old, but in good working order.

So far.

Bolan had moved his gear up to the floor behind the driver's seat, anticipating that he might require the Steyr AUG or some other tool on short notice, without pulling over to open his trunk. Plates were switched, and he'd considered running the car through one of Warri's all-night paint shops, but he didn't have the time to spare.

Besides, why treat the Honda to a new skin, then place it in harm's way before the paint was fairly dried?

"The first list is for Ekon Afolabi and his Itsekiris."

"MEND, in other words," Bolan said.

"Yes. The second has addresses for Agu Ajani and his Ijaws."

"Where do you fit in?" Bolan asked, frankly curious.

"I don't," Umaru said. "I'm Igbo—what the West mistakenly calls 'Ibo.' Distantly related to the Ijaw, but entirely separate."

"The odd man out," Bolan observed.

"Always, it seems. You need not worry that I'll suddenly switch sides."

"It hadn't crossed my mind," Bolan replied with less than total honesty. "My problem is that, strictly speaking, you weren't meant to have a side in this. Translation, basic guide work, drawing up a list or two like those. That was supposed to be the end of it."

Umaru shrugged. "Plans change," he said.

"But you can still get out of it," Bolan told him. "There was no choice on the first round, since they came for you. That changes now. I'm carrying the fight to them, both sides. If you mix into that, you're marked."

Another restless shrug. "Am I not marked already?" his companion asked. "The Itsekiri tried to kill me without knowing you existed. I assume they know my home address, may have been watching it for days. I can't just step out of this car and back into my life. It seems now that I have none."

"Don't write it off just yet," Bolan replied. "You're in the middle of a shake-up, but that doesn't mean you won't come out the other side alive. A change of scenery might be advisable, but don't assume the worst. So far, we're one-for-one."

"And they'll be hunting us."

"I'm counting on it," Bolan said. "It keeps them occupied while *I* hunt *them*."

"Where shall we start, then?" Umaru asked.

"If you're in—"

"My choice is made." Umaru cut him off.

"Okay. MEND took the first hit," Bolan said. "I yanked a hostage out from under them before I met you. We don't know who pulled the ambush in the marketplace, so it won't count. Next up, a little something for the Ijaw team."

"And hit them where it hurts?" Umaru asked.

"As hard as possible."

"In that case," his companion said, "I have a place in mind for us to start."

"THE RUSSIANS SEEM to think they own Nigeria," Daren Jumoke said.

"They may," Agu Ajani answered, "if we aren't cautious in our dealings with them."

"But we need their money," Jumoke said sourly.

"For now. It's only temporary, and it doesn't mean we are subservient to their wishes."

"Does Sidorov know that?" Jumoke asked, frowning.

"In time, he will," Ajani said. "For now, it serves our purpose for him to believe he's in charge. Calling the shots, as the Americans would say. He won't expect it, later, when the shots are aimed at him."

"He will divide us, if we let him."

"At the moment," Ajani said, "Sidorov and Uroil worry more about the Chinese and their ties to MEND. It's why they give us guns and money, to ensure that China National Petroleum does not secure the lion's share of oil."

"Did you believe Sidorov?"

"About what?" Ajani asked.

"Denying that he freed the hostage held by Afolabi's men."

Ajani gave a lazy shrug. "What difference does it make? He lies to us when it suits him. I care no more about the oilman's daughter than I do for any other cockroach scrabbling in the dirt. Her rescue wounds the Itsekiri, so it makes us stronger."

"Afolabi needs to die. His pet gorilla, too," Jumoke said.

"We've tried that."

"Why not try again?"

"I don't object, on principle," Ajani said. In fact, some said he *had* no principles, but that was slander from his enemies. "It would be helpful, though, if the suspicion fell on someone else."

"Such as?"

"Who hates him most, today?" Ajani asked his second in command.

"The list is long, Agu."

"But at its top, I would expect to find the man whose daughter was abducted, terrorized and violated by the Itsekiri."

"Violated?"

"It's a rumor," Ajani said. "I just started it myself."

Jumoke laughed at that, a rasping sound, more like an aging smoker's cough.

"Revenge," he said, nodding.

"The oldest motive in the world."

"It *is* the sort of thing Americans would do. Perhaps snatch Afolabi from the street, fly him to Egypt or some other country for interrogation to the death."

"We don't have time for all of that," Ajani said.

"A simple execution, then. I like it," Jumoke said.

"Not so simple. As you pointed out, we've tried before."

"Not hard enough."

"His death will be a victory, of course," Ajani said. "And better still if it is staged in such a way to further damage MEND and the Chinese."

"You have a plan in mind?"

"Not yet. Ideally, they should have a public falling out. Eliminate each other, for the greatest possible embarrassment to all concerned."

"I don't know any Chinese killers," Jumoke said.

"It was just a thought," Ajani said, smiling. "We can't have everything we want."

"I'll see what I can do, Agu."

"Nothing impetuous," Ajani cautioned. "To be done correctly, this must be well-planned, coordinated, carried out with surgical precision."

"And if that's not possible?" Jumoke asked.

"Well then, we simply smash him like a cockroach," Ajani replied. "I believe in being flexible."

"Whiskey?" Jumoke asked.

"Why not?"

CHAPTER NINE

The Ijaw drug lab was located in a warehouse on Warri's north side abutting railroad tracks and a stagnant canal. According to Umaru, the plant processed khat and marijuana from the stalk to packaging, cut imported supplies of processed cocaine and heroin for street sale and cooked up variable quantities of ecstasy, LSD and methamphetamine.

One-stop shopping for pushers.

Most of the product was wholesaled to "Area Boys," street gangs who fought for turf in Nigeria's urban centers. Ranging from twelve to thirty-odd years old, the "boys" were everywhere. United Nations monitors had counted 35,000 in Lagos alone, while doubtless missing many more. Aside from trafficking in drugs, the gangs sold "protection," stole cars and ran errands for established syndicates, which might include murder for hire.

Ironically the rise of the Area Boys since the late 1990s had sparked a vigilante countermovement, known as the Bakassi Boys. Originally limited to members of the Igbo tribe, Bakassi Boys had expanded to recruit members of other clans, advancing from use of ju-ju hexes on their enemies to execution via gunshot and machete.

Taking out a single drug plant wouldn't stop any of that. If pressed, Bolan wasn't even sure that it would count as a step in the right direction. What it *would* do was jab a long thorn in the side of Delta State's Ijaw warlord, while granting Bolan an opportunity to divide and conquer.

"You will blame Ekon Afolabi for the raid?" Umaru asked as Bolan parked their stolen car downrange from the warehouse.

"Seems like the way to go," Bolan replied.

"So that Agu Ajani will declare war on the Itsekiri."

"They're already feuding," Bolan said. "I want to ramp it up a bit."

"Creating a diversion?"

"That's part of it. And if the contenders take each other out, less work for us."

"It all sounds dangerous."

"That's what I've been explaining," Bolan said. "Nobody signed you up for frontline duty on this thing. You want to pull a fade right now, it's fine with me. Take off, with no hard feelings."

"I don't wish to leave," Umaru said. "I mean, I *do,* but there is nowhere safe to go."

"One of your contacts could arrange something," Bolan suggested. "Not the locals. Try the Company."

"I have," Umaru said. "Voice mail."

"You think they'd cut you loose?" Bolan inquired, prepared to answer that himself based on his personal experience.

"Why not? I was a pair of eyes and ears. They must have hundreds—maybe thousands—in Nigeria. Why waste their precious time and money on a renegade who brings them nothing but embarrassment?"

Bolan was on the verge of pointing out that he'd obtained Umaru's name from Langley, once removed through Hal Brognola and Stony Man, but kept it to himself. Umaru clearly recognized the CIA's penchant for dodging scandal, even if it meant the sacrifice of contract agents in the field.

Another typical snafu.

Langley had run the same back-stabbing, cutthroat game plan time and time again, for over sixty years. Why should it ever change?

The alleyway where he had parked the Honda Civic was pitch-black and deep enough to hide the car from passersby unless they probed it with spotlights. Bolan had also checked the alley out from end to end for sleeping vagrants and found none.

They were alone as he began to suit up for the raid, donning his web gear that supported ammo pouches, frag grenades, his Ka-Bar fighting knife, first-aid kit and various surprises that his enemies would only glimpse in the last fleeting seconds of their lives. His lead weapon was still the Steyr AUG assault rifle.

Umaru looked distinctly underdressed, holding his Chinese pistol, with no other weapon visible. It was a decent weapon, but it held a maximum of sixteen rounds.

"You have spare magazines for that?" Bolan asked.

"One," Umaru said, flashing a nervous little smile.

"Okay. With any luck, you should be able to pick up something that suits you when we get inside. They're bound to have plenty of guns."

Which would be pointed straight at Bolan and Umaru once they showed themselves. But why belabor the negative? the Executioner thought.

"Perhaps a rifle or a submachine gun," Umaru said.

"Once again, I have to say—"

Umaru cut him off, shaking his head.

"Unless you order me to stay outside," he said, "I'm going with you."

"Fair enough," Bolan said as he locked the car and started toward the alley's mouth. "Let's get it done."

"YOU HAVE ENOUGH supplies for the moment?" Valentin Sidorov asked.

The drug plant's manager, Olumbe Otah, nodded. "Everything came in on schedule this time," he replied.

There had been problems, recently, with late deliveries to Afolabi's cutting plant in Warri. Sidorov had done his best to make things right, using his contacts in the SVR, the Medellín Cartel and one of Mexico's three largest heroin-producing rings to tighten up the slack.

All things considered, it seemed only fair.

Sidorov had to earn his five percent somehow.

He wasn't sure what Eltsin and the Moscow bureaucrats would say about his little fling at private enterprise. Some of them had done worse during the Cold War and since communism's infamous collapse, but that wouldn't prevent the worst of them from sacrificing Sidorov to help themselves save face.

But if he wasn't caught, there would be nothing to explain.

And Sidorov was an expert at not getting caught.

He had imported a Bulgarian to help Agu Ajani build the drug plant, dropping in to supervise construction as it went along, taking a decent kickback from Ajani's purchases of lab equipment. The result, if not spectacular, was both efficient and discreet.

Within the old, abandoned-looking warehouse, each drug cut or processed had its own specific area. There was no cross-contamination, and the risk of an explosive accident in any of the cooking rooms was minimized by constant supervision and the use of relatively new equipment. Lookouts on the roof stood watch around the clock, regardless of the weather, while a team of well-armed men inside the plant stood ready to repel invaders.

Short of uprooting the plant and flying it to Mother Russia, with a staff selected personally, Sidorov could think of no way to improve the operation.

"You're always watching out for strangers, yes?" he asked.

A small twitch at one corner of his mouth betrayed Otah's irritation. "Of course," he replied.

"And you heard what happened to the Itsekiris?"

"With their hostage, yes," Otah said. "We all mourn for them, of course."

Sidorov recognized the joke, despite Otah's deadpan delivery. "The thing is," he continued, "that may not be the end of it."

"More trouble for the Itsekiri?" Otah said. "You're trying to amuse me now."

"It may not all be their trouble," Sidorov said. "I've warned Ajani that we may have unknown players in the game. Wise men use extra caution during troubled times."

"You're a philosopher," Otah said, barely smiling now.

Sidorov longed to slap him, wipe the sly smile from his face, but it would be bad for business. It might even prove to be his last mistake, if Otah's people turned on him. Sidorov knew he could take a few of them before he fell, but what a stupid waste it all would be.

Instead of lashing out, he said, "I've dabbled in philosophy. But I'm an expert on survival."

"In which case," Otah replied, "I thank you for your generous advice."

Sidorov knew he should leave before his temper and contempt for all things African betrayed him. Putting on a smile that never reached his eyes, he bid good-night to Otah and retreated toward the nearest exit from the plant.

BOLAN SPOTTED a sentry on the warehouse roof and reckoned that there had to be more to cover all sides of the building. After pointing out the watchman to Umaru, Bolan sought a path through shadow toward the warehouse loading dock.

Two cars were parked there, with a motorcycle and an old Dodge cargo van that had begun life in Detroit at least a decade earlier. No guards were visible, no cameras in evidence, no rooftop watchers currently in place to see them cross the twenty yards of open pavement from the darkness to their destination.

"Follow me," he whispered, and broke cover, sprinting for the concrete steps located at the west end of the loading dock. Umaru got there just behind him, and they both flattened against the wall.

Waiting.

If they'd been seen in transit, Bolan reckoned that they'd be aware of it in nothing flat. There might be no alarm, but spotters on the roof were bound to tip off men inside the plant and bring them spilling out with weapons at the ready.

Bolan braced himself to meet them, but they didn't show.

So far, so good.

They had a choice of doors. One was the normal kind, man-size; the other was a roll-back loading bay contraption that would wake the dead before they got it open while exposing them to fire from a dozen interior angles. The choice was elementary.

The door, as expected, was locked.

"Eyes peeled for any company," Bolan said as he knelt in front of the lock, palming a set of picks.

"I have it," Umaru said, standing with his pistol braced in a two-handed target-shooter's grip.

Bolan attacked the lock and beat it in a little under thirty seconds. It hadn't offered any great security to those inside, but he assumed the plant was never left unguarded or unoccupied, which cut down on the need for dead bolts that could withstand Judgment Day. Because there was no handy window in the door—a nod toward privacy—he wouldn't know if ambushers were waiting for them until they had stepped into the line of fire.

"Ready?" he asked Umaru.

"Yes." No hesitation in the other's voice.

"Okay, then. Here we go."

Bolan had slung his AUG and had the sound-suppressed Beretta in his hand before he turned the doorknob, felt it yield and eased the door open. When he wasn't gunned down at once, he felt a cautious surge of optimism, but they hadn't cleared that great first hurdle yet.

Only when he was standing on the open threshold, with Umaru at his back and both of them still breathing, did the Executioner relax enough to breathe. A heartbeat later they were both inside, but only just. A blank wall separated Bolan and Umaru from the warehouse proper, passing them along a narrow corridor devoid of decoration, scented with an odd, off-putting mix of sweat and other chemical aromas.

There was only one direction they could travel. Bolan paused to shut the unlocked door behind them, in a quick concession to appearances, then led the way along that corridor, toward voices and the busy sounds of people working, growing louder, step by cautious step.

UMARU TRAILED his American contact along the hallway, taking special care to breathe through his nose without gasping like a marathon runner. His heart pounded against his ribs, and he'd have been afraid to check his blood pressure just then, for fear that he might be on the verge of a stroke.

But he wasn't afraid.

Somehow, between his prior combat experience and Cooper's air of confidence, Umaru thought they had a chance. It might not be a great one, but they had beat the odds already once and might again.

Dividing his attention between Cooper and the corridor behind them, where they'd passed two closed and silent doors, Umaru nearly missed their first encounter with the enemy.

The man—a guard, presumably, with a slung rifle—emerged from yet another door on Cooper's left. Umaru had a split-second glimpse of urinals, and then Cooper was spinning toward the stranger, squeezing off a muffled round from his handgun.

The bullet drilled his target through the forehead, textbook perfect, and the man collapsed backward without a sound. Before he hit the concrete floor, the big American had moved to catch him, his free hand clutching at the corpse's shirt, helping him settle gently to the deck.

"In here," Bolan said as he dragged the body into the lavatory.

Umaru followed, checking the two toilet stalls by reflex, finding them empty. When he turned back, the American was offering him the guard's rifle, saying, "This should help."

Umaru stowed his pistol, accepting the weapon. He recognized the standard-issue Daewoo K-2 assault rifle used by many Nigerian soldiers, including himself, for a time. It was chambered for 5.56 mm NATO rounds, fed from 20- or 30-round magazines at a full-auto cyclic rate of 700 to 900 rounds per minute. The rifle weighed seven pounds, and with its folding stock collapsed, as now, it measured twenty-eight inches from muzzle to pistol grip.

Surprisingly, it felt like home.

"Yes, this is better," Umaru said.

"He's got a couple extra magazines." Bolan nodded toward the dead man's weighted pockets. "We can likely find more as we go along."

Umaru switched the two mags from the corpse's pockets to his own, then double-checked the Daewoo. He confirmed a live round in the chamber, released the safety and set the fire-selector switch for burst mode, which would send three slugs downrange with every trigger pull.

Somewhere inside him, the tension eased.

He couldn't have explained why that should be the case, and didn't question it. A measure of relief would steady both his hand and eye when action was required. Umaru still might miss a shot—he hadn't fired a rifle since he left the army—but at least it wouldn't be because he trembled like a frightened child.

"Ready?" Bolan asked.

"Yes."

"We're out of here."

He waited for a beat while Cooper checked the corridor, then followed him out of the men's room that had been converted to a morgue. The sounds of voices that had lured them this far were louder now. Umaru had the sense that he would glimpse their owners in another moment, find them weighing, measuring, bagging, whatever happened in a drug-production plant.

And when they met, he knew, the killing would begin in earnest.

Some of those he faced would certainly be armed. As for the rest, employees paid a pittance by the hour to process and package poison for sale on the streets or abroad, he supposed most of them wouldn't be trusted with weapons. Some might even be women, or, God forbid, children.

Guilty or innocent?

How would he judge those deserving of death?

Armed men first, he decided. And beyond that, he would try to follow Cooper's lead, while keeping both himself and the American alive.

And suddenly the men with guns were there.

VALENTIN SIDOROV was halfway to the exit, looking forward to his first drink of the night at his apartment, when he heard the first gunshots. They echoed through the sprawling plant, but he was reasonably sure they'd issued from the general direction of the loading dock and nearby room where khat was chopped and bagged for sale to the Area Boys.

The Russian drew his pistol without thinking, didn't have to think about a safety switch, since it was built into the trigger where his index finger rested. He was moving toward the source of the sounds when he caught himself.

What was he thinking?

If the plant was under attack, it could only be by police or one of Agu Ajani's enemies, perhaps a flying squad sent by Ekon Afolabi. In either case, one pistol wouldn't help Sidorov's side, and he could only harm himself by lingering to join the fight.

Discretion *was* the better part of valor, after all.

And medals were for "heroes" who had thrown their lives away.

Keeping the GSh-18 firmly in hand, Sidorov turned back toward the side door that would take him out into the night. His car was parked nearby, waiting. If anyone should try to intercept him, they wouldn't live to regret it.

It distressed him to suppose that he might lose his secret income from the Warri drug trade, but on balance, he saw no reason why that should happen. Even if Ajani's plant was overrun and looted, the demand for drugs—and Sidorov's dependable suppliers—still remained. The traffic might be interrupted for a moment, but it wouldn't end.

And neither would his stipend on the side.

The night was hot and muggy, but it held no grim surprises for Sidorov as he jogged the last few yards to his vehicle. A moment later he was roaring off toward his home in Warri, with the warehouse dwindling in his rearview mirror.

Thus, he saved himself and missed the best part of the show.

THERE WAS ONLY ONE guard in the khat-packaging room, a twentysomething rifleman whose bored expression vanished at the sight of Bolan and Umaru barging in. The shooter tried to raise his weapon, but a silenced round from Bolan's pistol bounced him off the nearest wall.

But even falling, he was trouble. A dead finger clenched the rifle's trigger, rattling off a burst that sent ricochets flying from concrete, evoking a chorus of panicky cries from the night-shift workers they had interrupted.

"Tell them to clear out of here," Bolan said as he palmed an M-15 white-phosphorus grenade and yanked its pin.

Umaru rattled off the order in a language Bolan didn't understand, and a dozen civilians bolted for the nearest exit. Bolan watched the last one disappear, then made an underhanded pitch into the nearest heap of khat, already backing out of there before it landed, with Umaru keeping pace.

The pop and whoosh of detonation told him when the charge went off. White phosphorus burned at 5,000 degrees Fahrenheit—enough to vaporize the drug, while burning through concrete and cinder blocks—and water wouldn't quench it. Even if he didn't have a chance to use another charge, the drug plant was already going up in smoke.

They double-timed toward the next nearest chamber, where wide-eyed workers had stopped bagging ganja to see what was happening. Two guards, this time, rushed toward the door as Bolan got there, with their automatic weapons at the ready.

But they weren't ready enough.

Bolan stitched them both with his Steyr AUG, discarding any bid for stealth. One of them fell at once; the other sagged against a table and was trying to return fire when Umaru hit him with a 3-round burst from his Daewoo K-2.

They didn't have to warn the workers in the ganja chamber. All of them were off and running as their second watchdog hit the floor. Bolan considered saving a grenade, letting the first one burn through from next door, but then decided not to skimp.

Pop! Whoosh!

The next chamber, a dozen paces down the hallway, was devoted to cutting and bagging cocaine. Another pair of guards emerged, hunch-shouldered, with their rifles clutched against their chests, when Bolan and Umaru were halfway to the door.

Umaru was the first to fire this time, shading Bolan by a fraction of a heartbeat. As it was, their rifles hammered both men down in something close to perfect synchronicity. A third white-phosphorus grenade went through the open doorway, and they moved on without looking back.

At least three labs or packing chambers remained, and they were meeting more resistance. Bolan didn't try to count the hostile guns assembled at the far end of the corridor, leap-frogging closer while their comrades covered them, because he didn't play the numbers game. He'd never notched a gunstock, and he wasn't starting now.

He chose a frag grenade this time and lobbed it down the hallway in a decent fastball pitch. His adversaries saw it coming, some of them recoiling while the others dropped or hunkered down to try to ride it out.

And failed.

No wind they'd ever faced before had come complete with shrapnel, ripping flesh and burying itself in bone, while smoky thunder sent bodies flying like bowling pins. Bolan and his companion rushed at the survivors, firing as they went, putting the wounded stragglers down and out.

How many left?

Bolan supposed they hadn't seen the rooftop lookouts, who would require some time to reach the warehouse floor and join their comrades on the skirmish line. And while he couldn't say for sure, there was at least a possibility of one or two slinking away to call for reinforcements while he finished blitzing out the plant.

So let them.

In the room reserved for cutting heroin, he added more white phosphorus to the white-powder drifts already piled atop stainless-steel tables. In the labs where meth was cooked, he sprayed the ether tanks with 5.56 mm rounds and ducked back out before they blew.

His ears were ringing as they backtracked toward the loading dock, both men holding their breath as they passed through successive drifting clouds of smoke and cloying vapor. Exiting the plant, Bolan allowed himself his first deep breath since taking out the meth lab. Umaru, beside him, spent a moment coughing, then seemed fine.

"We're still alive," the Nigerian said, all smiles.

"So far," Bolan replied, keeping a keen eye out for snipers as they crossed the open ground toward dark, concealing shadows.

No one tried to stop them. He supposed the sentries were already well inside the blazing funeral pyre or else had managed to escape somehow. It didn't matter which.

"Ajani must blame someone for his loss tonight," Umaru said.

"You're right," Bolan agreed, nodding. "And I think I know a way to help him focus. Let's go find a pay phone, shall we? Somewhere nice and quiet, near downtown."

CHAPTER TEN

Agu Ajani valued self-control. He recognized intemperance as weakness, and was proud that even when he flew into a violent rage, he always knew what he was doing. Every move, however savage, had been calculated for its maximum effect. He spoke through clenched teeth now, fighting an urge to scream.

"Tell me again how this could happen."

Standing at parade rest, with hands clasped behind his back, Daren Jumoke said, "Two men were seen. One white, one black. They got inside the plant somehow, past the lookouts."

"Which was supposed to be impossible," Ajani said.

"Yes, sir." Jumoke knew better than to adopt first-name familiarity under the present circumstances. "We had four men on the roof, as usual. Three now are dead. The fourth is missing."

"And his name?"

"Robert Ndibe. Not a new man. He's been on the payroll for three years."

"Missing, you say."

"Not with the other dead," Jumoke clarified.

"Or burned up in the fire?"

"It's always possible. Not likely, though."

"Why not?"

"The other three on roof-watch with him all came down and died together, at the west end of the plant. Ndibe's not among the men we found there. Also, none of those who fled remembers seeing him."

"Ask them again," Ajani said. "More forcefully. I want this runaway. He may have seen something. If nothing else, he can explain his failure and apologize before he dies."

"Yes, sir."

"And Sidorov. I need—"

A blare of music overrode Ajani's thought. He grimaced, cursing at the ring tone he'd programmed into his cell phone one night after drinking too much whiskey. The last thing he wanted to hear at the moment was "Eye of the Tiger."

Ajani drew the phone out of his pocket, flipped it open and studied its display screen. Its LED readout said Number Unknown.

Beyond irritation now, Ajani snapped, "Who is this?"

"Honestly," a voice answered him, "what's in a name?"

"I'm in no mood for games just now," Ajani warned.

"And I'm not playing one—unless you want to call the fireworks exhibition at your plant a game."

Ajani stiffened, felt as if his teeth would crumble into powder if he clenched them any tighter.

"You have information on that subject?" he inquired.

"I ought to," the caller said. "I was there."

"With a black friend, perhaps?"

"Discrimination is for amateurs."

"And now, you call to gloat?"

"Not even close."

"What, then?" Ajani heard the anger mounting in his voice and struggled to contain it.

"I'm a businessman," the caller said. "I never double-book or back out of a contract, but I'm not a one-trick pony, either."

"I don't—"

"Follow me? My bad. How's this—I know who hung the target on your back. For a consideration, I'll supply the name and full particulars."

"Betraying your employers?"

"They hired me to do a job. It's done. You're out of business at the old location. I held up my end."

"And now you want a bonus from the other side." Ajani was surprised to find himself laughing.

"Okay, forget it," the caller said. "If you're doing well enough to laugh it off, more power to you."

"I already know who wants me out of business," Ajani said.

"You might be surprised. But, hey, I'm on the next flight out of here. No skin off me."

"Wait! What are you suggesting?"

"Only that your friends may not be quite as friendly as they seem. You want more, there's a price tag."

"So, I pay you for a name. And why should I believe you?"

"I can't think of one good reason in the world," the caller said. "Except that I have everything on tape. Give it a listen, and you shouldn't need me to supply the names."

"We'd have to meet," Ajani said.

"It's doable, as long as you play straight and bring the cash."

"How much?"

"I'll make it easy on you, since you've hit a bad patch. Say a hundred grand, U.S."

"FURTHER DISTURBANCES last night, I understand," Huang Li Chan said.

Lao Choy Teoh nodded. "The destruction of an Ijaw drug-processing plant," he said. "Our man with the police believes that Ekon Afolabi is responsible."

Huang closed his eyes and spent a moment breathing deeply through flared nostrils.

"Why would he choose this moment, of all times, for such a thing?"

Lao could have claimed responsibility, at least in part. He had been doing everything within his power to increase the animosity between Ijaw and Itsekiri during recent months, convinced that triumph of the larger, stronger tribe would ultimately aid Beijing's ambitions in Nigeria, but he wasn't prepared to offer a confession at the moment.

Instead he answered, "It may be that Afolabi blames Ajani's people for the Ross fiasco. Add that to the history of tribal animosity…"

"And what of Uroil?" Huang inquired.

"Moscow's abandonment of socialism paved the way for chaos," Lao replied, citing the party line. "Russia is on the verge of bankruptcy, controlled by gangsters of the lowest order. They despise China because our own example offers daily proof of their incompetence and avarice. The KGB has passed away in name only. Men like Sidorov will do anything to undermine those they perceive as enemies or competition."

"As might we, perhaps?" Huang asked.

Lao smelled a trap and stepped around it. "Certainly, if challenged, we defend ourselves accordingly," he said.

Huang nodded, looking weary. "You believe the Russians are involved in this drug trafficking?"

"Based on their past performance, sir, from Cuba to Afghanistan, it does seem logical."

"I find the whole thing most distasteful."

"Of course, sir."

Lao had no intention of reminding Huang that Chinese

opium, cultivated in Guangdong and Yunnan provinces, rivaled worldwide supplies from the so-called Golden Triangle of Laos, Vietnam, Thailand and Myanmar. There was reason, after all, why Asian heroin was known as "China white."

"And yet—"

Before Huang could complete his thought, a buzzing emanated from the black phone on his desk. It was his private line, the one accessible directly from CNP headquarters, and, if the rumors were true, from certain politicians occupying rarefied positions in Beijing.

Huang frowned at the telephone, then picked up midway through its second ring. He answered first in Cantonese, then switched to English.

"Who is this?"

A pause for listening, and then, "I do not understand. What do you—"

Another interruption, this one longer, which turned Huang's frown to a scowl.

"You ask me to believe this, but—"

The caller cut him off again. Lao resisted an impulse to wriggle forward in his chair to try to eavesdrop.

"Anyone may make such claims," Huang said at last. "Without some proof—"

Lao waited, restless, while the caller tried to plead his case. He marveled that Huang would spend so much time talking to a stranger—and a rude one, by the sound of it.

"I will consider it," the CNP executive declared. "And if I need to get in touch with you—"

Some final comment set Huang's frown in stone before the line apparently went dead. Huang cradled the receiver, stared at it for several seconds longer, then looked up to meet Lao's gaze.

Lao bit his tongue to keep from asking any questions.

"Someone wants us to believe the Ijaw and their Russian friends blame *us* for last night's raid," he said.

"Someone?"

Huang shrugged. "A man, perhaps American. Who knows? He claims to have more details, but demands payment."

"A crank," Lao said dismissively.

"Who knows my private number?"

"We can try to trace the call, sir."

"Yes, do that. And in the meantime, I must ask headquarters if we wish to play his game."

"You mentioned payment, sir."

Huang actually smiled at that. "Oh, yes. One hundred thousand U.S. dollars, for the names of those responsible."

"And once we have the names?"

"That, I suppose, is up to us," Huang said.

"IT IS DIVIDE and conquer, yes?" Umaru asked.

"Something like that," Bolan replied.

"You hope that they will fight each other?"

"Not immediately," Bolan said. "At least, the Russians and Chinese should have a bit of self-control. But if we run with the assumption that they're backing rival sides in what's been happening, they both have vested interests in the outcome."

"But you do think Afolabi will attack Ajani?"

"Or vice versa," Bolan confirmed. "They were feuding when I got here. I'm just helping it along and taking out some of their major enterprises in the process."

"There are many public figures in Nigeria who stand with one side or the other," Umaru said. "Far too many, and too well protected, for you—for *us*—to strike them all."

"There's no such thing as a clean sweep," Bolan advised him. "If I knew a magic word that would make every crooked cop and politician in the world vanish today, you'd have a whole new crop of them in place tomorrow. Human nature hasn't changed in—what's the estimate, these days?—fifty or sixty thousand years. I don't expect that anything I do will change it in the next few hours."

"But you still go on," Umaru said, sounding confused. "If you don't believe in victory—"

"Who said that?" Bolan challenged. "Every soldier needs at least a hope of victory. Hell, I've had hundreds. But my point is, they don't last. Even if you confront a certain enemy and wipe him out to the last man, smart money says you'll have to fight again someday, guarding the same things that your old dead enemies were out to plunder or destroy."

"Ah. You are a fatalist."

A shrug rolled Bolan's shoulders. "Call it what you like. It's still a fact of life. You can kill men, but not emotions or ideas. You can't kill hatred, greed or plain old everyday insanity."

"But you devote your life to the pursuit of something you cannot attain," Umaru said.

"Most people do," Bolan replied, "unless they suffer from a limited imagination. Cops spend their lives fighting crime, without believing it will ever go away. Doctors— the good ones, anyway—are dedicated to elimination of disease. Sometimes they win, but Evil's like a germ that mutates, learns to live on penicillin. So you need new medicine, new treatments, for the next stage of the fight."

"Knowing that you can never win."

"Knowing that *someone* had to try it, and you gave it your best shot."

"And then? When you are finished?"

"Then," Bolan replied, "you wait to see what happens.

So-called holy men have been debating it since they invented speech. I'll let them stew about it, while I do my job."

Umaru mulled that over for a moment, nodding, then asked Bolan, "Who's next?"

"I don't want anyone to feel neglected," Bolan answered, opening his cell phone. "Let's give Uroil equal time, shall we?"

ARKADY ELTSIN felt as if he'd aged five years within as many hours. That was curious, since neither he nor Uroil had been damaged by the recent violence in Warri, but he understood the intricacies of his job and knew that things were always happening behind the scenes that might rebound to harm him, even if he hadn't authorized them or been made aware of their occurrence.

So it was that he had summoned Valentin Sidorov once again, to face his second in command across the spacious desk, searching the younger man's pale eyes for any hint of treachery.

"I take it that you are aware of the most recent incident in Warri?" Eltsin asked.

"The warehouse incident?" Sidorov nodded. "It has come to my attention."

"It was owned by one of our associates, I understand."

"Agu Ajani. Yes."

"And not, strictly speaking, a warehouse," Eltsin said.

"As far as that goes, sir—"

"In fact," he interrupted Sidorov, "it was some kind of drug lab, shipping center, or what have you."

Sidorov's shrug was casual.

"I don't know," he replied. "But say it's true. Why should we be surprised? Ajani is a criminal. We knew that when we first began supporting him against the Itsekiri."

"For our own advantage," Eltsin said. "Do you remember that, as well?"

"Of course, sir. It's the reason we do everything."

"And how do you suppose that it will help us now, to be associated with a known narcotics trafficker?"

"It shouldn't be a problem," Sidorov replied, "unless someone discovers the connection."

"And you don't suppose they will?"

"I won't pretend that it's impossible," Sidorov said. "Ajani could expose us, but for what reason? How would it help him? There's no paper trail connecting Uroil to the Ijaw. Nothing can be proved."

"Sometimes, suspicion is enough," Eltsin replied. "If my superiors suspected half of what's been done here—"

"Nothing has been done, sir. Uroil came and offered riches to a nation hamstrung by corruption, mired in tribal warfare. Obviously, since we're not a charity, it was in hope of earning profits. Anyone in Europe or America who now condemns that motive is a lying hypocrite."

"You know how these things work," Eltsin replied. "When the Americans cash in, they're 'spreading freedom.' When we follow their example, they all cross themselves and moan about an Evil Empire."

"Hypocrites, as I just said."

"But in the world view—"

Eltsin's cell phone chose that moment to disturb him. Frowning, he retrieved it from a pocket, opened it and saw that the incoming number had been masked. Against his better judgment, then, he answered.

"Yes?"

"Arkady Eltsin?" asked an unfamiliar voice.

"Who's this?" Eltsin demanded.

"A friend."

"I know my friends by name," Eltsin replied. "Goodbye."

"Before you hang up," the caller said, "I'm just wondering. How badly do you want to stay alive?"

"So now you threaten me?"

Eltsin felt angry color rising in his cheeks.

"A simple question. But you're right. There *is* a threat. Unfortunately, there's a good chance you'll be looking in the wrong direction when it hits you."

"I have no time to waste on childish riddles," Eltsin said. He saw Sidorov leaning forward in his chair, trying to work out what was happening.

"I'll come straight to the point, then," the caller said. "Someone close to you has sold you out. You're on the skids, and you don't even know it yet."

"Because you say so?"

"In your shoes," the caller said, "I might not buy it, either. But you're smart enough to see what's happening, assuming that you look below the surface."

"If you have a point—"

"Last night, your buddy's drugs went up in smoke. What's next? *Who's* next? Is it a tribal thing or something that's been cooking since the sixties? You remember Mao? Those territorial disputes when Khrushchev called the shots?"

"That's ancient history," Eltsin said.

"Maybe so. But then, you have to ask yourself who's paying me to take you out."

And then, as Eltsin felt the color drain from his face, the line went dead.

"A DOZEN DEAD, you say?"

"At least," Taiwo Babatunde said. "Maybe more."

The confirmation put a smile on Ekon Afolabi's face. In fact, he felt like leaping from his chair and breaking into dance, some tribal rhythm signifying triumph over mortal enemies.

The only problem was, he hadn't done a thing.

He had considered taking out Ajani's drug plant more than once, but something always made him hesitate. He wouldn't call it fear, but *apprehension* was a decent word. If he attacked Ajani and was beaten, it would injure Afolabi in a host of ways beyond the simple loss of men and weapons. It could ruin him in Warri, and throughout the state.

"Who should we thank for this?" he asked, half joking.

"No one seems to know," Babatunde replied. "The drug agency suspects we did it, but the witnesses describe two men, one of them white."

"Another white man?"

Afolabi felt his tension mounting, heard the thumping of his pulse inside his ears as his blood pressure spiked.

"Maybe the same one," Babatunde said, rolling his massive shoulders in a shrug.

"Why would you say that, Taiwo?"

"Well, how many white soldiers would you expect to find in Warri, Ekon?"

"The Americans and Russians all have mercenaries posing as security," Afolabi said.

Babatunde nodded. "And we know them, yes? We have their photographs on file before they've packed their footlockers. Our witnesses deny that any of them took the Ross girl."

"But you suggest the same man hit us *and* Ajani. What sense does that make?"

"Who knows the white man's mind, except another white man?" Babatunde countered. "All I know is that we cannot trust them."

That was true enough. But still—

The shrilling telephone distracted Afolabi, but he let one of his soldiers answer it. A man in his position was at no one's beck and call. He was about to dissect Taiwo's logic when the soldier—in this case, one Anthony Okotie, all of seventeen years old—approached him cautiously, clutching the cordless phone against his chest as if he feared it might escape.

"Sir, it's for you," the young man said.

"Who is it?" Afolabi asked.

"He will not give his name."

"Tell him to fuck off, then."

"He says it's vital, sir. For your survival."

Afolabi extended a languid hand, received the phone and brought it to his ear.

"Who is it that disturbs me?" he demanded.

"Someone who can help you stay alive," a voice said.

"You are a healer?" Afolabi asked sarcastically.

"Prevention's more my style," the stranger said. "I thought you'd like to know that someone wants you dead."

"That isn't news," Afolabi said. "Many people wish to see me dead."

"Okay, then. If you'd rather wing it without knowing how they'll come at you, good luck. Sorry to waste your time."

"Wait, now. What is it that you have to say?"

"That all depends. How much is your life worth to you?"

"So you want money?"

"Just a fair exchange. I didn't get as much for picking up the lady as I might've liked," the caller said.

A grimace twisted Afolabi's face. His stomach lurched.

"You took her?"

"Nothing personal. A job's a job."

"How do I know you speak the truth?"

"I'm guessing that your people found the bike I borrowed, where the chopper picked us up. That would have been the second search party. Your first one didn't make it."

"And you call me now because…?"

"I answered that already. When I got my paycheck, it was short. I'm settling accounts before I get the hell out of Dodge."

"I don't know Dodge," Afolabi said.

"Never mind," the caller answered. "Do you want to know who pinned the target on your back or not?"

UMARU HAD PREPARED a list of targets in the Warri area that covered both Ijaw and Itsekiri factions, plus some operations run by criminals who stood outside the bloody snarl of tribal conflict. Bolan, scanning through the roster, spied a commonly recurring name and asked, "Who's this?"

Umaru followed Bolan's pointing finger, frowned and said, "Idowu Yetunde. He's a wealthy gangster. What we call a godfather."

"You're kidding, right?"

"Why be surprised? Your films are popular throughout Nigeria. *The Godfather* had great influence on our criminals. They crave respect, which they obtain by force or bribery. Our godfathers support and counsel politicians who will serve them. Those, we call the godsons. Most of them are stupid, greedy men, but they are loyal to those who place them in the government. Disloyalty is the only sin. Its penalty is death."

"Small world," Bolan said.

And it all sounded familiar, sure. Back in the States, some members of the old-line Mafia had been afflicted with "Godfather syndrome" after Brando won his acting award for portraying Vito Corleone. The top man in New York's Five Families insisted that the movie's haunting theme be played each time he walked into a restaurant or nightclub.

No one with an instinct for survival laughed.

"So, tell me more about Yetunde."

"As I said, he is a major criminal. Much of his money comes from drugs, illegal weapons, prostitution, gambling. For the past ten years or so, he's also made a fortune from the Internet."

"How so?"

"You've heard of 419 confidence games?" Umaru asked.

"Advance-fee fraud," Bolan replied.

"Correct. Named for Section 419 of Nigeria's criminal code, governing fraud. E-mails go out around the world, offering fabulous rewards to someone who will help the sender with some private difficulty. Details vary. He's in prison, or has wealthy relatives in custody. His bank account is frozen by the state, or he must pay a legal fee to claim a great inheritance. He asks a perfect stranger for some small—or not-so-small—amount of cash, and promises to split his fortune with the benefactor he has never met when all has been arranged."

Bolan had never tackled organized con men, but he knew they duped gullible millions worldwide with their 419 scams, also called the "Nigerian letter" technique for its most frequent point of origin. According to the last report he'd seen from Justice, 419 scammers raked in eight billion dollars every year, and their haul was increasing, despite public warnings to would-be investors.

The urge to get rich in a hurry, without working, seemed to be a universal human weakness, and the rip-off artists loved to milk their cash cows dry.

Bolan pointed to an address on the hit list that was decorated with a penciled asterisk. "Is this his main hangout?" he asked Umaru.

"Yes. Yetunde has an office and apartment there, above his largest boiler room. Is that the proper term?"

"It works for me," Bolan replied, imagining a cyber-sweatshop where Yetunde's minions worked keyboards around the clock, mass-mailing pleas for cash around the globe.

"You wish to visit him?" Umaru asked.

"It's like you read my mind," Bolan replied.

CHAPTER ELEVEN

Idowu Yetunde lit his first cigar of the morning and swirled its fragrant smoke around inside his mouth before exhaling a gray cloud. Each cigar cost him roughly the equivalent of three dollars, U.S.—but Yetunde believed he got his money's worth.

It was a subject near and dear to him: the acquisition and distribution of wealth. Like most Nigerians outside the country's ruling dynasties, Yetunde had come up from nothing, running wild through Lagos with a gang of urchins, living by his wits and nerve. Experience soon taught him that the stronger boys were often less intelligent than he, and they could be persuaded to protect him— even serve him—if he proved his worth.

Of course, it hadn't been as easy as it sounded. He was scarred from battles nearly lost but nearly didn't count, as long as he came out on top at last.

And Idowu Yetunde always came out on top.

He had been reasonably wealthy when the oil boom lured him from Lagos down to Warri. At the same time, idle conversation with an old-school swindler had enlightened Yetunde to the wonders of cyberspace. A relatively small investment got him started, and today he ranked among the top five con men in Nigeria, if not all of West Africa. Yetunde could retire tomorrow, never work another day, and still live out his life in luxury.

But what would be the fun in that?

The truth was, he enjoyed preying on human weakness, whether through long-distance fraud or catering to other vices—drug addiction, sexual frustration, the compulsive need to gamble. You could say that human frailty made Yetunde strong.

But he wasn't invincible.

Yetunde never got himself confused with Superman. He knew that bullets wouldn't ricochet on contact with his body. That he couldn't walk through fire unharmed, or ride the shock wave of a bomb blast with a smile etched on his face. And he couldn't survive in prison with the perverts.

To avoid such things, Yetunde had a private army of enforcers, plus the law-enforcement officers who sold their badges and their honor for a little something extra on the side. He had the godsons he had sponsored in political careers, ready to take his calls at any hour of the day or night and do as they were told.

Invulnerable? No. But well protected, certainly.

And yet, he worried that it might not be enough.

The intertribal violence in Delta State was constantly increasing. The authorities couldn't control it; some of them no longer tried. Yetunde purchased peace of mind by shelling out protection payments to both sides, juggling his books to make the loss look tax-deductible, but as the local rate of violence increased, he doubted that appeasement could protect him.

Not that he considered shutting down. Far from it.

On the contrary, he had considered different ways to get

the greedy bastards off his back, from helping the authorities convict the rival leaders, to eliminating them himself. So far, there had been no clear opportunity. But if the mayhem escalated any further, he imagined that it would be relatively simple to kill Afolabi and Ajani, planting evidence to blame each for the other's death.

It helped, of course, to have police on his payroll.

Before the week was out, with any luck, Yetunde might be liberated from his bondage to the warring tribes. But first, he had more pleasurable business to conduct in his apartment two floors up from what he called the Warri Data Center, where his lackeys worked around the clock to swindle idiots in every time zone on the planet.

Waiting in his bedroom at that very moment was a delicious eighteen-year-old.

Yetunde couldn't keep from smiling as he waited for the private elevator that would take him to his quarters. Everything, he thought, was looking up.

"YETUNDE OWNS the building, top to bottom?" Bolan asked again, determined to confirm it.

"That's correct," Umaru said.

"He doesn't rent out space to anybody else? No one inside but his employees?"

"Guards. Computer operators. Staff for his apartment, I assume."

Bolan had parked his stolen car behind the Warri Data Center, half a block downrange and partly shielded by a large overflowing garbage bin that smelled ripe enough to rate a dozen health code violations.

"When's their trash pickup?" he asked.

Umaru blinked and frowned at that. "I'm sorry, I have no idea. If I had known—"

"Forget it. They have room to work around us if they come while we're inside."

Worst-case scenario, they might emerge with shooters on their heels, to find a garbage truck obstructing their retreat. The obvious solution: deal with any gunmen on the premises before they left.

No sweat—unless Yetunde had an army waiting in the square, four-story red-brick building. In which case, they could wind up sweating blood.

"Ready?" he asked Umaru.

In the shotgun seat, Umaru double-checked his Daewoo K-2 rifle, making sure he had a live round in the chamber and the safety off. Bolan did likewise with his Steyr AUG, confirming that the see-through plastic magazine was fully loaded, the rifle's fire-selector switch set for 3-round bursts.

The alley he had chosen was deserted as they stepped out of the Honda, carrying their rifles slung and more or less concealed from any distant passersby. A few more seconds and it wouldn't matter who was watching. Bolan wondered if Yetunde's lair was soundproofed to prevent eavesdropping by competitors or the police, but in the last analysis it didn't matter.

They were going in. Case closed.

Bolan assumed that few, if any, of Yetunde's keyboard lackeys would be shooters. If they started coming up with guns, he'd drop them where they stood, but it would work to his advantage if they fled, bearing the story of a mixed-race hit team striking at the city's foremost godfather, after the raids on MEND and the Ajani drug lab.

Anything that helped confuse his adversaries was a bonus for the Executioner.

He counted on the back door being locked, so that was no surprise. He picked the outer locks, Umaru standing by to watch his back, but when that job was done, the door still wouldn't open.

Bolted on the inside.

They'd reached a point where it was time to raise or fold, and Bolan didn't plan on turning back before he had a look inside the Warri Data Center.

"Step back while I blow the bolt," he cautioned, waiting while Umaru moved around behind him.

Bolan thought it was a toss-up whether they'd installed a bolt above the doorknob or topside, inserted in the upper frame. To play it safe, he fired short bursts at both spots, then stepped forward, kicked the door and slammed it open with sufficient force to strike the wall behind it.

Startled voices spoke excitedly from inside as Bolan crossed the threshold, but the ones that he could make out didn't sound like soldiers. He was half a dozen paces in before a door flew open on his left, disgorging a young man armed with a pistol.

Bolan shot him in the face before he had a chance to use it, didn't need to wait to see if 5.56 mm tumblers fired at point-blank range had done their job. The guy was down and out, but from the sound of running feet, he hadn't been alone.

Bolan sidestepped into the open doorway, found his cover there and waited for his enemies to show themselves.

IDOWU YETUNDE had his pants around his ankles when he heard the first gunshots. Preoccupied with the woman kneeling at his feet, it was tempting for Yetunde to dismiss them as a car backfiring in the street.

But he knew better.

He had heard enough gunshots and backfires to realize that exhaust pipes didn't stutter in short bursts like automatic weapons. No, someone had to be shooting, but that didn't mean—

"A moment please," he said regretfully.

Hobbled and muttering profanity, Yetunde waddled like a penguin to the nearest tinted windows facing the street three floors below. No one outside could see him, but his view was unobstructed.

Nothing.

And it hadn't really sounded as though the shots were coming from the street outside the Warri Data Center. Possibly in back? The alley was—

More shots, slightly less muffled than before. They were inside the building now, ground floor. Yetunde stooped to grab his slacks.

"Get dressed!" he snapped at his companion. "We're in danger!"

Not that he was overly concerned about Abebi, as lovely and compliant as she was. Yetunde understood that no one would invade his property to kill a prostitute.

He was the target. There could be no doubt of that.

Yetunde didn't know if he was being robbed, or if he was a target for assassination, and it made no difference at the moment. Either way, he could be killed within the next few moments if his guards downstairs failed to contain the enemy.

Yetunde crossed the spacious bedroom, gripped a painted landscape by its frame and swung it outward on a hinge fastened along the left-hand side. A safe was thus revealed, with numbered buttons in place of the traditional dial. Even in this extremity, Yetunde shifted his position to prevent Abebi from glimpsing the combination.

Inside the safe, there sat thick wads of cash, banded in blocks equivalent to ten thousand U.S. dollars. In fact, most of the currency with which Yetunde stuffed his pockets now *was* dollars, siphoned from the black-market economy of Delta State to form Yetunde's nest egg.

His escape fund.

Beside the cash rested a Skorpion vz.61 machine pistol, loaded with twenty 7.65 mm rounds in a curved magazine, its wire stock folded topside to reduce its length. Two extra magazines went underneath Yetunde's belt, in back, before he palmed the weapon, closed his safe and locked it, then replaced the landscape that concealed it.

Grimacing as the reports of gunfire echoed through his bedroom floor, Yetunde crossed the room to reach his walk-in closet. There, he first slipped on a Kevlar vest, then donned the jacket he had recently removed, which matched his pants.

Ready.

Yetunde left the woman as she dressed, passing from the bedroom to his so-called study, where his private elevator was concealed within another closet.

It would take him down to the garage, below street level, where his cars sat waiting. All of them were bulletproof, at least in theory, and his pocket jangled with the keys for all of them. A few more minutes and he would be safe— at least, for now.

Then he would take the necessary steps to find out who dared threaten him at home.

And once he knew their names, God help them all.

THE GUARDS were well-armed, mean-looking—and out of practice. If he had been forced to guess, Bolan would have surmised that none of them had fired a shot in anger for at least a year, perhaps a good deal longer. Their reaction time was on the sluggish side, their movements rusty.

So they died.

They weren't exactly sitting ducks, of course. A lazy soldier could be dangerous, and even untrained amateurs could make a lucky shot. It took only one bullet, rightly placed, and Bolan would be twitching in his death throes on the floor.

He took no chances with the hired help, knocking down the guards as soon as they appeared in front of him. Umaru had his left flank covered, cutting down a couple of Yetunde's shooters when they popped out of a smoky lounge on that side, television blaring in the background.

Umaru put a bullet through the big set's picture tube and silenced the frenetic game show that was playing. Turning back to Bolan with a little shrug, he said, "I can't stand all that noise."

The noise of gunfire rattled on, coupled with the panicked sounds of Idowu Yetunde's keyboard operators scrambling for the nearest exit. Bolan watched them long enough to know that none seemed threatening, then focused on the dwindling group of men who meant to kill him.

There'd been something like a dozen when he started, less than half that many standing by the time the last of the computer con artists had vanished from the killing floor. They rallied toward the end, after retreating to the conference room where they were cornered, but a frag grenade killed two of them and left the three survivors wounded, stunned, no challenge for their executioners.

"Penthouse," Bolan said, hoping they might find Yetunde waiting for them in his pad. They took the service stairs two at a time, passed no one on the way and didn't hear the building's central elevator running in its shaft beside the stairwell as they climbed.

But they were still too late.

A startled-looking, half-dressed woman was waiting for the elevator when Bolan and Umaru reached the fourth floor. After noting that the woman was lovely and unarmed, Bolan brushed past her to invade Yetunde's quarters through a door that had been left ajar.

And found it hastily vacated by its tenant.

"We have missed him," Umaru said.

"Not by much, the way it looks," Bolan replied.

But gone was gone.

A far-off siren wailed, still faint with distance. Bolan couldn't tell if it was headed his way, but he knew that they were out of time. They took the stairs again and reached the ground floor just in time to see the shaky woman exit the building.

All clear now.

Bolan unhooked the next-to-last of his white-phosphorus grenades and left it smoking in the middle of Yetunde's boiler room. By the time they hit the alley, double-timing toward their waiting ride, white smoke was pouring from the exit, trailing after them.

A moment later they were rolling. Bolan merged with traffic, watched his rearview mirror, while he ran Umaru's list of targets in his head. The shotgun rider's voice distracted him.

"I may be able to locate Yetunde," Umaru said.

"Oh?"

"I have informants of my own. As in the food chain, you might say."

"Contacting them means that you'd have to surface," Bolan said.

"It could be useful."

"Could be dangerous."

"I'll risk it," Umaru said.

"All right, then," Bolan replied. "Where are we going?"

UMARU HAD a system for his extra eyes and ears in Warri. As his handlers gave him cash for information, so he paid the men and women who provided much of what he sold to the NDLEA, the NPF, the NIA and the Americans. On a hot tip he might clear two, three hundred U.S. dollars after covering his people on the street.

But not this day.

Umaru understood that he was playing for his life this time. He had been targeted for execution, and he didn't know if it was linked to his collaboration with Matt Cooper, on the CIA's behalf, or whether someone had been stalking him for days, seeking to punish him for helping send a relative or friend to prison.

Either way, he soon learned that the word was out.

Umaru made five calls, each to a different informant. Three were shunted off to voice mail and ignored. A fourth hung up without a word the second that he recognized Umaru's voice. The fifth was brave enough to speak, though not for long.

"You're poison, you," the petty thief and drug dealer declared. "If you know what's good for you, go somewhere else. Don't call anymore."

Bolan had waited through the round of calls, silent, until he sensed Umaru giving up. "Doors closing on you now?" he asked.

"So it would seem."

"Bad luck. But we can get along without them."

"There's one more I can try," Umaru said.

"Go ahead, then."

"Not on the telephone. I need to see her."

"Her?"

"My best informant, if she'll help me now."

Sophie Adagoke had been more than an informant of Umaru's—still was, on occasion, if the truth be told—but after living in his flat for six months, two years back, both had agreed they needed "space." Umaru wasn't sure exactly what that meant in Sophie's case, but for his own part, he was happy to resume the bachelor life that might strike some as lonely, but that somehow gave him peace of mind.

Sophie continued to supply him with good information,

gleaned from tipsy patrons at the Dragon's Den, a night-club where she doubled as a singer and hostess. Many of the customers were criminals of one sort or another, but the prices kept out petty thieves and other trash. When they spent the odd nostalgic night together, normally at her place, it was almost like old times.

Almost.

Umaru gave directions to the Dragon's Den and Bolan followed them, after explaining why he thought the drop-in was a bad idea.

"Somebody's on to you," he said. "They could be onto her. We could be walking into trouble that's avoidable."

"Not we," Umaru said. "No whites go to the Dragon's Den."

"I'm in a time-warp now," Bolan replied. "Is this Nigeria or Mississippi in the sixties?"

"You would be allowed inside," Umaru said. "But then, no one will speak to me. Perhaps forever."

"There goes the neighborhood. I get it," Bolan said. "I wouldn't want to cramp your style."

They parked a block from the club, behind a service station that had shut down for the night. Umaru made the walk alone, thankful for the QSZ-92's solid weight at the small of his back. Along the way, Umaru felt as if a dozen pairs of eyes were tracking him, perhaps watching him over gunsights, waiting for the signal that would let them cut him down.

Then he was at the club, paying his cover charge, passing from muggy air that smelled of car exhaust into a world of lights and noise, fogged by tobacco and at least a touch of ganja.

Sophie Adagoke wasn't near the door or up onstage. Umaru drifted toward the bar, guessing that she was on a break or maybe changing outfits between sets. He could afford to wait, at least a little while.

The sense of being watched had followed him inside the Dragon's Den, but this time it was no illusion. He could see heads turning, tracking him across the smoky room. Facial expressions ranged from mild surprise and curiosity to something very much like rage.

Umaru had almost decided he should leave, for Sophie's sake, when a deep voice behind him said, "She's gone."

Wiping his face clean of emotion as he turned, Umaru said, "Who's gone?"

"Your bitch," the stranger told him, sneering underneath a sad excuse for a mustache. "Don't worry, though. You'll join her soon."

The man was reaching for his pocket when Umaru drew his pistol, jammed it hard into the stranger's gut and snarled, "You have a choice to make. Will you die here, or come outside with me?"

"You won't shoot," the other man said. "I'm not alone."

"If that's the case," Umaru challenged him, "what have I got to lose?"

The stranger saw death in his eyes and nodded, then.

"Outside," he said, and let Umaru guide him toward the door.

BOLAN HAD THOUGHT Umaru would return alone. A long-shot second option had him turn up with the woman he had come to meet. The very last thing Bolan had expected was Umaru hurrying along the sidewalk with another man, gripping his sidekick's arm with one hand, while the other very obviously held a gun against the stranger's ribs.

"Who's this?" Bolan asked as Umaru shoved his grim companion into the backseat, climbed in beside him and began to rifle through his pockets.

"He's a liar," Umaru said.

"Ah. Just what we need."

A sharp metallic snap behind him drew Bolan's eyes to the rearview, where he saw Umaru brandishing a wicked switchblade.

"And stupid, too," Umaru said. "He brings a knife to a gunfight."

Bolan already had the car in motion when he asked, "What was the lie, again?"

"'I'm not alone,' he said." Umaru mimicking a voice that Bolan hadn't heard as yet. "Where are your friends, then?" he demanded, jabbing with the knife.

"You'll meet them soon enough," the man said.

"And were you lying about Sophie?" Umaru asked.

"That's your own fault," the prisoner said. "Seducing her to be your spy. Your little cockroach."

Bolan heard Umaru strike him, followed by a squeal that brought his eyes back to the rearview. There, Umaru had the switchblade's tip buried a quarter-inch or so into the captive's cheek.

"Watch out for bloodstains on your clothes," Bolan advised, then focused his attention on the flow of traffic.

"You are right," Umaru said after a long, tense moment. "We must take him someplace where the blood won't matter."

"I'm not going anywhere with you," the stranger said, half whining.

"We're halfway there," Umaru said. "Your only choice is whether you survive the night or not."

"So," Bolan asked from the driver's seat, "we're halfway *where*, again?"

Umaru gave directions to a west-side neighborhood, if you could call it that, where vacant lots stood between dilapidated houses like gaps in a mouth filled with half-rotten teeth. One of the houses had a small carport on its north side. Bolan nosed into it, as he had been directed, switching off the Honda's lights and engine.

"You might say this is my home away from home," Umaru told him as he dragged their unexpected guest out of the car. "We shall have privacy, I think."

"For what?" Bolan inquired, as if he didn't know.

"To ask my friend some questions," Umaru said. "I assure you that he will cooperate."

CHAPTER TWELVE

"Now, is everyone entirely clear about the plan? Questions from anyone? On anything at all?"

A dozen pairs of somber eyes regarded Ekon Afolabi as if he were God Almighty, issuing commandments from on high. It was an attitude that he appreciated—and demanded—from his soldiers, but he sometimes worried that the awe they felt for him prevented them from asking questions if they were confused. And that could get them killed.

Or, more important, keep Afolabi from achieving his intended goal.

He glanced at Taiwo Babatunde, standing to his left, and raised one eyebrow. They had known each other for so long that the man could read Afolabi's face better than he could read a printed page.

"The man asks if there's any questions!" Taiwo snapped at the assembled gunmen. "If you got them, ask them now. No time for wondering when you're up in the middle of it, eh?"

Still nothing from the troops.

"All right, then," Afolabi said, forcing a smile that radiated confidence. "Remember that the man you seek must not be harmed. If he resists, after his guards are dead, you have the stun guns, yes?"

Four of the soldiers answered, "Yes, sir!"

"And they're fully charged?" Afolabi asked.

"Yes, sir!"

"Show me."

Four hands dived into pockets, brandished objects that resembled cheap electric razors. Four thumbs pressed the triggers. Tiny bolts of lightning crackled between blunt electrodes, treating Afolabi to the scent of ozone.

"Good," he said. "I will accept no other injury to Jared Ross. Whoever harms him may expect to share his pain tenfold."

Twelve voices, this time, barking, "Yes, sir!"

"You are dismissed," he told them. "Go and make our people proud."

When the twelve soldiers had departed, Babatunde said, "Perhaps I should go with them, after all."

"Do you not trust the one you put in charge?"

"I do, of course."

"We have no problem, then."

"Something could go wrong, Ekon. There's always something."

"In which case, you would be jeopardized, old friend."

Babatunde blinked back at him, as if confused by Afolabi's words.

"It is my job—"

"To choose the best men for the team, as I requested. Have you done so?"

"Yes. But if they kill him—"

Afolabi fanned the air with one hand, a dismissive gesture. "We would lose the ransom," he replied. "But our point would still be made. Others will not defy us with the grim example set before them."

"Ah. I understand now."

"Either way, we win," Afolabi said.

"As you say."

"This time tomorrow, Jared Ross will either wish that he had paid his daughter's ransom, or he will have no wishes at all."

"A lesson," Babatunde said.

"It's always best to be the teacher, rather than the student," Afolabi said.

"I always hated school."

"The six years you were in it?" Afolabi teased him.

"Six *long* years, it seemed to me."

"But all behind you now. And see how far you've come."

"I should go back and find my teachers," Babatunde said.

"To boast of your success?"

"To cut their throats."

"Perhaps another time. We're busy at the moment, yes?"

"Of course."

"But when we've taught our lesson to the white men who run K-Tech, well, perhaps you will have cause to celebrate."

"I shall look forward to it," Babatunde said, beaming.

"The simple pleasures," Afolabi told his old friend, "are the best."

THE CAPTIVE'S NAME was Simon Aguba. Beyond that, he wasn't inclined to disclose anything, but Umaru was light-years beyond taking no for an answer. After they'd secured Aguba to a straight-backed wooden chair, Umaru asked for time alone with him, to help Aguba recognize the error of his ways.

Torture revolted Bolan at a primal level, but he'd used pain in the past to squeeze a vital bit of information out of this or that maimed predator, when time was of the essence.

The Reader Service — Here's how it works:

If offer card is missing write to: The Reader Service, P.O. Box 1867, Buffalo NY 14240-1867

NO POSTAGE
NECESSARY
IF MAILED
IN THE
UNITED STATES

BUSINESS REPLY MAIL
FIRST-CLASS MAIL   PERMIT NO. 717   BUFFALO, NY

POSTAGE WILL BE PAID BY ADDRESSEE

THE READER SERVICE
PO BOX 1867
BUFFALO NY 14240-9952

Get FREE BOOKS and a FREE GIFT when you play the...

LAS VEGAS
GAME

Just scratch off the gold box with a coin. Then check below to see the gifts you get! →

YES!
I have scratched off the gold box. Please send me my **2 FREE BOOKS** and **gift for which I qualify.** I understand that I am under no obligation to purchase any books as explained on the back of this card.

366 ADL E4CE   166 ADL E4CE

FIRST NAME   LAST NAME

ADDRESS

APT.#   CITY

STATE/PROV.   ZIP/POSTAL CODE

7	7	7	Worth TWO FREE BOOKS plus a BONUS Mystery Gift!
🍒	🍒	🍒	Worth TWO FREE BOOKS!
🔔	🔔	♣	TRY AGAIN!

Offer limited to one per household and not valid to current subscribers of Gold Eagle® books. All orders subject to approval. Please allow 4 to 6 weeks for delivery.

Your Privacy—Worldwide Library is committed to protecting your privacy. Our privacy policy is available online at www.ReaderService.com or upon request from the Reader Service. From time to time we make our lists of customers available to reputable third parties who may have a product or service of interest to you. If you would prefer us not to share your name and address, please check here ☐. **Help us get it right**—We strive for accurate, respectful and relevant communications. To clarify or modify your communication preferences, visit us at www.ReaderService.com/consumerchoice.

Drawing a moral line between himself and those he hunted was a fine idea, in theory, but his own experience in war had taught him that the line was hard to see when you were peering through a veil of battle smoke.

He left Umaru to it, went into the fenced backyard and waited for what seemed like ages, but was only twenty minutes on the clock. Instead of agonizing over what was happening inside the house, he pushed his thoughts downrange, to the remaining targets on his list.

Assuming he could pull it off, how many would he have to blitz before one of his adversaries cracked? And would the men who'd promised money to a nameless stranger in return for information keep the rendezvous they'd scheduled? If Bolan bothered showing up, would he be greeted by a bagman or a squad of shooters sent to take him out?

A faint sound from the house made Bolan pause, half turning, but he shrugged it off. Umaru had been through a lot since they found each other in the marketplace, and he was grieving the loss of a friend, a lover, whatever. Simon Aguba might not be responsible for that himself, but by his own account he knew who was. And Bolan had a strong hunch he would talk before he died.

He heard the back door open, turned to find Umaru standing on the tiny concrete stoop, two steps above the weedy yard. His face revealed no lessening of anger or anxiety.

"You find out where Yetunde went?" Bolan asked.

"No. This one was Itsekiri, part of MEND. He told me who killed Sophie. I will find them someday, if it takes a lifetime. But we have to hurry now."

"Why's that?" Bolan inquired.

"To stop a kidnapping."

Umaru saved the rest of it until they had the Honda rolling back toward downtown Warri. He had left Simon Aguba's body in the house with the doors unlocked.

"I'm finished with it, anyway," Umaru said.

Bolan assumed he meant the house. He asked, "So, who's the target this time?"

"Jared Ross," Umaru said. "It seems that Afolabi has been brooding over Ross's daughter and the ransom that he lost. He reckons that K-Tech Petroleum will pay a good price for its man in Warri, and for peace. Of course, no matter what they pay, there'll be no peace with MEND."

"There'll be no kidnapping if I can help it," Bolan said.

"We may already be too late. I'm sorry for the wasted time," Umaru offered.

"Look at it the other way around," Bolan replied. "Without our side trip and your grilling, we'd have no idea that Ross was on the spot."

"Still, if I had been more capable—"

"And how would that work?" Bolan asked him. "You got unexpected answers when you didn't even know the questions. Cut yourself some slack."

"All right. But if we *are* too late—"

"Then we revise Plan A. Focus on rattling cages until someone tells us where they're holding Ross, or else agrees to give him up. I've played this game before."

He didn't mention that in several cases, where a friend's life was at stake, the answers he required had come too late. But if that happened here, Bolan's response would be the same.

Scorched earth.

"I STILL SAY this is too damned risky."

Jared Ross had heard it all before from his chief officer in charge of plant and personal security.

"There's risk in everything we do here, Clint," he said. "The only way we can avoid it is to barricade ourselves inside the compound, or pack up and leave the country."

"Sir, I understand the normal risks," Clint Hamer said. "I've got those covered. But it hasn't been a day yet since your daughter got away from kidnappers who planned to kill her. Now you put yourself at risk. For what? A dinner party with the Russians and Chinese? They hate each other, and they both hate us. Why bother?"

Ross smiled and answered, "You're a soldier, not a businessman. Part of my job is making nice with folks who hate me—while I try my best to stab them in the back."

"I'm with you on the last part," Hamer said.

"The whole thing should be over in two hours tops," Ross said. "So, if you're ready?"

"Yes, sir. Everything's in place."

Hamer walked him to the white stretch limo, one of three that K-Tech kept on-site, and Ross found five men waiting. He knew all of them were armed, although he couldn't see the weapons underneath their tailored jackets. Then again, maybe their heavy weapons were concealed inside the limousine.

When they were buttoned up inside and moving, Ross took one more stab at getting Hamer to relax.

"It doesn't make much sense, when you consider it," he said.

"What's that, sir?" Hamer asked.

"That anyone would make a move on me so soon, after they lost Mandy and had their asses handed to them on a platter."

"Mr. Ross, we're not exactly dealing with a stable crowd. Mix greed, fanaticism and whatever dope they're smoking this week, you can pretty well expect the unexpected."

"Which is your department, Clint. You have my every confidence."

"I blew it with your daughter, sir."

"Nonsense. She slipped out of the compound on her own, and damn near paid the price. Thank God she didn't suffer any worse than being dragged around the countryside by lunatics."

"Yes, sir. But—"

"No buts. That's an order. Let's get through this silly smile-fest and—"

Inside the armored limousine, the first shots sounded like a string of distant firecrackers exploding, then Ross heard the bullets striking bodywork and three-inch laminated glass.

Despite the fact that they were shielded from incoming fire, Hamer dragged Ross to the limo's floor and crouched beside him, gun in hand. The other guards were busy drawing compact submachine guns, turning toward the long car's nearest gun ports.

"We have one car in pursuit," a guard said from the driver's side.

"Two cars," another answered from the other side.

"Assume that we're outnumbered," Hamer told them. "Leave the gun ports shut unless you have a dead-bang target, and remember that the cops here take a dim view of civilian casualties."

The plainclothes soldiers grunted in response, focused on their pursuers. Hamer didn't have to tell the driver he should step on it and shake the chase cars, if he could. Not that a stretch limo in Warri downtown traffic had much chance of ditching two midsize sedans.

"You get a chance to sideswipe either of these bastards," Hamer called out to their wheelman, "take it!"

"Be my pleasure, boss," the driver said.

Damned if he wasn't smiling.

"Clint?" Ross spoke up from the floor.

"Yes, sir?"

"If it comes down to it, I want a gun."

Hamer removed his backup pistol from its ankle holster, handing it to Ross.

"Just keep your finger off the trigger now," he warned. "Glock hides the safety there. I'll tell you when it's time to go for broke."

THE LATE Simon Aguba hadn't known how many soldiers would be going after Jared Ross, but he'd revealed that MEND would make its move with Ross in transit to or from some kind of party at the Delta Petroleum Institute, located half a mile from K-Tech's downtown headquarters. The Honda's dashboard clock told Bolan that Ross had to be on the road, unless he wanted to be fashionably late.

Instead of driving past the K-Tech compound and pursuing Ross from there, Bolan picked up his likely route of travel two blocks east of headquarters and started weaving through the traffic toward the oilman's destination. Since he didn't know if Afolabi's men had planned on jumping Ross before or after his appearance at the institute, he might be forced to park somewhere and wait the party out.

Or, as Umaru feared, they might already be too late.

"Up there!" Umaru said, pointing, a heartbeat after Bolan saw the running fight in progress.

"Got it," Bolan answered.

It was hard to miss the white stretch limo barreling through traffic, with a pair of chase cars flanking it, bright muzzle-flashes winking from their open windows. Bolan took it as a given that Ross had bodyguards on board, but they weren't returning fire so far. A wise decision, overall, since one stray bullet striking a bystander could provoke an incident as lethal for the company as any threat to Jared Ross himself.

Bolan accelerated, racing to catch up, and heard the traffic sounds grow louder as Umaru powered down his window.

"If you get a shot," Bolan advised, "take it."

"There is a risk to bystanders," Umaru said.

"Same thing if they keep firing wild," Bolan replied.

He'd closed the gap to thirty yards, no problem staying with the K-Tech limo, but the chase cars veering back and forth prevented him from pulling even with them. Bolan drew his 93-R from its shoulder rig and held it cradled in his lap, driving right-handed, hearing bleats from angry horns mixed with the sharp staccato rap of automatic weapons.

"Almost there," Umaru told him as he eased the muzzle of his Daewoo out the open window. "Just a little to the left."

Bolan tried to accommodate him, checking out his side and rearview mirrors as he changed lanes, drifting. He was ready for the racket when Umaru fired his first short burst, bullets gnawing their way across the right-hand chase car's trunk.

Not bad.

The target swerved, a startled face framed in the wide rear window, then Umaru's second burst frosted the glass and blew some of it back into the car.

Not bad at all.

Bolan was busy on his own side, then, aiming with his Beretta toward the chase car on the K-Tech limo's left-hand side. He sent a 3-round burst downrange, saw two slugs scar the right rear fender, while the third punched through a window on the passenger's side.

That made the driver swerve to his left, but he recovered swiftly, veering back to bring the limo under fire. One of the backseat shooters tried for Bolan, firing at an awkward angle with a stubby SMG, but he was off by six feet, easily. A van behind the Honda took those bullets through the windshield, while the driver locked his brakes and lost it in a noisy, tumbling roll.

So much for traffic coming up behind them in the next block, anyway. Someone inside the limo, or along the route of battle, would have phoned for the police by now, but Bolan couldn't let it go. He couldn't let the hunters have an unobstructed shot at Jared Ross.

And he suspected that their snatch plans had gone out the window now.

From that point onward, they'd be going for a kill.

"GET OFF THIS street, for Christ's sake!" Jared Ross commanded, feeling stupid even as he said it, from his prone position on the floor.

"They'll have guards at the institute," Clint Hamer said. "We need to—"

"No!" Ross interrupted him. "You think I went to roll up to the gates like this and start a firefight on the street outside the goddamned institute? Get on the radio for backup *now,* and find someplace where we can either sit it out until they come or deal with this ourselves!"

Reluctantly, Hamer addressed the limo's driver. "Well, you heard the man! What are you waiting for?"

"An opening in traffic," the driver said, then he swerved abruptly to the left, gunning the stretch through an intersection Jared Ross couldn't see.

He heard the horns blaring in protest, however, and braced himself for a collision that seemed imminent. Somehow they made it through, and then were running south, the two pursuit vehicles keeping pace.

"Three cars now, damn it!" one of Hamer's guards announced. "Hey, wait. The new guy's shooting at the others! What the—"

"Are you sure?" Hamer demanded, leaving Ross's side to press his face against one of the tinted windows on the driver's side.

"Hell, yes! Look! There! He's firing, but it's not at us."

"Who could it be?" Ross queried no one in particular. "Did you already call for help?"

"Not me, boss," the driver said. "I'm on top of that, right now."

"Then who—"

More bullets raked the limo, making no impression beyond ruining its paint and putting scuff marks on the three-ply windows. It would take more than assault rifles to crack the vehicle that sheltered him.

And Ross was worried that his would-be killers might be packing more, just waiting for an opportunity to use it. He supposed they couldn't fire a rocket launcher from a speeding car without endangering themselves, but—

Christ! What was he thinking?

"Hold that backup call," he ordered. "Turn back to the K-Tech compound, while you get the cops moving. If these shits want to fight, we'll do it at our own house."

"Roger that, sir!" said the driver.

Ross stayed where he was, clutching the borrowed Glock, and prayed that he would have a chance to use it soon against the bastards who had dared to touch his little girl.

"WHAT'S THIS?" Umaru asked. "Where are they going now?"

"Evasive driving," Bolan said as he squeezed off another 3-round burst from his Beretta. "Maybe waiting for police to intercept them. Maybe heading home."

"To K-Tech?"

"Why not? They must have reinforcements there. It makes more sense than leading this bunch to a dinner party with the competition."

"Saving face, you mean?"

"Or saving lives," Bolan replied. "Maybe Ross wants to spring a trap."

"Can he succeed?"

"I don't tell fortunes," Bolan said. "It's possible, I guess. But we don't want to be there when it happens."

"Why not?" Umaru asked.

"Cops and K-Tech's shooters swarming all over the place? If we can't take these guys out first, we need to disengage."

"So let us take them," Umaru said with a crooked grin.

Bolan floored the accelerator, closing up behind the nearer of the two chase cars. One of the men inside was leaning from his window, lining up a shot at Bolan's Honda, when Umaru hit him with a short burst to the head and face that sent his weapon flying while his corpse slumped back inside the sedan.

Instead of backing off, Umaru kept on firing, stitching holes along the driver's side of the pursuit vehicle, his bullets knocking shiny divots the size of silver dollars in its faded paint. Bolan was watching when the driver took a hit and toppled over to his right into the shotgun rider's lap. That startled shooter grabbed the wheel, but there was no way he could reach the brake or the accelerator with a body sprawled across his thighs.

Umaru fired a parting burst after the chase car as it leaped the curb and plowed into the plate-glass frontage of a restaurant. Some of the diners might be hurt or worse, but Bolan couldn't stop to help them.

It was his job to wreak havoc, not repair it.

They were riding on the second chase car's bumper now, faces shouting curses at them through the shattered rear window. Bolan triggered another burst from his selective-fire pistol and saw one of those faces rupture, dropping out of sight. The others quickly ducked below his line of fire, while someone raised a gun and started rapid-firing blindly toward the Honda.

Bolan swerved to miss the worst of it, giving Umaru the angle he needed to rake the car's trunk and rear driver's side. One of his bullets found a tire, somehow, and it collapsed into a wallowing rumble, throwing the driver off stride.

Bolan reversed direction in an instant, coming up along the passenger's side of his target, Beretta extended through his open window. He started firing before the cars were lined up side by side, blasting 3-round bursts at the driver and his huddled passengers.

And somewhere in the midst of it, he scored.

The chase car swerved away, into oncoming traffic, and collided head-on with a bus. Bolan had floored his brake pedal before the echoes of the crash had time to fade, reversing until he was level with the crumpled ruin of the chase car.

There was no point letting any of the shooters get away to fight another day. Killing them now would save him time—and just might save the rest of Warri's residents a world of future hurt.

Umaru ran around the car to join him, just as Bolan leaned inside and saw two of their enemies still moving. Bolan shot one through the head, then stepped back as Umaru drilled the other with a Daewoo double-tap.

And they had turned back to the Honda when he saw the white stretch limo idling in the middle of the street, a short block farther on. A second later its backup lights winked at him, the behemoth rolling in reverse toward where he stood with gun in hand, while terrified pedestrians sought cover anywhere they could along the street.

The limo stopped a dozen paces from the Honda. Two armed men the size of football linemen stepped out of the car, their automatic rifles looking almost toylike in their hands. Next came the boss, wearing a dazed expression on his face.

"It's you again," Jared Ross said.

"I don't really have the time to socialize," Bolan replied.

"You saved *my* ass this time."

"Looks like it," Bolan said. "But I'm trying to meet a schedule, so I can't keep doing that."

"Just tell me how you knew. I mean, that they'd be after me today. And where to find me."

"A friend of theirs spilled it," Bolan explained. "Now, if you're good—"

"Hey, wait!"

"Can't do it. Hear those sirens?"

"Right. Okay. But I still owe you, big-time."

"I'll keep that in mind," Bolan said as he slid behind the Honda's steering wheel.

He left the oilman to decide if he should flee the scene or wait and talk to the police. Whatever happened, Bolan had a list of targets waiting for him, and he was checking it twice.

Everyone on the list had been naughty, in spades.

CHAPTER THIRTEEN

"Would you care for coffee? Tea, perhaps?"

As agitated as he was, the simple courtesy grated on Ekon Afolabi's nerves, but he had spent enough time with the Chinese to know he couldn't rush them if they sought to drag their feet.

"Nothing, thank you," Lao Choy Teoh replied.

"Straight down to business, then," Afolabi said. "That is good."

"I much prefer it," Lao informed him.

"Have you listened to the news this evening?"

Lao stared at Afolabi, blank-faced, as he said, "Another failure to assassinate K-Tech Petroleum executives."

"This is precisely why I hate the media," Afolabi said. "I had no intent to kill him whatsoever."

"All that shooting can be misinterpreted so easily."

Did Lao intend to mock him? Afolabi felt an urge to leap across his desk and slap the man's bland face, but he managed to control himself.

"My men were sent out with specific orders to—"

Lao raised a hand to silence him.

"I don't care what you meant to do," he said. "Results are all that matter. And you failed. Again."

"But I—"

The soft, infuriating hand came up again.

"In fact," Lao said, "I wonder why you called me here to tell me this. Surely you don't pretend that any Chinese agency—much less executives of CNP—encourage criminal behavior in the nations where we're privileged to operate?"

Afolabi gaped at Lao and asked, "What are you saying?"

"Simply that you must be seriously, *fatally* mistaken if you think that the People's Republic of China supports gangsterism in any way, shape or form. Believing such a thing—or sharing that delusion with your fellow countrymen—would damage your relations with Beijing beyond repair."

And Afolabi caught up to his guest at last. He understood what Lao was doing to protect himself.

"You think I bug my own office?" he asked the man. "Why would I? For what purpose?"

Lao shrugged without changing the nonexpression on his face. "How should I know? Ask any U.S. president why he would tape incriminating conversations."

"Would you like to search the room?"

"I didn't come here to redecorate," Lao said.

"Well, then, why did you come?"

"I must assume that you invited me to talk about some problem you've been having, yes? Perhaps the contributions CNP has made to MEND are insufficient for your present needs?"

"Money? Well, since you mention it—"

"Or were you interested in hiring some of the security consultants that we sometimes make available to valued friends?"

"Security consultants? Um—"

"They are adept at problem-solving, whether it be

personal, political or corporate. They have my personal endorsement."

Afolabi wondered how his men would take it if he used Chinese soldiers to kill the bastards who'd been running rings around them since the shootout at the marketplace. Aside from momentary disappointment that they couldn't personally kill their unknown enemies, he guessed that most of them would be relieved.

"Your offer is most generous," Afolabi said. "I am pleased to accept it."

Smiling thinly for the first time since he'd entered Afolabi's office, Lao said, "Naturally, the firm you will be dealing with is private, unconnected to the CNP or People's government in any way."

"Of course. I understand."

Deniability.

"And as a private company, they must charge for their services."

"As to the price—"

"Another ten percent," Lao said. "On top of our original agreement."

Afolabi nearly winced, but caught himself in time. He could afford the payment if he was victorious. And if not, well, Lao could collect it from his corpse.

"Agreed."

Lao took a cell phone from his pocket, opened it, touched two buttons, then spoke in rapid-fire Chinese for thirty seconds. When he'd closed and stowed the phone again, he said, "They should arrive within the hour. Until then, you should relax. Do nothing that would place you or your men at risk."

Do nothing.

It was sounding better all the time.

"CAN YOU EXPLAIN what's happening?" Agu Ajani asked his visitor.

The Russian had arrived with questions of his own. Ajani couldn't answer them, and now it seemed that he would find no resolution to his own troubling inquiries.

Sidorov sipped vodka from a square crystal glass, then spent several seconds staring at its contents.

"It is confusing," Sidorov declared at last, stating the obvious. "First, Afolabi is attacked, his hostage liberated. Next, your plant goes up in smoke. Then, someone challenges Yetunde—at his home, no less. And now, it seems they're back to Afolabi, killing off more of his men."

"You think it is the same group?" Ajani asked.

Sidorov's shrug was indolent, almost insulting. "How would I know? Your soldiers and Afolabi's have used Warri as a shooting gallery for years."

Ajani stiffened in his high-backed swivel chair. "I tell you that I didn't do these things. I didn't order them. And even if I had gone after Afolabi, why would I attack Yetunde?"

"That's the puzzler," Sidorov replied. "That, and the phone calls placed by someone who appears to know a great deal about all of this."

"A white man," Ajani said. "Anyhow, the one who spoke to me, demanding money."

"Have you paid him yet?" Sidorov asked, half smirking.

"I'm following his orders, doing nothing. Waiting for instructions on the drop."

"And when you get them?"

"We shall see who walks away with money…and his life."

"At least that's settled. But I've been thinking." Sidorov paused before continuing. "What if it is the same man calling everyone? Yourself, my boss. How many others have been contacted? Is Afolabi waiting for instructions, too? And what of the Chinese?"

"Who could it be?" Ajani asked.

"Consider this—four incidents, so far, and two of them involve Jared Ross or his daughter at K-Tech Petroleum. Perhaps he has what men of the cloth call a guardian fairy."

"Angel," Ajani said, correcting him.

"Whatever. If someone, an outsider, wished to destabilize Warri, he's going about it the right way, I think."

"But why?"

"A name, I can't provide. But think about which country has a stake in K-Tech? Which would like to see both Russians and Chinese expelled from Warri—or Nigeria itself? Which country had condemned militant action by both major tribes in Delta State, from CNN to the United Nations?"

One answer covered everything. "America!" Ajani blurted.

Sidorov nodded, seeming pleased for once.

"Now," he said, "all we have to do is find out who they've sent and neutralize him."

"Oh, is that all?"

"For the moment. In the process, there's a possibility that we may profit from his actions."

"And how do we do that?" Ajani asked.

Sidorov smiled. "I have a few ideas," he said.

"SHALL WE CONTINUE with rotation on the targets?" Umaru asked.

"I'm considering a change-up," Bolan said. "A little razzle-dazzle."

"Sorry. I don't understand."

"Just when they start to see a pattern, you discard it. Double back and hit them in the same place where you hit the last time, or go long with something none of them expect. Like that."

"I see." Umaru's tone left Bolan in some doubt.

"Our last two hits were Afolabi's people, if we count the guy at your safehouse."

"I count him," Umaru said.

"So do I," Bolan replied, "although it's possible nobody's missed him yet. Whatever, there are two ways we can go—hit Afolabi a third time to increase the paranoia, or pick someone else and keep stirring the pot."

"More phone calls?" Umaru asked.

"Shouldn't be required," Bolan said. "If we have a living witness we can talk to, I'll leave him a message. Otherwise, who knows? Graffiti? Mash notes at the scene?"

"Mash—"

"Never mind. It was before your time. Some kind of written message, I'm suggesting."

"Ah, yes. Good. Should I prepare one?"

Bolan thought about it, then asked, "How much paper do you have?"

Umaru pulled a notebook from an inside pocket of his windbreaker. It wasn't large—about the size detectives often used in the United States for crime-scene notes—and bound on top with spiral wire. Umaru read the cover and told Bolan, "Fifty sheets."

"Okay. Write five notes, then."

"Five notes?"

"One each to the Ijaw and Itsekiri, to the Russians and Chinese, and to Yetunde."

"Yes, of course. What should I say?"

"I'd keep it simple," Bolan said. "For the Itsekiri, something on the lines of 'MEND must go!' Maybe some kind of tribal insult for Ajani. For the rest, if we get to them, warning them to leave town ought to be enough."

"I think the Russians and Chinese should leave Nigeria completely," Umaru said.

"Works for me," Bolan replied. "Go with your gut. Block letters, by the way, and simple words. To mask your handwriting and make it easy on whoever finds the notes, in case they're not great readers."

"Yes, I have it."

"Do Ajani first," Bolan suggested. "I don't want him out there pouting, thinking that he's been forgotten."

"No," Umaru answered with a cunning smile. "We can't have that, can we?"

"And on the way," Bolan went on, "we need to find another set of wheels. This ride's been seen by Afolabi's men, and there's a chance they could have tipped off headquarters by cell phone or a two-way radio."

"No problem," Umaru said, already engrossed in drafting his first threat. "I know a place where there are many cars and no closed-circuit cameras."

"WHAT DO I pay you for, if not protection?" Idowu Yetunde asked the officer of the Delta Police Command.

"You've received protection," the officer said defensively.

He was a captain, the third-highest rank within his department. His name was Johnson Mashilia, as if that mattered. To Yetunde, he was just another greedy bastard with his hand out, always wanting more for this or that good cause. Money well spent, as long as the police performed—or failed to perform—as Yetunde required.

But now…

"Protection, you say?" he challenged the captain. "When gunmen can invade my home and kill employees there?"

"We are police, not full-time bodyguards," the captain said. "Most certainly, we cannot see the future or read minds."

"And how, if I may ask, is your investigation of the raid proceeding? Do you have suspects? A name? Affiliation? Anything?"

"As you must know, Mr. Yetunde, there are no surveillance systems in your home or…place of business."

"So you're telling me what, Captain?"

Mashilia shrugged and spread his empty hands. "We have no pictures of the men responsible. No useful fingerprints, thanks to the fire and water damage. We have a sketch artist working with your various employees to prepare sketches but—"

"They barely resemble living people, much less someone you are trying to arrest."

"The quality is variable, I admit," the captain said.

"The quality is shit!" Yetunde raged at him. "One black, one white. They could be anyone."

"You see my problem, then."

"*Your* problem? Did they burst into *your* home while you were entertaining guests? Are *you* losing an average two thousand U.S. dollars hourly, because the boiler room is closed?"

"I only meant—"

Yetunde fanned the captain's words away to silence him, the fat cigar he held between his first two fingers trailing smoke in crazy spirals. Suddenly, Yetunde felt the anger draining out of him, as if someone had pulled the plug on a simmering tub of venom.

"All right," Yetunde said. "How *can* you help me? Surely you must have informers on the street. You can find out which gang is the most envious of my success. I only need a pointer, Captain."

"It may not be quite that simple," the officer said.

"I'm sure you are aware of the attacks on other, um, targets, occurring recently?"

"Trouble between the Ijaw and the Itsekiri," Yetunde said. "What has that to do with me? I'm friends with both of them, a simple businessman."

"We have begun to think," the captain said, "that the attacks suffered by either side are not mere tribal warfare. Witnesses from each scene speak of two men—one black, one white."

"The same men?"

"That I cannot prove, but I would say the odds against two interracial murder teams working in Delta State are nothing short of astronomical."

"So, you can locate them!"

"If they were staying at a hotel or a licensed rooming house, of course. We're checking those and moving out into the suburbs, but so far," the captain said, "we have found no evidence that they are staying anywhere."

"I don't care if they're sleeping in a car, or in a highway culvert, Captain," Yetunde said. "I still expect my money's worth from you, and don't forget it!"

"I'm not likely to," the captain muttered.

"Two more hours. That's your deadline," Yetunde said, rising from his chair to end the meeting. "If you don't have something for me then, I'll speak to your superiors."

And as Yetunde left the coffee shop where they had met, leaving Mashilia at their corner table by the broad front window, he thought that at least two-thirds of the men in Warri had to be superior in some respect to the brow-beaten captain.

Yetunde was surprised to find himself smiling as he retreated to his waiting car.

"WHAT WORD from the Ijaw?" Arkady Eltsin asked.

"They're agitated, as you might expect," Valentin Sidorov replied.

"Of course. How may we calm them?"

"I do not believe it's possible," his number two replied.

Eltsin could only frown at that. "Why not?"

"Ajani wants revenge, not compensation from third parties," Sidorov explained. "He won't be satisfied until he's killed the men responsible for shaming him."

"He sounds more like a Russian gangster every day," Eltsin replied.

"Beneath the skin, they're all the same," Sidorov said. "Obsessed with pride."

"Has he become a liability to us?" Eltsin asked.

Sidorov considered that, then shook his head decisively. "Not yet," he said. "If Afolabi falls—perhaps I should say *when* he falls—we want a friend taking his place. It will be good for Uroil. Good for Warri, all around."

"Replacing one beast with another, eh?"

"Our beast," Sidorov said. "Responsive to our needs and our suggestions."

"So you hope, at least," Eltsin said, sounding skeptical.

"Of course, there are no guarantees, sir," Sidorov replied stiffly.

"You understand how these things work," Eltsin said. "Guarantees or not, there will be consequences if you fail. The Uroil board can't fire Ajani when they won't admit hiring him to start with. In a case of costly failure, scapegoats must be found. You don't expect the company's directors to dismiss themselves, surely?"

"No, sir."

Sidorov's eyes told Eltsin that he'd been around this track before. The contents of his hefty dossier confirmed it.

"If it's any consolation, Valentin, you won't go down alone."

"None of us need go down at all, sir, if we win."

"Then I suggest you do precisely that," Eltsin replied. "By any means available."

"Deniable, of course," Sidorov said, not quite smirking.

"Deniability and positive results are all we ever ask,"

Eltsin said. "If Ajani manages to do the job without your help, more power to him. If he needs assistance, there must be no ties between him and yourself. No link to anyone from Uroil."

"Understood," Sidorov said.

"I'll leave you to it, then, and hope for swift results."

"Yes, sir."

Sidorov left the office without shaking hands or glancing back. He closed the door softly, gently, when Eltsin thought he longed to slam it.

Never mind.

Sidorov knew his place. He would perform as he was ordered to, like an attack dog. And when he had outlived his usefulness to Uroil, he would be put down exactly the same way.

"I AM DISTURBED," Huang Li Chan declared, "by the increasing incidence of violence in the city."

Lao Choy Teoh considered his response, then settled for, "This *is* Nigeria. Nigeria's worst state for crime, in fact."

"Surely you don't pretend the recent outbreaks are a normal thing?"

"No, sir. I do believe that the relations between hostile tribes are breaking down, becoming worse each day. Which need not necessarily discourage us."

Chan frowned at his subordinate. "I realize our people have a global reputation for inscrutability," he said. "But here, at least with me, you may speak plainly."

"Yes, sir. Simply stated, I believe that this unrest may work to our advantage, if we back the winning side."

Chan's frown deepened. "Go on."

"MEND and the Itsekiri are more numerous, it's true. But they opposed all foreign drilling for petroleum, which marks them as enemies of the state and economic progress.

Their foolish jingoism—*Nigerian oil for Nigerians*—fails to account for the lack of domestic technology, training and knowledge required to succeed. In short, they're doomed to fail."

"And so?"

"If we support their opposition, we support the present government. When MEND collapses—and it will, taking the Russians with it—China fills the void."

"While I admire your confidence," Chan said, "I do not understand how you can guarantee that Uroil will be driven out, along with MEND."

"I still have friends inside the Ministry of State Security," Lao said. "They have prepared back-dated documents on Uroil stationery that will indicate financial and material support for MEND's outrageous criminal activity. The locals could arrest Arkady Eltsin, but they'll probably expel him and his people from Nigeria."

"Which still leaves the Americans," Chan said.

"Already shaky, following attacks on Jared Ross, his daughter and their various facilities throughout the state. If they're convinced the government supports Agu Ajani and his Ijaws—"

"Who, in fact, the Russians have supported, have they not?" Chan interrupted.

Lao waved his words away. "No one knows that, except the Russians and ourselves. Ajani will defect from the Russians soon enough, if we adopt him as a special friend."

"And if your plan succeeds?" Chan asked.

Lao shrugged. "We have no further need for him or his guerrillas. I predict a brief but thorough internecine conflict that will decimate Ajani's ranks. He'll likely be among the first to die."

"I thought these days were over," Chan observed. He sounded weary, looked exhausted.

"Subterfuge and scheming have no end, sir."

"No. It seems you are correct. At least you'll never want for work."

"No, sir."

A momentary silence hung between them, broken when Chan cleared his throat.

"We have another matter to discuss."

"Yes, sir?"

"The phone call I received, demanding money."

"Yes. Sadly," Lao said, "I was unable to identify the telephone. It is a satellite model, meaning the man could have called from Beirut or Bombay."

"But he didn't. We know that," Chan said.

"Probably not," Lao granted. "But the caller blocked his phone number from caller ID, and we cannot triangulate on his location unless he should call again."

"In short, you failed," Chan said.

"You are correct, sir."

"If I approve the plan you have explained to me," Chan cautioned him, "you must not fail again."

"No, sir. We won't."

"Not *we,*" Chan said, correcting him. "It's your plan, and its execution is your sole responsibility. If you fail, expect no mercy or consideration."

"Understood, sir."

"Good. Then, I suggest you get to work."

"WE DID THE DRUG THING last time," Bolan told Umaru. "Now, Ajani needs a wake-up call."

"I still think it's too dangerous," Umaru said.

"Don't worry. All you have to do is drive around the block and be there when I need you for a lift out."

"I meant dangerous for you."

Bolan had already considered that. It *was* risky, but it

would also be the last thing that his Ijaw enemies expected. With a bit of luck, they might relax enough on their home turf to let their guard down just a little.

He could work with that.

"Just work the plan," Bolan replied. "We'll be all right."

"And if you don't come out? What then?"

"You drive away. Simple."

"Drive *where,* in this?"

The second car they'd stolen, from another shopping center, was a four-door Subaru Impreza, five or six years old.

"You could try reaching out for your contact," Bolan said. "I mean the Agency, not locals. If you'd rather not try that, it's about two hundred miles from Warri to the U.S. consulate in Lagos, maybe three hundred to Abuja and the embassy. Or you could keep on going to the border, if you have your passport with you."

"Always."

"The flip side of it is, I may get lucky at Ajani's, and your worry's all for nothing. Either way, you won't be on the inside when it hits the fan."

"Of course. You will be careful, yes?"

"Count on it," Bolan said. "I've still got miles to go before I sleep."

CHAPTER FOURTEEN

Agu Ajani's walled estate on Warri's west side was spectacular by postcolonial Nigerian standards, but it would have been considered small and somewhat shabby in various parts of California, Nevada or New York.

And it wouldn't keep Mack Bolan out.

The eight-foot wall was topped with broken glass instead of razor wire or something more elaborate. Bolan beat that obstacle with a blanket he found in the Subaru's trunk and dropped into the grounds that could have harbored guard dogs, but didn't.

There were two-legged watchdogs, but they didn't seem to take their duties all that seriously, wandering around the property without any apparent system, pausing often for impromptu conversations that were long on smiles and cigarette smoke, short on any evidence of focusing on business.

All the better for an uninvited visitor.

If Bolan had intended to assassinate Ajani, he would have been forced to penetrate the house. But since that wasn't his intention, he was free to strike at random, raise whatever hell he could within a short time and get out again while the getting was good.

In a pocket, he carried one of Umaru's five hand-printed notes. It read: YOUR TIME IS COMING. MEND PREVAILS.

Not subtle, but he wasn't dealing with Phi Beta Kappa types or code-breakers from Mensa. In the present circumstances, he was opting for the most direct approach.

Like blunt-force trauma.

He started with a gardener of sorts, lip-synching to the music from a personal stereo while trimming a half acre of lawn with a riding mower. The guy had an H&K MP-5 submachine gun slung across his back, but had no time to reach for it as Bolan appeared in front of him, drilled his startled face with a silenced round from the Beretta 93-R and left him slumped over the mower's steering wheel, embarked on a last ride to nowhere.

Bolan jogged toward the house. He holstered the Beretta, palmed a frag grenade and yanked its pin as he closed to throwing range. The nearest window was, in fact, a sliding-glass door that opened onto a flagstone veranda, where someone had built a brick barbecue pit. The door stood open, sparing Bolan any need to smash it as he made his pitch, then he was off and running with the Steyr AUG in hand before the blast echoed behind him.

That brought sentries on the run, and he was ready for them, firing 3-round bursts that should be enough for any target, unless he did his garment shopping at a Kevlar outlet. And Ajani's men weren't sporting body armor.

Some of them weren't even wearing shirts.

When he'd used half of his first magazine to drop five men, Bolan began retreating toward the point where he had scaled the wall. His blanket from the Subaru was waiting for him, but he wasn't finished yet. He hadn't left Umaru's note, and if he didn't pass the word, he would be leaving the job incomplete.

One of the sentries made it easy for him, springing from

a bank of untrimmed shrubbery and brandishing a pistol. If he'd thought it through, a shot from ambush would've been the way to go, but something made him think it was more manly to confront his enemy, give up the sweet advantage of surprise.

Bolan was tumbling through a shoulder-roll before the guard triggered his first shot, high and wide. The AUG stuttered another triple burst, stitching his target left to right above the belt line. The guard was breathing when he fell, but he'd forgotten all about his gun and what he'd planned to do with it.

Bolan stood over him just long enough to place the note dead center on his chest. By that time, respiration had already dwindled to a flutter, and it wouldn't last much longer.

Bolan slung his weapon and hit the wall running, seized the dangling blanket in both hands and scrambled clear before his furious pursuers could respond. Once on the other side, he whipped the punctured blanket free and draped it over his left shoulder, covering the AUG.

No sweat.

The Subaru came into view, with Umaru at the wheel. Bolan was in the shotgun seat before his wheelman finished braking. They were clear before Ajani's men got organized enough to scramble through the gate.

"No problems, then?" Umaru asked him.

"Nothing that I couldn't handle," Bolan answered. "Let's drop in and have a look at Uroil."

No BUILDING was impregnable, if a would-be intruder had sufficient time and money to invest in penetration, but the Uroil offices in Warri had enough security in place to make Bolan revise his plans. Instead of picking up a suit somewhere and trying to bluff his way past the armed guards with a bomb or whatever, he went back to his roots.

He'd earned the "Executioner" nickname in uniform, as a U.S. Army Special Forces sniper with ninety-seven confirmed kills. He'd lost none of the skill he'd gained when his war turned private, and he'd often used it to reach out and touch someone, as snipers liked to say among themselves.

Uroil's office block stood on a downtown street lined with similar buildings, none topping its eight-story height, a few shorter by one or two floors. Bolan chose a seven-story structure across the street and let himself in through the back, wearing a jumpsuit that would stall interrogation long enough for him to draw a gun or strike a blow, lugging a toolbox that contained his disassembled Steyr AUG.

Steyr made a sniper's version of their classic assault rifle—the AUG HBAR-T—with a universal scope mount cast into the receiver, supporting a Kahles ZF69 6x42 optical sight, but Bolan would make do with the standard-issue AUG. Its topside carry handle contained a 1.5x telescopic sight made by Austria's Swarovski Optik, which featured a simple black ring reticle with a basic range-finder, designed so that a man of average height—say, five foot ten—completely filled the reticle at three hundred meters.

In fact, he'd be firing from less than one-tenth of that range, no sweat for the Steyr's standard sight. And no problem at all for the armor-piercing 5.56 mm rounds he'd loaded in the rifle's plastic see-through magazine to pierce Uroil's "shatter-proof" windows.

All security was relative.

Bolan made it to the roof and was relieved to find he had it to himself. He knelt, opened his toolbox and assembled the Steyr within seconds flat. Crouching behind the building's parapet, he scanned Uroil's facade and found the corner office he was seeking on the top floor, where Arkady Eltsin could look down and watch the people whom he bought and sold each day scurry along the street like insects, chasing meager paychecks he would never need.

Eltsin was at his desk when Bolan spotted him, telephone receiver wedged between his right ear and shoulder, saying something that seemed to amuse him. Bolan put his crosshairs on the Russian's smiling face and felt the Steyr's trigger start to move with gentle pressure from his index finger.

It would be so easy, but it wasn't Bolan's plan.

Not yet.

Sliding away from Eltsin's moon face, Bolan sighted a photo of a dour-looking woman that was planted on a corner of the Russian's desk. Clearly, whatever he might do in private, Eltsin hadn't bothered to collect a trophy wife.

"Say cheese," he whispered to the woman he would never meet.

And fired.

"I WOULD HAVE liked to see him dance," Umaru said. "That must have been a sight."

"Not much to see," Bolan replied. "He dropped behind the desk after the first three rounds, and that was all I saw of him. I used the rest to renovate his office."

"And you left the note?"

"Anchored with empty brass, across the street."

The Russian's men or local cops would find it soon enough, a simple matter of calculating where the shots had come from and tracing them back to their source. Unless it rained before they found the note, whoever spotted it would see the message Umaru had printed in big block capitals: YOUR TIME IS FINISHED IN NIGERIA.

It was direct and to the point, but still unsigned. Enough, in short, to keep the Uroil honcho wondering who hated him enough to spoil his penthouse view of downtown Warri.

"Yetunde next, is it?"

Nodding, Bolan replied, "But not another boiler room. He's got some other operations on your list, there."

"Yes, indeed," Umaru said. "Two brothels, a casino, an opium den—"

"Now you're talking."

"Which one?"

"Let's start with the dope," Bolan said. "Point me toward it."

Umaru gave directions, and in twenty minutes they were parked outside a shabby hotel, standing three-quarters of a mile from Uroil's downtown headquarters.

"Which floor?" Bolan asked as he primed the Steyr with a fully loaded magazine.

"The basement," Umaru said. "But, in fact, we have two targets underneath one roof. The addicts go downstairs. The other floors are filled with prostitutes."

"Two targets for the price of one," Bolan replied, smiling.

"If you have time," Umaru said.

"I'll make time. Where's the note?"

Umaru passed it to him. Bolan read: YETUNDE, YOU ARE FINISHED.

"He shouldn't have a problem understanding that," Bolan observed. "I'll see you in a bit."

Umaru shifted to the driver's seat as he got out, propping the Daewoo rifle between his left knee and the door, where it was out of sight but easily accessible.

Bolan jogged across the street, holding the Steyr against his right leg, scanning in both directions as he crossed. A few pedestrians were visible, but none appeared to notice him. He guessed this was a neighborhood where turning a blind eye to strangers qualified as a survival skill.

The entrance to Yetunde's opium den lay below street

level, accessed via steep concrete stairs in an alley west of the hotel. Bolan descended, knocked, then kicked the door in when a shadow blocked the peephole set chin-level in front of him.

Entering the drug parlor, he found its first guard struggling to rise from the floor, multitasking as one hand groped for a holstered sidearm. Bolan drilled the shooter's forehead with a single 5.56 mm round and stepped across his twitching corpse as half a dozen of Yetunde's workers panicked, breaking for a hidden exit while their groggy customers examined Bolan through a drifting haze of smoke.

"The party's over," he informed them, causing two or three to lurch out of their bunks. When no more showed an inclination to get moving, Bolan sprayed the ceiling of their smoky cave with automatic fire, rewarded with a scramble toward a door somewhere in back and distant screams from somewhere overhead.

Leaving a frag grenade behind to aggravate the damage he'd already caused, Bolan retreated to the alleyway and double-timed around the corner to the hotel's main street entrance. He'd reloaded by the time he reached its dingy lobby and was ready for the two gunmen who met him there, cutting them down with 3-round bursts before they had a chance to fire.

More women's screams at that, and male voices shouting in anger or panic, he wasn't sure which. Bolan shouted back at them, mounting the nearby stairs as females dressed in next to nothing started rushing past him, trailed by johns who clutched their pants and shoes in shaky hands.

The whorehouse madam met him on the second-story landing, hands on chubby hips, showing more nerve than anyone he'd met so far that day.

"What in the hell you think you're doing?" she demanded.

"Burning down the house," he told her as he primed a fat white-phosphorus grenade, then tucked its pin into her ample cleavage with Umaru's note to Idowu Yetunde. "Give that to your boss, with my regards."

"He's going to kill you, man!" she shouted after Bolan as she headed for the street.

"Tell him to get in line," the Executioner replied, and pitched his smoking canister into the stairwell overhead.

"I WANT HIM DEAD!" Ajani stormed. "I want him dead today, before another hour passes!"

Daren Jumoke watched Ajani circling his desk, resembling a hungry panther in a cage. "Of course," he said, eager to please. "But...who, again?"

Ajani rounded on him, his lips drawn back from teeth that could have been a snarling animal's.

"Who? *Who?* Who do you think I mean, Daren?" Before Jumoke could respond, Ajani answered his own question. "Afolabi, damn you! Who else could I mean?"

"Yes, sir." Meek, now, when it could save his life.

"His pigs came to *my home,* Daren. You understand? They might have killed me, just as easily as those baboons I pay to guard the house. How many dead, was it?"

"Seven, so far. Dr. Bassir can't promise that Hakim will live, with so much shrapnel in his guts."

"Hakim? Who's this Hakim?"

"One of the men, Agu. It's not important."

"Idiots! They let this white man climb the wall, attack *my house?* They're lucky I let any of them live."

"As I informed them."

"Good. And this." Ajani dropped the crumpled note into Jumoke's lap. "It seems that Afolabi signs his work now."

Jumoke read the note again.

YOUR TIME IS COMING. MEND PREVAILS.

"He didn't actually sign it, Agu. Have you thought that possibly, just maybe, someone else wrote this?"

"One of his men, you mean? What diff—"

"No, no." Jumoke knew that interrupting could be dangerous, but he was anxious to communicate his thought. "I mean, someone outside MEND who wants you hunting Afolabi when you should be looking elsewhere."

"What are you saying, Daren?"

"Someone who would profit from a war between yourself and Afolabi, without risking anything himself."

"Such as?"

Jumoke shrugged. "I don't know. It's a thought, Agu. If I knew who it was, I would be handing you his liver on a plate right now."

Ajani thought about it, for perhaps a second and a half, then shook his head.

"No, Daren. It is good to have imagination in the bedroom, or when playing with your children. In the real world, we rely on facts. That note from MEND tells me all that I need to know."

"*If* it was sent by MEND," Jumoke said.

"And you can't tell me who this someone else might be. Someone who has a white man do his killing for him?"

"Put it that way, and it doesn't sound like Afolabi, either," Jumoke said.

"Don't allow yourself to be distracted by a fantasy," Ajani said. "I need you now, with all your wits about you."

"Yes, Agu."

"I need you to go out and bring me Ekon Afolabi's head."

HUANG LI CHAN was running late. He'd lingered over paperwork and now urged his chauffeur to get him home with all dispatch.

Before Tupele arrived at his condo.

The doorman always phoned up when she came to visit Chan, intent on making himself look efficient, no matter how often Tupele came calling. Chan didn't mind the little game, but he knew well enough that if he wasn't home to take the doorman's call, Tupele would be left to wait downstairs or turned away entirely.

That would put her in a sour mood, and would affect his own pleasure adversely.

He'd met Tupele Bayewu at a fashion show, of all things. Chan knew less than nothing about women's clothes, but he had been invited to the function by a local businessman, and had been surprised to learn that they had fashion shows in Warri, where the public emphasis was all on oil and heavy industry. Tupele had been modeling— Chan still recalled the dress, a thing of gossamer and lace that someone might have painted on her body—and she had been bold enough to introduce herself after her catwalk turn, while models circulated through the audience.

Chan had surprised himself by asking her to join him at his home for dinner, and she had agreed without pretense that she would have to check her social calendar. The next night was convenient for them both, but Chan, prepared for disappointment, had steeled himself for the possibility that she might stand him up.

In fact, she had arrived ten minutes early, and had stayed all night. Since then, she'd come to visit him at least two nights per week, on average.

Chan didn't delude himself with any fantasy that he had been transformed into a sex machine, nor did his mirror lie to him. Still, while he had an opportunity to revel in Tupele's firm young flesh, why not take full advantage of the situation while it lasted?

They reached his building with minutes to spare. Chan dismissed his chauffeur with a reminder to pick him up promptly at eight o'clock in the morning, and passed the doorman with a bare acknowledgment of his greeting. The elevator seemed slower than usual, but Chan knew that had to be an illusion.

Emerging on the sixth floor, Chan frowned at the empty hallway. Two security men watched his condo while he was at work, and their short list of duties included greeting him when he disembarked from the lift. Growing more irritated by the second as he moved along the hallway, digging in a pocket for his key, Chan turned his mind toward fitting punishments for dereliction of such simple tasks.

He used the key and stepped into the foyer of the condominium, barking their names.

"Guan! Tang! Where—"

"They can't hear you," a grim voice said just behind him as an unmistakable gun barrel kissed the flesh behind his left ear. Chan imagined that the steel was warm.

"This way," the intruder directed him, toward his own spacious living room. But it was a *dying* room now, with Guan Xi and Tang Mei sprawled in separate armchairs, their brains leaking out of their skulls.

Chan felt his knees about to buckle, but the gunman's free hand caught his collar, held him upright, as the killer said, "You get to live this time. At least, a little while. But Mr. Eltsin has a message for you."

Eltsin? Huang Li Chan's mind was racing. Who was Mr.—

Just as it came to him, the gunman released his collar and pressed something into Chan's left palm. It felt like folded paper as he clutched it.

"If you want to live," the killer said, "don't turn around until you hear the door close. Read that when I'm gone, before you call for help."

An age later, it seemed, Chan heard the front door to his

condo open then close with a snap of its self-locking latch. Against all instincts, he did as he'd been told, raising the paper and unfolding it to read its two-line message.

LEAVE NIGERIA ALIVE OR DEAD. THE CHOICE IS YOURS.

"NEXT STOP," Bolan said. "I don't want our buddy Afolabi thinking that he's been forgotten."

"This will hurt him. I've no doubt," Umaru answered from the Subaru's passenger seat, "but we cannot be sure how he'll react."

"It doesn't matter," Bolan said. "He's bound to take a run at someone on our list. One's as good as another to me."

"You specialize in chaos," Umaru said, his lips stuck somewhere between a frown and a smile.

"It's a useful tool sometimes," Bolan replied. "Confused enemies mount ineffective defenses."

They were approaching the target by then, a drab two-story building in Warri's northwest quarter that served as a barracks for Afolabi's off-duty gunmen. Sizing it up, Bolan guessed it would sleep a hundred men or so, but he thought MEND's warlord would have most of his able-bodied men on the street today, kicking ass and taking names.

The wrong names, granted. But still…

"I'll take the note," he said, giving it a glance as Umaru passed it over.

It read: MEND IS FINISHED. GIVE UP AND GO HOME.

Which ought to have roughly the same effect, he thought, as throwing rocks at a hornet's nest. But when he finished in the drab gray two-story, Ekon Afolabi would have lost a few more hornets.

"If any cops come by—"

"I leave," Umaru said. "And come back when they're gone."

"Strike one," Bolan replied. "If cops come by and *stop,*

you *don't* come back. Leave your cell phone on for an hour, and if you don't hear from me, do what we talked about."

"Lagos or Abuja," Umaru stated. "Possibly the border."

"Right," Bolan said. "Don't forget it."

As he stepped out of the stolen car, Umaru shifted to the driver's seat and left the engine running. It crossed Bolan's mind that he was wasting lots of gasoline this time around, leaving an ugly carbon footprint on the Earth, as conservationists might say.

He shrugged it off.

This was a clean-up mission, not some slacker's holiday. And when he finished here, the footprints that he left would all be etched in blood.

Clutching the AUG against his hip, Bolan steeled himself for the killing to come and pushed off toward his target.

CHAPTER FIFTEEN

"What do I want from you?" Ekon Afolabi raged. "I want action. I want you to do your goddamned job for once, and solve this problem now, before we lose another man! Is that so much to ask?"

Taiwo Babatunde stood in front of Afolabi with his broad shoulders hunched, cringing as if his old friend's words were lashes from a whip. He'd asked the question innocently, but it only served to anger Afolabi more, after the fresh report of soldiers gunned down by a white man.

And the note infuriated Afolabi most of all.

"You know who wrote this, don't you?" he demanded.

"No, Ekon," Babatunde replied, although he guessed what Afolabi wanted him to say.

"Well, *I* do. I can see the bastard smirking as he wrote it, thinking he could twist the knife and make me lose my grip!"

He nearly had, Babatunde thought, but he bit his tongue to keep the words inside. There was no "right" thing to be said when Ekon flew into one of his rages. It had to simply be endured.

The big man didn't stop to think that he could wrap one hand around Afolabi's throat and shake him as a dog might shake a rat. It would have been so easy, given the disparity in size between them, but the notion literally never crossed his mind. Somehow, the pattern of their interaction had been fixed in childhood, and Babatunde couldn't seem to escape it now.

He found the strength to ask, "What should I do?"

"Strike back!" Afolabi snapped. "Hit Ajani anywhere you can, and keep on hitting him until his blood runs in the street, with that of every bastard who belongs to him. Kill all of them, and make me proud!"

Babatunde wasn't convinced that he could do it, or that such a thing was even possible, but he responded with an ardent, "Yes, Ekon! I will!"

"Go now," Afolabi said, "and don't return until you have good news."

"One other thing—"

"What now?"

"About the caller and his hundred thousand dollars," Babatunde said. "I have the money."

"You believe I ought to *pay* him?"

Afolabi was about to launch into another tirade when his second in command replied, "No, Ekon."

"But—"

"I said I *have* the money, not that we should give it to him."

"Then why even mention it?"

"Because, when he calls back, we can arrange to meet him. Lay a trap. Whoever comes to claim the money, we surprise him. If we can take him alive, he will certainly tell us who's behind him."

"I already know—"

"And it will hurt Ajani to lose his point man. Perhaps it will be Ajani."

Afolabi stared at him with narrowed eyes, letting the best part of a minute pass before he spoke again.

"That's good," the warlord said. "You're thinking now, with your whole brain. Has someone called with the payoff instructions yet?"

"No, but they will. And I'll be ready."

For the first time in twenty-four hours, Ekon Afolabi seemed almost happy. He still paced the floor, but with a different kind of energy now, radiating anticipation rather than pure unadulterated fury.

"Make me proud, Taiwo," he said. "Bring me the bastards who have caused this trouble. Bring them before me, and let me hear them scream!"

"A WHITE MAN," Lao Choy Teoh repeated, as if the concept was foreign to him.

"That's what I said," Huang Li Chan replied.

"Russian?"

"If so, he's lost his accent. I'd have guessed American. Perhaps an Englishman who's spent much time away from home."

"And he left this," Lao said, not asking, as he poked an index finger on the note that lay between them in the middle of Chan's ornate coffee table.

They were seated on the long couch in Chan's living room. The corpses of Guan Xi and Tang Mei had been carried out, together with the matching chairs in which they died. The carpet had been scrubbed clean with some chemical that made Chan's nostrils twitch and sting.

"I've told you that already," Chan reminded him. His patience with the younger man was swiftly drawing to an end.

"From Eltsin."

"As I said. As *he* said. 'Mr. Eltsin has a message for you.' There was no mistake on my part."

"No, sir. I'm simply thinking that a Russian might have phrased it differently."

"I didn't call you here to seek instruction in the Russian language," Chan said stiffly. "I don't claim that Eltsin wrote the words himself, or even spoke them to another. He undoubtedly has others to perform such tasks."

As I do, Chan thought, then dismissed it.

"Certainly," Lao answered. "But I wonder, sir, if this—" he waved a hand to indicate the note, the missing chairs and corpses of Chan's bodyguards "—has anything to do with Eltsin and the Russians, after all."

"Who else?" Chan asked.

Lao's shrug was casual enough to be infuriating.

"I don't know, sir. I'm simply curious."

"And while you whet your curiosity, assassins wait to kill me."

"I have tripled your security," Lao said. "You are as safe as you can be in Warri, at the moment."

"Meaning what?" Chan challenged his subordinate. "That I should leave? And say what to Beijing? That I'm afraid a Russian may creep into my bedroom?"

"By no means, sir. I think we should retaliate," Lao said. "But against whom?"

"You really don't believe the Russians are responsible?"

"They may be," Lao replied. "Of course, they'd all be thrilled if CNP abandoned Warri and Nigeria. But something troubles me about the white man's words. Would Eltsin give his name, then let you live?"

"Why not?" Chan asked. "Humiliate me in my own home, hoping that I'll be frightened enough to leave. Letting me know who was behind it would be frosting on his cake."

"Or, it could start a war that Eltsin might not win. We have more men in Warri and across the country than the

Russians do," Lao observed. "A phone call can double their number in twenty-four hours."

"You're thinking of the man who called me," Chan said, "offering to sell the names of those behind the recent violence."

"I am," Lao said. "And have you heard from him again?"

"I would have mentioned it," Chan said, frowning.

"I know it's difficult, but can you possibly recall the killer's voice?"

"I am not likely to forget it!"

"And, perhaps, compare it to the voice from that telephone call?" Lao asked.

"I'm trying," Chan replied. "They could be similar. Beyond that, I can't say."

"Perhaps you'll have another chance to hear the phone voice soon," Lao said. "Meanwhile, I'll increase security at all of our facilities. If you have any other special orders, sir…?"

It would have been so easy, then, to speak the words. Send gunmen for Arkady Eltsin at his home, office, wherever they could find him. Somehow, at the final instant, he restrained himself.

"Not yet," Chan said. "But hold a team in readiness in case I change my mind."

"Yes, sir," Lao replied. "And now, I leave you to your rest."

Chan almost laughed at that, but thought it would have made him sound hysterical, and bit his tongue instead.

THE TARGET WAS a gambling club on Warri's southeast side, owned by Idowu Yetunde. Another boss might have shut down in the face of the losses he'd suffered, but not Yetunde. He was open for business and ready to rake in the cash.

Which made Bolan's job easier, at least in theory.

"There will be more guards than usual," Umaru cautioned as they made their second drive-by at the club.

"Most likely," Bolan said. "Of course, the smart move would've been to close."

"He can't afford to lose face with his people," Umaru replied. "To lose *and* run away would be the end of him in Warri. Everyone would test him, then. He might as well dress up in women's clothes."

"Sounds good to me," Bolan replied. "As long as he keeps setting targets up, I'll knock them down."

He parked the Subaru a block downrange, stepped out and let Umaru scoot across to take the driver's seat. Bolan was wearing a light plastic raincoat to cover the Steyr AUG he carried under his right arm, slung muzzle-down. The Beretta 93-R was snug in his left armpit, while his pockets bulged with spare magazines and grenades.

Just another night on the town for the Executioner.

There were no guards on the street outside Yetunde's club, which seemed to have no name. Government-licensed casinos operated freely in Abuja and Lagos, but Yetunde's club appeared to be an off-the-radar kind of place, where cops were paid to look the other way and taxes somehow never made it to the revenue collectors.

Bolan didn't care about all that. Legitimate or otherwise, the club was shutting down this night.

The front door opened to his touch, and Bolan was inside, absorbed into a miniversion of the smoky world offered by Monte Carlo and Las Vegas, among other "gaming" spas. A doorman built like King Kong's little brother moved to intercept him, but a glimpse of Bolan's rifle sent him backpedaling into the main casino proper.

That was where all hell broke loose.

The doorman shouted to a couple of his buddies on the sidelines, both of whom drew stubby SMGs from underneath their baggy sport coats as they spotted Bolan. He was quicker, feeding each a 3-round burst that left them wallowing in blood, before he caught the doorman reaching for a hidden piece and made it three for three.

And somewhere in the midst of that, the screaming started, players breaking for the nearest exit, some of them delayed by frantic efforts to sweep chips and cash from the felt-topped tables.

Bolan fired a ceiling burst to keep them moving, then began a prowling circuit of the room, watching for other guards along the way. He met two just emerging from an office at the northwest corner, framed in the doorway with guns at half-mast when he stitched them both with 5.56 mm manglers and moved on.

Most of the gambling crowd had found its way outside as Bolan doubled back toward the main street entrance, double-tapping one last shooter who had tried to hide in a tiny coat room. The last few vanished through a back door that was marked with warning signs but had no functioning alarm in place.

All clear.

The Executioner primed an incendiary grenade and pitched it toward the middle of the room, saw it bounce across a roulette table before it detonated, spewing white-hot coals and streamers across the casino. Overhead sprinklers came on at the first hint of fire, but they couldn't douse white phosphorus. Their output was steaming, turning the place to a sauna as Bolan pushed back through the street door and into what passed for fresh air in Warri.

Umaru spotted him and cut the Subaru through a tight U-turn to meet Bolan at curbside. The Executioner let himself in on the passenger's side, riding shotgun.

"Next stop," he told Umaru. "Let's do it."

"How many men can we gather on such short notice?" Agu Ajani asked.

Daren Jumoke considered the question and finally said, "By sunrise, perhaps 150."

"That's all?" Ajani seemed surprised and angry, all at once.

Jumoke risked a shrug. "We've suffered losses," he reminded Ajani. "And since the trouble started, there have been desertions."

"Bastard scum! I want their names put on a list for punishment."

"I'm keeping track of who they are," Jumoke said. He didn't bother to explain that finding those who'd fled might be extremely difficult, particularly if the tribe's ranks suffered any more attrition from assaults by unknown enemies.

"Name three," Ajani ordered, staring from across his desk, prepared to catch Jumoke in a lie and vent his wrath on someone close at hand.

Jumoke drew a small notebook from his pocket, opened it and read the first three names he'd written there. "Jimoh Dangote. Ladi Ibrahim. Femi Dantata. Shall I go on, Agu?"

"No. I would have sworn Ladi, at least, would be loyal to the end."

Another shrug, more confident this time. Jumoke saw no need to mention that he'd filled four notebook pages with the names of those who'd run away, or that the list was growing by the hour.

"All men have a breaking point," he said.

"I'll break them, when I get my hands on them again," Ajani muttered.

"In the meantime, first things first, eh?"

"Yes! How soon can we mount the attack on Afolabi's home?"

"Agu—"

"Don't tell me why we shouldn't do it! All I want to hear from you is the deadline."

"Perhaps midnight," Jumoke said.

"That's fitting. And the Chinese?"

"As I've said—"

"No arguments!" Ajani roared at him, slamming his fists onto the desktop with sufficient force to make his telephone and pistol jump.

Startled, Jumoke swallowed hard and chose his next words carefully.

"There's been an incident with one of the Chinese, apparently. Huang Li Chan, the man in charge. We don't have details yet, but something happened at his condominium. He and the rest are heavily guarded."

"So, kill the guards," Ajani said.

Daren Jumoke knew that if he tried to calm Ajani, reason with him, he might never leave the room alive. In self-defense, he nodded and replied, "Midnight it is."

"Go, then, and make the final preparations. I will join you when the time arrives."

Jumoke left the office thinking that the first thing he should do was pack two bags. One filled with money and the other with enough clothes for the road.

UROIL'S FIELD office in Warri had taken on the air of an armed camp. All leaves, time off and normal hours had been canceled for executives and personnel involved in plant security. Men armed with automatic weapons circulated through the hallways, and patrols on Uroil's property outside the city had been doubled. That force was supplemented by small units from MOPOL, the Nigerian Mobile Police, flying squads nicknamed Kill-and-Go by some observers in the 1990s.

Arkady Eltsin didn't care what they were called—or

who they killed, for that matter—as long as they protected him, his job and Uroil's property, in that order of priority. In fact, the more of Uroil's enemies who lost their lives, the better he would like it.

But they had to find the bastards first.

And so far, that had proved impossible.

Hence, Eltsin's order that Valentin Sidorov should meet him in the basement, where there were no windows to accommodate snipers. Eltsin's first brush with sudden death would also be the last for many years, if he had anything to say about it. He would rather live belowground, tunnel into sewer pipes and travel thus around the city than expose himself to one more instant of the living hell he'd suffered when his office window shattered in a hail of automatic rifle fire.

"What progress, then?" he asked Sidorov in the glare of harsh fluorescent lights.

"This compound is secure," Sidorov said. "As are the pumping fields and the refinery. That doesn't mean they can't be attacked, of course. But if they are, we should prevail."

"Should, or will?" Eltsin demanded.

"Sir, I can't predict the future. Every man and weapon we possess is presently assigned and will remain on duty until we have resolution of this problem."

"I have been in touch with headquarters," Eltsin observed.

Sidorov nodded, as if he expected nothing less.

"They are disturbed and disappointed, as you may imagine."

"Yes, sir."

"I expect that if our situation hasn't been resolved by, say, this time tomorrow, you and I will be in search of new positions."

"Twenty-four hours?"

"Who can say?" Eltsin replied. "'Tomorrow,' I was told, which could be one minute past midnight, our time."

"It's to be expected," Sidorov told him. "The nature of bureaucracy."

"And yet, I would prefer not to begin job-hunting at my time of life," Eltsin observed, allowing just the right amount of acid to flavor his tone.

"Understood, sir."

"So when I ask about progress," Eltsin continued, "I hope to hear something more than security estimates. Progress, to me, means identifying and locating the sons of bitches who tried to kill me in my office upstairs! Understood?"

"Perfectly," Sidorov said. "Unfortunately, wishing for a thing doesn't make it appear."

"And yet, as luck would have it, while I hold this post I can make certain things—and people—disappear. I have my deadline, Valentin, and you have yours. Midnight. If there are no significant results by then, you may expect to be replaced."

For just a heartbeat, Eltsin thought that Sidorov might smile. It would have been the last straw, but he caught himself in time.

"I'd best be going, then," he said.

"Yes," Eltsin replied. "I'd say that's wise."

"ANOTHER DRUG PLANT," Bolan noted as he parked the stolen Subaru a long block from their target on the north side of Warri.

"Khat only, here," Umaru clarified. "The bales of leaves come in. Yetunde's people chop and bag it for his retail dealers."

The target was a duplex, heavy curtains drawn across its windows, no light showing from inside. Which didn't mean the cutting plant was closed, by any means. Bolan would have to wait to see about that when he made his way inside.

There was no foot traffic to speak of on the street as Bolan crossed, leaving Umaru with the car. A couple crossing farther down the block spared him a glance, then picked up speed, continuing along their way.

Bolan considered the front door, then passed along a strip of worn-out grass between the duplex and its neighbor on the west, ducking below a pair of curtained windows as he passed them, just in case. He saw nothing suggesting cameras in place, or any other kinds of sensors on the property, and made it to the northwest corner without incident.

Two gunmen occupied the back stoop, smoking cigarettes that had a funny smell about them. Bolan hoped their final high was worth it as he leveled the Beretta 93-R from a range of twenty feet and dropped them both with silent head shots.

The dead men had been armed with folding-stock Kalashnikovs. Leathering the Beretta, Bolan removed their magazines, flung them into the night, then stood in front of the back door they had guarded carelessly in the last moments of their lives and unslung the Steyr.

Knock, knock, he thought, and kicked it in without trying the knob. A heartbeat later he was standing in what once had been a kitchen, now converted to a basic packaging setup, with heaps and cases of plastic bags standing to one side, bundles of khat leaves on the other.

Two middle-aged women were stuffing the bags when he entered. They gaped at him, blinking, hands raised, until Bolan stepped clear of the doorway and waggled the AUG's muzzle to get them moving. Another moment and he had the kitchen to himself.

"What's all this noise?" a harsh male voice demanded,

moving toward him from beyond the kitchen doorway opposite where Bolan stood. He waited with the Steyr leveled, ready when a husky gunman filled the doorway, stopping short to blink at him.

"That would be you, dying," Bolan replied, and stitched the gunner with a 3-round burst that punched him backward, out of sight.

More voices, then, and feet running in his direction. Bolan primed a frag grenade and pitched it through the doorway, crouched beside tile-topped kitchen counter as it blew, then followed in a rush before the echoes finished rattling through the duplex, raining plaster from the walls and ceiling.

Shock waves reached out to his enemies in hiding, giving them another taste of Hell on Earth, before their final meeting with the Executioner.

CHAPTER SIXTEEN

Captain Johnson Mashilia surveyed the smoking ruins of a former duplex—or, as he understood it now, a house devoted to the packaging of khat for dealers on the street. The mix of smells—charred wood and roasted flesh—told him that someone had died in the fire.

The fire inspector found him, read the question on Mashilia's face and said, "Four dead inside. They burned, but I can't tell you how they died. You'll need an autopsy for that."

More damned delays. There was no medical examiner in Warri, and Mashilia frankly didn't trust the Delta Police Command's surgeon with much beyond first aid. He was certainly no pathologist, and any report he prepared would be highly suspect.

"It's Lagos, then," he said disgustedly.

"And if you put a rush on it, you might hear something back within a month," the fire inspector answered as he lit a thin brown cigarette.

"Doesn't it bother you to smoke around all this?" Mashilia asked.

"Why?" the fire inspector countered. "I'm already

breathing smoke and human ash all day. What difference can it make?"

He had a point, at least where the futility of trying to accomplish anything in Warri was concerned. It had been years since Captain Mashilia qualified by any standard as an honest cop, but there were times he would have liked to do his duty simply and efficiently.

Like now.

He should at least be able to determine how four people had been killed. Then he could pocket any bribes that were forthcoming to conceal the truth about their deaths, content to realize that someone knew the facts, even if they couldn't be publicized, the guilty never brought to justice.

And what was justice, anyway? There'd been a time when Mashilia thought he knew the answer to that question, but a life of compromise and lies had stolen even that from him.

He knew the burned-out duplex had belonged to Idowu Yetunde. Mashilia would be forced to hear another tirade, field more questions that he couldn't answer, promise a solution he couldn't deliver. Even thinking of it made his stomach start to cramp.

But there was something he *could* do. In a crisis where no adequate response was feasible, the wise police commander made a point of seeming to be busy. There were orders to be given, witnesses to be interrogated, squads of men on standby, waiting to race here and there around the city in pursuit of leads.

"Some kind of gang war, you suppose?" the fire inspector asked.

Now it was Mashilia's turn to shrug. "Who knows? I'll have to trace the deed, for whatever that's worth, or wait to find out who was killed."

"Good luck," the fire inspector told him, drawing deeply

on his rancid cigarette. "I still have three more scenes to visit. One's a market. Seven people trapped inside."

"Why do we do it?" Mashilia asked.

"Have you forgotten? For the fame and fortune."

Laughing to himself, the fire inspector walked off, trailing smoke.

And he was right, at least in part. Captain Mashilia had banked a small fortune from bribes in the past thirteen years, but fame was the last thing he wanted. Any undue publicity would mark him as an officer for sale, and while that hardly made him special in Nigeria, exposure might compel his equally corrupt superiors that it was time for a cosmetic change.

The recent spate of violence threatened Mashilia's peace of mind, and while he might not have the power to stop it, he could certainly appear to try.

His cell phone chirped and the captain scowled. No matter who was calling him, it had to be bad news.

"Hello?"

"Where are you?" Idowu Yetunde's too-familiar voice demanded.

"Looking at the ashes of your khat house," Mashilia said.

"And do you know who is responsible?"

The captain snorted. "I can't even tell you who's been killed."

"No one important," Yetunde said. "I need answers, and I need them now. Come see me."

"When I can," the captain said.

"Don't keep me waiting, Mashilia. That would be a serious mistake."

The line went dead.

I wonder, Captain Mashilia asked himself, if I could get away with murder.

And the answer came back silently. Why not?

"Police," Bolan said as he drove the Subaru Impreza past the target he had chosen for their next drop-in.

"I see them," Umaru replied, riding shotgun.

It would've been hard *not* to see them, with a marked Land Rover parked outside the bar and brothel owned by Ekon Afolabi, patronized on any normal day by troops from MEND. Bolan counted five uniforms, four of them standing by with automatic rifles while the fifth harangued a clutch of people whom he took to be employees.

"So, they're catching on," Bolan observed.

"Or Afolabi missed his bribes this week," Umaru said.

"Not likely," Bolan said. "Let's try the next place on your list."

"Another Afolabi spot?" Umaru asked.

"Whatever's handy," Bolan said.

"In that case," his navigator replied, "there's a small apartment building nearby, where MEND folk sleep."

"I doubt if anybody's home," Bolan replied, "but we can have a look. What else?"

"Another brothel. This one is Ajani's. It's…distasteful. Children."

"Now you're talking."

"Yes," Umaru said. "I was, but—"

"Sorry," Bolan interrupted him. "Figure of speech."

"I see."

"The address?"

Umaru directed Bolan to a street of smallish shops, with an aging hotel at one end of the block. It wasn't much to look at: square, three stories tall, flat-roofed, with nothing in the way of decoration but a sign in front that marked it as the Hotel Hêbê.

It took Bolan the best part of a minute to recall his Greek mythology from high school.

Hêbê. The goddess of youth.

"Somebody has a sense of humor," he observed, unsmiling.

"This," Umaru answered, "is an evil place."

"It's going out of business," Bolan answered as he circled once around the block to find a parking place.

There were no guards in evidence, no traffic in or out of Ajani's slime pit. Bolan supposed it might be closed for the duration, but that didn't mean he couldn't burn it down just for the hell of it.

"What will you do if there are children here?" Umaru asked.

Bolan considered that. He didn't have the rolling stock to transport any minor hostages, nor could he think of anyplace that would accept them.

"Call the cops, I guess," he said at last. "But not until I settle with their keepers."

"I'd like to help you," Umaru said. "This is…personal for me."

It meant leaving the Subaru unguarded, but it wouldn't be the first time. "Come ahead, then," he replied. "Be careful with your fire through walls, though. Just in case."

Umaru grabbed his Daewoo rifle from the floorboards, tucked it underneath his arm and followed Bolan at a jog across the street. With each step closer to their goal, he felt a mounting sense of urgency. If there were children suffering inside this house of horrors—

Bolan heard the pop and whoosh of an RPG round somewhere above them, glancing up in time to see the rocket-propelled grenade streak from an open third-floor window of the Hotel Hêbê. They were too close for the shooter to hit them, but another heartbeat told Bolan that he was aiming for their car.

And Bolan couldn't fault his marksmanship.

The Subaru erupted into flames and sprayed the street

with smoking shrapnel, sinking on melted tires into a lake of blazing gasoline. While windows rattled up and down the street, the front door of the Hotel Hêbê opened, spewing gunmen from its lobby to the sidewalk, firing as they came.

UMARU REACTED on instinct, a heartbeat behind his comrade in arms. He didn't know or care how long the trap had been in place, or whether more teams had been placed throughout the city, waiting for a chance to kill him and the tall American.

To hesitate under the gun meant death.

Cooper had dropped one of Ajani's gunmen by the time Umaru raised his stolen Daewoo rifle and sprayed the hotel's facade with 5.56 mm NATO rounds. Two of the opposition fell—one stitched across the chest, the other clutching at a wounded arm—before the rest returned fire, driving Umaru under cover behind a parked car.

He saw Cooper priming a grenade and nodded when the tall man said, "Be ready when I make the pitch." A second later, Cooper lobbed the lethal egg over the low roof of their bullet-punctured shelter, ducking back and down before it blew.

The blast was trailed by cries of pain, but Umaru had seen Ajani's gunmen fanning out before Cooper had pitched the grenade. He guessed that some had managed to escape its full effect, so he came up with the Daewoo seeking targets, aping Cooper's movements with his Steyr AUG.

Three men were standing as he rose, and Cooper nailed the first two with a pair of 3-round bursts at something close to point-blank range. Umaru caught the third turning to bring the white man under fire, and slammed a short burst through his rib cage, shredding heart and lungs to leave a dead man tottering, eyes blank, before he fell.

"Come on!" Bolan snapped, and they ran westward

along the empty street, past cars that might have had ignition keys in place, but would have cost them precious time. Umaru didn't know if there were more gunmen inside prepared to chase them, but the rocketeer upstairs was still in play, firing another RPG just as they reached the nearest intersection.

This time, his missile struck the curb and ricocheted beneath an ancient pickup before it blew, the shock wave nearly dropping Umaru to all fours. He scrambled through it, deafened for a moment by the blast, but found his footing and ran after Cooper, north along the side street going—where?

They needed wheels, as Cooper would say, before another squad of gunmen overtook them or police arrived with sirens screaming to infest the neighborhood. If they were forced to stop and search for hidden keys or to hot-wire some old junker, Umaru believed they might be finished, here and now.

Just then, a BMW MINI Cooper turned onto the street ahead of them, its driver slowing as he saw the smoke and flames ahead. Cooper didn't hesitate, Umaru saw, lunging into the street and leveling his rifle at the driver's startled face, pulling the door open to drag him from behind the wheel.

Umaru ran around the car and hurled himself into the passenger's seat as Cooper floored the clutch to keep from stalling the engine, shifted down and gave the little car some gas. He found a lever underneath the driver's seat and shoved it back to full extension, driving with the Steyr AUG across his lap, its muzzle angled through the open driver's window.

"Here they come!" he said as half a dozen gunmen raced around the corner, spotted the car and raised their weapons in the semblance of a firing squad. "Hang on!"

Umaru ducked his head as Cooper whipped the MINI Cooper through a squealing U-turn in the middle of the street while bullets flew around them. They were halfway down the block and taking scattered hits before Umaru realized that he was laughing like a madman.

"What's so funny?" Bolan asked him.

"This car! A MINI *Cooper*," Umaru gasped in reply.

"Hilarious," the American said. "When you get over it, you want to watch for any chase cars on our tail?"

VALENTIN SIDOROV took a last drag on his cigarette, tossed it away and stepped out of his car. He looked both ways along the street, not merely glancing, but examining the shadows that surrounded him. It was a lifelong habit of survival.

And this night, it wouldn't help him.

He was meeting with the enemy, a meeting he'd requested, and Sidorov knew a dozen unseen snipers could be tracking every move he made through night-vision scopes without revealing themselves to his unaided eyes. Still, he reached beneath his jacket and stroked his GSh-18 pistol in its holster, just for luck.

Which he would need, if he was going to survive the night.

Crossing the street, Sidorov passed into a dimly lit alleyway and moved halfway along its length until he reached a bright red, freshly painted door. The men who flanked it were Chinese. The weapons they carried were Type 95 assault rifles, the 5.8 mm bullpup design introduced by China North Industries in 1997.

Sidorov didn't speak to the guards, nor they to him. One of them knocked on the red door, and it was opened seconds later by another Chinese, this one with a shaved scalp and a handlebar mustache. He left the guards in place and led Sidorov down a narrow corridor, to reach an office on the left.

"You're armed?" he asked Sidorov when they reached their destination.

"Certainly," the Russian said. "Are you?"

The bald man stared holes in his skull for thirty seconds, then opened the door without knocking and ushered Sidorov into the presence of Lao Choy Teoh.

"He has a weapon, sir," the guard announced.

"We all have weapons, Shin," Lao replied.

"Is this a suicide mission, Comrade Sidorov?"

"Hardly. And we don't call each other comrades anymore."

"Good. No comrades here, then. Shin, bring…vodka? Whiskey? Beer?"

"Coffee," the Russian said as he sat in the lone chair facing Lao's small desk.

When Shin had closed the door, Lao said, "I admit that you surprised me when you asked to meet. It is…unorthodox."

"We're living in confused and troubled times," Sidorov said.

"Indeed. And my superiors have reason to believe the troubles are your fault."

"My boss is of a similar opinion," Sidorov replied. "Someone has taken pains to make him feel that way."

"Meaning?"

"Meaning I *know* that none of the attacks on CNP were ordered or directed by Uroil. Whoever told you otherwise is lying through his teeth. I'm willing to believe the same about the claims that you and Mr. Chan have sponsored hostile actions against Russian interests in Warri."

"You believe in cutting to the chase, as the Americans would say."

"I don't have any time to spare," Sidorov said. "If I'm mistaken, and you *are* behind these incidents, then I'm as good as dead. Case closed. But if there's someone out there, stalking both of us for reasons I don't fully understand, our interests would be better served by joining forces than by stabbing one another in the back."

"You are aware of the attack on Mr. Chan, at his home?"

Sidorov nodded. "As I'm sure you are aware that someone fired on Mr. Eltsin in his office."

"Yes."

"And Mr. Chan received some kind of warning, I assume?"

"He did."

"Which implicates Uroil in the invasion of his privacy?"

"Perhaps."

"And prior to that, a telephone demand for money."

"Mr. Eltsin, also?"

"Someone's playing us," Sidorov said. "And not just us. Whoever this is has the Ijaws and the Itsekiris at each other's throats all over town. You will have noticed that, no doubt."

"It's come to my attention."

"I suggest," Sidorov said, "that we can win this bastard's game if we join forces. Change the rules. Surprise him, them, whoever it may be."

"And how would we accomplish that?" Lao inquired.

Sidorov smiled and said, "I thought you'd never ask."

"THERE. THE MIDDLE of the next block," Taiwo Babatunde said. He pointed with one massive hand, while the other clutched his SIG SG 543 carbine.

The weapon, stock folded, resembled a toy in Babatunde's hands, but it was lethal all the same, a selective-fire assault rifle chambered in 5.56 mm, one of half a dozen standard-issue small arms used by Nigeria's army. With a full-auto cyclic rate of 800 rounds per minute, it could shred a man before his lifeless body hit the ground.

And if that man was Agu Ajani, why, so much the better.

Babatunde had taken his master's order to heart. He couldn't return without "good news," which meant Ajani's death, or, at the very least, some major blow against the Ijaw warlord that would leave him reeling, vulnerable to a coup de grâce. All Babatunde had to do was to find Ajani, penetrate his personal defenses, kill him and return alive with evidence to satisfy his oldest living friend.

Simple? Not quite.

On any other night in Warri, Babatunde and his dozen gunmen, packed into three sleek sedans, could have driven straight to Ajani's home and hoped for the best. Do or die. Kill or be killed.

But someone else had already raided Ajani's estate, leaving chaos and corpses behind. That strike had driven the Ijaw commander deep underground, thus far beyond the reach of Babatunde's most trusted informants. Thus, the hunt became more complicated.

And more urgent.

Babatunde had squeezed an address from one of Ajani's confederates, snatched off the street while a woman distracted him and driven to a neighborhood where screams were commonly ignored. He'd been a long hour dying, but he had revealed the information Babatunde needed.

If only it were true.

According to the dead man, Agu Ajani had a "special" lady who resided in the house their little convoy was approaching. His attachment to this woman verged upon obsession, to the point, perhaps, where he might risk his life to see her in the midst of war.

It was a lead, at least, and all that Babatunde had.

If Ajani wasn't at the woman's apartment, perhaps she would know where he was. Failing that, she might make a useful hostage.

"Here!" the giant told his driver. "Stop in front."

The three sedans parked nose to tail, engines still running as the doors began to open. Babatunde had one size-fourteen shoe on the pavement when lights blazed around him, from the house and two of its neighbors, followed by an amplified voice from a bullhorn.

"Stop where you are!" the voice commanded. "Lay down your weapons!"

The first shot sounded from somewhere behind Babatunde, instantly multiplied by a dozen or more as weapons chimed in from all sides. A bullet cracked the windshield, inches from his face, as Babatunde raised his carbine, firing toward the lights that nearly blinded him.

"Get out of here!" he barked at his driver. "Hurry up!"

His car screeched away from the curb on command, slamming Babatunde's door on his extended leg. He cursed and grappled with the door, dragging his injured limb into the car before he slammed it shut. Behind him, his companions followed in their vehicles, all taking hits as they retreated from the battleground.

And there were more headlights behind him, now, as other cars gave chase. Not squad cars, he decided, since they had no flashing lights or sirens, but a trap.

He'd blundered into it, and now the question was, would he survive that grave mistake?

"I HAD BEGUN TO THINK you wouldn't call again," the voice in Bolan's ear declared.

"I've had a busy night," he told Huang Li Chan. "And so have you, from what I hear."

"Indeed. Given the recent progress of events—"

"You'd rather call it off?" Bolan suggested. "Hey, no problem. Keep the hundred thousand. Maybe it will tide you over while you're looking for a new position."

"Wait! I have the money, and I need the information we discussed. Now more than ever, it appears."

"Well, if you're sure," Bolan said.

"Absolutely. How soon can we meet?"

That tipped it over. With his recent near-miss fresh in mind, Chan shouldn't be that quick to volunteer for any meeting with a stranger, much less an extortionist.

"How's midnight sound to you?" Bolan inquired.

"Midnight?" Repeating it for someone else's benefit, perhaps. Delaying long enough to get the nod. "Yes. That is satisfactory," Chan said. "And where?"

"I'll call back thirty minutes prior and let you know."

"But—"

Bolan broke the link and turned to face Umaru.

"Suddenly, Chan's hot to pay and play," he said.

"A trap?" Umaru asked him.

"Absolutely."

"You'll avoid it, then."

"And keep him waiting? That's just rude," Bolan replied.

"But if he's waiting for us—"

"Chan can't set a snare unless he knows where to expect me. Neither can the others. If we bring them all together…"

"Can you do that?"

"Only one way to find out," Bolan said as he keyed another private number on his cell phone.

Three calls and seven minutes later, he closed and pocketed the phone, smiling. "All aboard," he told Umaru. "Seems they can't wait to get in the game."

"You didn't call Yetunde."

"He's a fifth wheel, literally," Bolan said. "I don't put him on anybody's side, except his own. The rest can pair off, feeding one another's paranoia while they wait for me to fix the meeting."

"And they'll all send gunmen."

Bolan nodded. "Sure. I'm counting on it."

"Will we even be there?" Umaru asked.

"I will," Bolan answered. "If you want to skip it, that's okay with me. You've done more than your share already."

"Just enough, it seems, to end life as I knew it."

"Change won't kill you," Bolan said. He almost added "necessarily," then let it go, hoping that the next few hours wouldn't prove him wrong.

"What shall we do until midnight?" Umaru asked as he reloaded one of his rifle's spare magazines.

"What else?" Bolan replied. "Turn up the heat and see who squeals."

CHAPTER SEVENTEEN

Bolan left the hijacked MINI Cooper at a housing project on Warri's west side, where he hot-wired a five-year-old Kia sedan and escaped without being spotted.

Cruising in the Kia, killing time until his enemies convened to kill him, Bolan kept his promise to Umaru. He was turning up the heat, intent on keeping everyone off balance, even as they schemed to trap him at midnight. He didn't know if any of them would be bringing cash, as ordered, but it made no sense to count on it.

The *narcotrafficantes* had a saying in Colombia: *plata o plano*.

Silver or lead.

It normally applied to situations where a bribe was offered, and refusal meant a bullet would be coming next, but Bolan thought he could adapt it to his current situation. He'd demanded cash from four men who could spare it, but who wouldn't give it up without a fight. Now, all four had agreed to pay him off at midnight, the location of his choice, but Bolan had a hunch they'd be long on weapons, short on cash.

Just as he'd planned.

The fun, if you could call it that, would come from seeing how the several groups reacted when they all showed up together—if they showed.

The trick, at least for Bolan, would be getting out of it alive.

But first he still had some time to kill.

And people, too.

"This is a place where stolen cars are kept and sometimes broken down," Umaru said.

"A chop shop," Bolan translated.

"On newer models, they may only change the registration numbers. Older ones, they sell for parts. The money goes to MEND."

It was the first junkyard, per se, that he had seen in Warri. Older cars than some of those he saw parked on the lot, behind a chain-link fence topped by a roll of razor wire, were bustling up and down the city's streets all day and night. The main shop was a structure made of corrugated metal, with a roof to match, that had to be an oven in the afternoons.

And it was going to get hotter in a few more minutes.

Bolan found the main gate padlocked, passed it by and cut a flap in the chain link, along the junkyard's north perimeter. He had already checked for dogs, scanning the lot and whistling softly, without getting a response. If there were any on patrol inside, trained not to bark or show themselves before a strike, he'd deal with them as they appeared and offer up a silent commendation for their souls.

He slipped inside the lot and held the flap of wire for his companion, who'd insisted on joining the party after their snafu at the Hotel Hêbê. Bolan would've liked to double back and burn that place, assuming it was closed to customers after the ambush, but he knew the risk would be too great.

New targets. New frontiers.

Someone was working in the shop, and they'd apparently forgotten to post guards. Maybe the chop-shop trade was deemed too insignificant to rate a hit. Maybe someone had simply dropped the ball.

In either case, he owned them now.

Bolan peered through a gap in the corrugated wall and saw four men working on a Volvo station wagon. One wielded a cutting torch, the other three had wrenches. Bolan found a window they'd left open, pulled the pin on a white-phosphorus grenade and lobbed the bomb through the opening, watching it bounce across the concrete floor and disappear beneath the front end of the Volvo.

Time to split.

As Bolan turned away, the shop went blazing white inside and people began to scream. The screaming didn't last long, but the fire he'd started would burn through the night, devouring flesh, concrete and steel.

A little something else for Ekon Afolabi to consider as he counted down the hours to midnight.

VALENTIN SIDOROV worried that he might have spread himself too thin, but what did he have to lose?

Only his life.

After his meetings with the Chinese and Arkady Eltsin, he was going back to see Agu Ajani one more time, to try to keep the lid from blowing off a city racked by violence.

Sidorov didn't like his chances, but he had to try.

Ajani was expecting him, the guards staked out around an old abandoned factory where he had gone to ground. It reminded Sidorov a bit of the drug plant their common enemy had already razed, but he guessed that Ajani wouldn't appreciate the comparison.

The sentries were expecting Sidorov and passed him through, after studying his face a moment longer than was necessary in the glare of three flashlights. Sidorov thanked them in a tone that left no doubt about his sarcasm, then trailed a slender guide past silent, rusty machines to reach a tiny office, where Ajani occupied a swivel chair without a desk to match.

"What news?" the Ijaw warlord asked before Sidorov had a chance to speak.

"First thing," Sidorov said, "I spoke to the Chinese. I don't believe they're behind the trouble you've experienced."

Ajani rose to pace the room. "All right," he said. "Who *is* responsible?"

"It may be MEND, or someone else."

A mocking smile twisted Ajani's lips.

"Is that supposed to help me?" he inquired.

"I'm hoping that you'll take a breath, calm down and let me work this out," Sidorov said. "We've been in touch with someone claiming he can solve this problem. I suspect, in fact, that he's behind it. We're supposed to meet at midnight."

"As am I," Ajani said.

"Wait, let me guess," Sidorov said. "He wants a hundred thousand dollars for the information?"

"It would seem that we are doing business with the same man, after all," Ajani noted.

"Yes. Except that I don't plan to give him any money," Sidorov replied.

"Nor I," the Ijaw tribal leader said. "If I can capture him alive, so much the better. And if not, at least I'll shake the stone out of my shoe."

"What if he's not the only stone?" Sidorov asked.

"I've thought of that. It's why I hope to bring him in for questioning."

"I see no reason why we can't cooperate on this," Sidorov said.

"You think I need your help to take one man?"

The Russian shrugged. "You haven't done so well with him so far. None of us has."

Ajani thought about that for another moment, then replied, "What is it you suggest?"

CAPTAIN JOHNSON Mashilia waited on the street corner outside a pawn shop where a steady stream of customers traipsed in and out, bearing heirlooms and trinkets that they swapped for petty cash. Each man and woman passing by paused long enough to eye his uniform with various expressions of suspicion or contempt, while Mashilia tried to ignore them, watching the street for his ride.

He had ordered his driver to drop him a block from the point where he stood, then park the squad car and wait until the captain called him back for a pickup. The driver, a sergeant, was told to ask no questions and to keep his mouth shut if he valued job security.

Now Mashilia waited, feeling painfully conspicuous. He had begun to wonder if Yetunde might be planning to eliminate him as an object lesson to the other officers who banked bribes and couldn't deliver satisfaction on demand.

He was about to give up waiting, actually had the cell phone in his palm, when he saw Yetunde's limousine gliding along the curb. He pocketed the phone, patted his holster just to reassure himself that he was armed and waited for the car to stop in front of him.

When he was seated in the back, facing Yetunde from his jump seat, the captain waited for the usual barrage of questions. What he got, instead, was simply, "Well?"

He knew that *"Well, what?"* would not serve him, and might even get him killed by one of Yetunde's four hulking gunmen. Instead of risking it, the captain said, "Regrettably, I have no further information. Since you called me here—"

"I called you here," Yetunde interrupted him, "because *I* have new information."

"Oh?"

"It is ironic, don't you think, that I must give you leads to find the people who have set out to destroy me?"

"Not just you," Mashilia replied. "There have been raids against the Russians and Chinese, against the Itsekiri and Ijaw."

"I know all that!" Yetunde snapped. "And I may know how you can find the men responsible."

"I'm listening," the captain said.

"I'm a businessman, as you're aware," Yetunde said. "I deal with Afolabi *and* Ajani, on occasion. It's useful to have eyes and ears inside both camps."

The captain nodded, hoping that Yetunde would get to the point.

"Tonight, those eyes and ears tell me that someone has approached both sides, claiming to know the individuals responsible for all their suffering. And, by extension, mine, as well."

"You have the name?" Mashilia asked.

"If I did, the bastard would be screaming in a basement now, spilling the names of those who hired him to torment me," Yetunde said. "No. But I'm informed that Afolabi and Ajani will be meeting this informant soon, to meet his price and find out what he has to say."

"When you say 'soon—'"

"Midnight," Yetunde told him, "if my information is correct. And if it's not, someone will pay."

"They've both agreed to meet this stranger, at the same time?" The captain thought that sounded foolish, even dangerous.

"Who knows if one suspects the other may be there?" Yetunde said. "Who even cares? My point is that you should be there, to capture the informant and deliver him to me."

"Snatch him from both tribes?" Mashilia scowled at that, envisioning a bloodbath.

"Why not?" Yetunde asked. "You have the authority, the men, the weapons. You can field an army, if you need one. In the process, if you confiscate the cash earmarked for the delivery, well, who's to say that it won't be misplaced?"

Mashilia saw the possibilities. He also saw the risks involved.

"Where is this meeting being held?" he asked.

"Ah, that's the problem. It remains unknown, at present."

"So—"

"You'll know as soon as I hear something, Captain. Be prepared to act upon a moment's notice."

"If you're wrong—"

"Then we'll try again," Yetunde said.

Or I may have to find another partner, Captain Mashilia thought. And feed you to the wolves.

Forcing a smile he didn't feel, the captain said, "I will be waiting for your call."

"So, YOU ARE DEALING with the Russians now?" The tone of Ekon Afolabi's voice was stark, accusatory.

"Dealings? No," Lao Choy Teoh replied. "We had a brief discussion of our mutual concern. If you are interested in hearing what I learned, so be it. If not…"

Lao had risen halfway from his chair when Afolabi waved him back. "Sit down and tell me this amazing thing," he instructed, "by all means."

"If I may have some tea…?"

Lao knew he was pushing it, but he refused to let a common thug from MEND dictate his actions when the bastard had his hand out half the time, begging for money. If Afolabi couldn't behave in a reasonably civilized manner, Lao would be pleased to abandon his cause on the spot and find someone else willing to help CNP reach its goals in Nigeria.

Lao waited for his tea and took a sip before he spoke again. It was inferior, but what could one expect?

"It seems," he said at last, "that your old adversary has received the same demand for money as you have. The same demand inflicted upon CNP and Uroil, for one hundred thousand dollars."

Afolabi blinked at that. "From the same man?"

"Perhaps. We don't have recordings of the other calls for voice comparison. But, at the very least, a single group attempting to profit from bloodshed in Warri."

"The same group, you think, who protects Jared Ross and K-Tech?"

Lao took another sip of tea, considering the question. "It is possible, of course," he said. "I have no great faith in coincidence."

"I should have killed him while I had the chance," Afolabi said.

"You have tried, if I recall, on more than one occasion. If you plan to try again, just now, I must advise against it."

"Who needs your advice?" the warlord snapped.

"In general," Lao said, "the same people who need my money to support their cause. If you were truly independent, self-sustaining, I wouldn't be here. In fact, we never would have met."

"You came to me, remember?" Afolabi challenged.

"When I recognized your need for help," Lao answered. Thinking to himself, And saw the possibilities for profit. "If the time has truly come when you no longer need assistance," he continued, "let me thank you for the tea and leave you to your planning for the days ahead."

"Wait, wait! Why are you always rushing off?" the warlord asked, forcing a smile that never reached his brooding eyes. "So hasty, all the time. Tell me, what are you planning with the Russians, to destroy these people who would rob us blind?"

"The payment deadline has been set for midnight, yes?" Lao asked.

"So I was told."

"It is the same for all of us. Myself, Uroil, Ajani and his people. We are waiting for directions to the payoff site."

"And when they come?"

"If we receive another call—and bear in mind, the whole thing may turn out to be a hoax—but *if* we are directed to a single meeting place, we may assume the plan is to ignite more violence among us. Rather than participate in mutual destruction, we must all collaborate to trap and punish our tormentors."

"Are you telling me the Russians have agreed to this?"

"They have," Lao said.

"And Agu? What does he say?"

Lao smiled. "I'm confident that he will see the wisdom of our plan before midnight."

"I don't share your confidence," Afolabi said.

"If I am mistaken," Lao replied, "then he will have to deal with all of us, including those he has betrayed at Uroil. Either way, we win."

A brighter smile cracked Afolabi's face.

"More tea?" he asked.

TAIWO BABATUNDE grimaced as the barmaid swiped a cloth moistened with alcohol across a shallow wound on his biceps. The bullet graze was painful, but he knew it wasn't serious.

Nothing like his precarious position, if he tried to get in touch with Ekon Afolabi.

His instructions had been simple and explicit: don't come back until he had destroyed Agu Ajani, or at least inflicted harm enough to cripple Ajani's army. The details might be open to debate, but Babatunde knew that getting ambushed, chased halfway across the city, and escaping only after he had lost two men would never be confused with victory.

He felt stupid for blundering into Ajani's trap. The error had cost him two soldiers, some skin and three cars marked with bullet holes now, which he'd have to replace. Altogether, a blunder that Afolabi would neither forgive nor forget.

The dead men, Sokari Tukur and Lawrence Ibeto, were simply unlucky, in Babatunde's opinion. Tukur had been in the third car, taking hits as they fled from the house of Ajani's mistress, and was struck in the head before traveling two blocks downrange. Ibeto had been riding in the backseat of Babatunde's own car, for God's sake, when a slug drilled the back window, halfway through their wild ride, and grazed his neck.

A minor wound, it seemed—no worse than Taiwo's arm, he would have said—until the blood began spraying and gushing from a carotid artery. There'd been no saving him from that point onward, while they raced through the streets willy-nilly.

And only luck had saved them in the end.

Luck and a bus filled with nuns and young children, which struck the lead chase car broadside, then rolled over and blocked the advance of two others while Babatunde and his men escaped.

To what?

He was in exile from the ranks of MEND until he carried

out his orders, and he still had no idea where they could find Agu Ajani. Once the damaged, bloodstained cars had been replaced, he could attempt to snatch another of Ajani's men, obtain new information on his likely whereabouts and try again.

And if he failed again?

Was this his life from now on, wandering the streets of Warri, searching for a ghost who constantly eluded him? Would he stumble on Ajani sometime, weeks or months from now, by accident? And if so, would he still have any soldiers with him? Would it be a stupid waste of time, by then, to carry out the contract he'd been given?

The barmaid was starting to bandage his arm when Babatunde's cell phone made its tinkling sound, like fairy bells. He snapped it open, checked the screen and was startled to see Afolabi's number displayed.

"Hello? Ekon?"

"Where are you?" Afolabi asked.

"Following orders." He knew enough of cell phones not to broadcast what those orders were.

"I need you back here now," Afolabi said.

"Back where?" Babatunde asked, confused.

"Headquarters. Hurry!"

"But you said—"

"Forget that, now," his old friend said. "I need my strong right arm."

"You have it," Babatunde answered, beaming like a child on Christmas morning. "I am on my way."

ANOTHER SAFEHOUSE, this one used to stash weapons, along with shooters in hiding. Umaru had fingered it as one of Agu Ajani's holdings, but Bolan didn't really care which side claimed ownership.

If he could take guns out of circulation, maybe even

score some extra ammunition for himself, so much the better. It was all in a night's work.

Bolan surveyed the target, another anonymous house in a poor neighborhood, with no guards visible. That might mean the place was deserted, or that his watchmen were keeping themselves out of sight. Either way, Bolan knew he would have to approach, if he meant to find out.

With the Kia hot-wired, Bolan had to leave it running or risk critical delay if they were in a hurry taking off. Therefore, he didn't ask Umaru if he minded staying with the car, just said, "I'll be back soon," and cleared the driver's seat.

Umaru covered him, crossing the street, but lost him, as Bolan passed along a shadowed strip of dirt between the target dwelling and its neighbor to the west. He ducked below dark windows, heard no challenge raised from either house and reached the tiny shared backyard without incident. There, he found a back door facing onto a porch lined with abandoned, rusted-out appliances.

The door was locked.

Bolan considered picking it, but first peered through a window to the left side of the door and saw a laundry room of sorts. Old sink against one wall, a metal rack for drying clothes directly opposite, peeling linoleum and wallpaper. No sign of life within.

Bolan retreated twenty feet into the yard, drew his Beretta from its shoulder rig and sighted on the back door's knob. The first round from his silenced pistol dropped the shattered doorknob to the wooden porch. He aimed another at the door's dead bolt, squeezed off—and staggered, as the world exploded in his face.

Some kind of plastic charge, he reckoned, wired to the door with a trigger set to blow if it opened. Maybe a mercury switch, or something as simple as a steel ball bearing in a plastic pill bottle, with needles through the lid, wires leading to a battery and blasting cap.

It wasn't just the first charge, though. That should have killed whoever had come prowling, but it would have left the arms stash in the house unguarded if the thief had backup standing by outside the first blast's lethal radius. Ajani or his armorer had thought of that, and opted not to leave their arsenal intact if it was breached.

The secondary blast caught Bolan crouching in the yard and slammed him over backward through a rolling somersault. In front of him, the little house appeared to swell, walls straining, roof trying to levitate, before it came apart and showered rubble for a hundred feet in all directions. Bolan missed the worst of it as he fell prone, but still sustained a bruise across his left calf when a smoking piece of lumber struck him there, then bounced away.

He was already up and running in a crouch as flames began to spread, consuming ammunition stashed within the house. Bolan could hear the rounds cooking off in the midst of the fire, bullets sizzling and hissing around him as he sprinted for the waiting car.

Umaru had the Kia moving as he got there, opening the door for Bolan's leap, then gunning it away from the demented sound of small-arms fire that popped and rattled in the night.

"A trap?" Umaru asked.

"It nearly worked," Bolan replied. "With any luck, Ajani will believe he bagged me."

It would be some time before firefighters could approach the blazing wreckage, search for bodies and report that there were none.

Meanwhile, the Executioner was blitzing on.

CHAPTER EIGHTEEN

The satchel—more of a small suitcase, really, made from old, cracked leather—sat in the middle of Agu Ajani's small desk. He walked around it, studying the object as if it was foreign to him, something that had suddenly materialized from out of thin air.

"There it is," he said at last. "One hundred thousand American dollars."

Standing on the sidelines, Taiwo Babatunde frowned. He was relieved to be present, forgiven for all of his failures, but a question still nagged at his mind.

"It's a trap for the blackmailer, yes?" he inquired.

Ajani nodded. "That's correct."

"Then, I'm afraid I do not understand, Agu."

"Understand what?"

"Why we're taking the money. I mean, since it's a trap, and all we plan to do is catch or kill these cockroaches, why take the payoff money in the first place?"

Ajani blinked as if the question hadn't occurred to him. He hesitated for a moment, frowning, then explained, "The others will be bringing money. If we don't, the others may suspect something is wrong."

"I see. But none of them intend to pay the blackmailer, correct?"

"Yes," Ajani answered. "Sidorov says they are all agreed on that."

"I still don't understand, Agu. If none of them intend to pay, why take four hundred thousand dollars to the meeting place?"

Ajani's frown revealed a hint of anger now. "In case something goes wrong," he said, "and we are forced to pay up, after all."

That made no sense to Babatunde. If the trap failed, he assumed their quarry would be running for his life, not dallying around the place to pick up four bags filled with cash. It seemed ridiculous, even to his distinctly limited imagination, but he dared not press Ajani on it any further and risk falling out of his old friend's good graces once more.

Instead he simply nodded and replied, "I see."

"You understand," Ajani said, "that many things can happen in a situation of this kind. We must be on alert, not only to the blackmailers, but also to our allies of the moment."

That made sense to Babatunde, absolutely. He had hated Ekon Afolabi and his Itsekiri brothers for as long as he could remember. Being thrown together with them now, if only for an hour, felt bizarre and absolutely wrong. He would most certainly be on his guard against betrayal by the MEND warlord and his Chinese associates.

"It is possible," Ajani said, "that once the trap is sprung, there may be some confusion. Ideally no one will be injured but the thieves who plan to rob us, yes? But there's a chance, however small, that some mishap may be upon our friends, as well."

When he said "friends," Ajani curled his lip into a sneer, his eyes glittering.

"It's possible, of course," Babatunde replied.

"If something should happen to Afolabi, for example, it would be our duty as his allies to protect the money that he carried to the meeting. We must guarantee that it doesn't fall into the wrong hands."

Babatunde was slow, and always had been, but he saw where this was going and it made him smile. "As you command, Agu," he said. "I will defend their fortune with my life, as if it was my own."

"I would expect no less," Ajani said, wearing his own smile now. "Of course, this accident—in theory, mind you—must be absolute. False accusations sully friendship. If the Itsekiri claimed we tried to steal their money, it would place another obstacle between us."

"I wouldn't attempt to guard their money while they lived," Babatunde replied. "No doubt, they'd be insulted."

"But if they were all dead, well…"

"There'd be no other honorable choice."

"Exactly. So, we understand each other, then?" Ajani asked.

"Beyond a doubt," Babatunde said, hoping he would have the chance to kill Ekon Afolabi himself.

"Do you believe that anyone will actually bring the money?" Obinna Umaru asked.

"It doesn't matter," Bolan said, "as long as they show up."

"With men and guns," Umaru said.

"Let's hope so."

"All prepared to kill us."

"All prepared to kill *someone*," Bolan replied. "Remember, two of them are mortal enemies. The other two are rivals and outsiders who've been making tension worse between the tribes, whether they planned on it or not. Put them together, it's a jug of nitro, waiting for someone to tip it over."

"Meaning us," Umaru said.

"It doesn't have to be," Bolan reminded him. "I told you once already, you've gone well beyond the call. You want to split right now, I'll help you bag a ride for old times' sake."

"Old times," Umaru said. "It hasn't even been two days."

"It feels longer," Bolan said, "when you're living large."

"It's all a blur, right now."

"Maybe that's better," Bolan told him. "Get out while you can, before it hits you."

Umaru shook his head. "No, I will stay," he answered. "To the bitter end, as you Americans would say."

"I'm hoping that it won't be bitter," Bolan said. "For us, at least."

"What if some of them actually *bring* the money?" asked Umaru.

Bolan shrugged. "It's fifty-fifty that we'll never even see it," he replied. "But if you get your hands on some, consider it a bonus for a job well done. Like overtime."

Umaru smiled at that, but only briefly. "Where do you intend to meet them?" he inquired.

"Someplace with combat stretch and cover," Bolan said. "Maybe a park nobody uses after dark. Someplace like that."

"Why not the football stadium on Cemetery Road?" Umaru asked. "It's closed at night, of course, but breaking in is simple. In addition to the field and parking lots, the stadium seats twenty thousand spectators."

"Sounds good," Bolan said. "We should go and check it out. But first…"

"More cages to be rattled," Umaru said.

"I wouldn't want the opposition getting settled," Bolan told him. "Having any time to plan and organize."

"Agreed. What's next?"

"We've worked through roughly half your list," Bolan replied. "Let's try something a little different."

"There is a bathhouse," Umaru said.

"And?"

"It's very private. Certain wealthy men and government officials go there to relax with friends. Young men, especially."

"It's a commercial operation?" Bolan asked him.

"Run by Ekon Afolabi."

"Worth a look, then, if you're up for it."

Umaru gave him the address, adding, "It's not far from the stadium, in any case."

"Two birds, one stone," Bolan replied.

He had no beef with anyone because of sex, unless that someone was a predator who forced himself on others, and the animosity some soldiers felt toward gays hadn't infected Bolan. This night's business was about crippling his enemies, putting them out of business, whether they were peddling drugs or fantasies, providing games of chance or squeezing money out of local merchants for "protection." Bolan didn't fault their customers—the weak, addicted or embarrassed—but neither would he let his sympathy for them divert him from his duty.

Which, this night, was shutting down the predators in Warri. If their operations opened up again tomorrow or the next day, with new faces in command, Bolan would neither be dismayed nor disappointed. He had come to terms with human nature long ago, and understood that every battle had a limited objective.

Evil was immune to unconditional surrender.

It would always bounce back, always find another angle of attack.

And while he lasted, it would have to face the Executioner.

CAPTAIN JOHNSON Mashilia stood outside Plato's Health Club, breathing smoke while the flashing colored lights of emergency vehicles stained his face red, blue and yellow. Firefighters were preparing to pack up and leave.

The arson investigator approached Mashilia, scribbling something on his clipboard as he said, "Just the two dead inside. Both with guns. They were shot."

"You can tell that, in spite of the fire?" Mashilia inquired.

"Neither one of them burned," said the other. His name eluded Mashilia, though they'd spoken at several crime scenes over the past year or so.

"Not burned?"

"The fire wasn't extensive, Captain. Someone used a hand grenade, or possibly a pipe bomb, but the place is mostly tile and concrete inside. Little to burn, except the drapes and furnishings."

The dead men would be guards, then, the captain thought. What health club needed gunmen standing watch?

"I've heard about this place," he told the arson officer.

"Who hasn't, eh? Rich people and their boys, pretending they come here for a massage and exercise. Some exercise!"

"There were no customers inside when your people arrived?" Mashilia asked.

"No one but the dead," the arson officer replied. "You've seen a lot of that lately, from what I hear."

"Too much," the captain agreed.

"Or maybe just enough, eh?"

"What?"

"Sometimes," the fireman said, "I think that we can only stand so much, you know? Society, the world. We reach a point where someone says, 'Enough! No more!' And when the smoke clears, we can start all over, mucking up our lives again."

"You'd call it fate, then? People being murdered in the streets?"

"I'd say it would depend on who's been murdered. Do

we need drug dealers, gunmen, perverts, revolutionaries? I think we can spare some of them, for the greater good."

"You'll put me out of business if that notion catches on," said the captain.

"Not a bit," the other told him, smiling. "You'll always have bad men to chase. Maybe the next lot can't afford protection, and you'll track them down more easily."

Those words struck home, but Mashilia saw no malice in the firefighter's expression, heard none in his voice. Even a blind man had to know the government in Warri was corrupt, as throughout all Nigeria. What fool believed that wealthy criminals were punished like common thieves and rapists?

No one.

Least of all a captain of the Delta Police Command.

"I'll have a word with my superiors," Mashilia said. "More murders, for the good of the community." He smiled to show that he was joking.

"It's a thought," the arson officer replied. "And now, I leave you to it. You should have a copy of my final report by sometime tomorrow."

Mashilia nodded, already planning the questions he'd ask of the "health club's" owner. Assuming he could locate Ekon Afolabi at this hour, on a day when the warlord was hiding to save his own life.

And why bother trying, when any serious investigation would lead him to powerful men with dark secrets they had to protect? How would he profit from confronting them, if he could even learn their names?

At least the club didn't belong to Idowu Yetunde, so he wouldn't have to hear another whining tirade about how police failed to protect the gangster's livelihood.

Small favors, the captain thought as he turned in the direction of his vehicle.

Before the night was over, he supposed that there would

be more murder scenes for him to visit. Some of them, perhaps, would be less sensitive. It would be a refreshing change if he could simply do his job, investigate a crime for once, without having to shield the guilty or concern himself about the reputation of the victims.

His dashboard radio was squawking when he reached the car. Snagging the microphone, he raised it to his lips and asked, "What now?"

FROM HIS ROOFTOP perch, Bolan surveyed the drab facade of buildings on the far side of the street. Directly opposite, the Simba Social Club was not exactly jumping, but it had a steady stream of hard-eyed men parading in and out of its front door, flanked by two body-builder types whose muscles weren't the only things bulging beneath their loose shirts.

After fifteen minutes on the roof, Bolan had seen no one but street soldiers enter or leave the Simba Social Club. *Simba* meant "lion" in Swahili, but the cats who frequented his latest target wouldn't qualify for singing roles in any animated Disney film.

In fact, they worked for MEND and Ekon Afolabi.

Bolan had no idea what they were doing in the club—receiving orders, stocking up on ammunition, simply killing time until their next deployment—and he didn't care. Each soldier he eliminated now was one less that he'd have to face at midnight, when his main targets lined up to kill him at the Warri football stadium.

Assuming any of them kept the date.

Bolan's Steyr AUG had a factory-standard grenade-launcher muzzle, but he hadn't brought any rifle grenades or blank cartridges with him when he parachuted into Delta State the previous day. Instead he had two white-phosphorus grenades remaining, and decided this would be an opportune occasion to use one of them.

It was a relatively easy pitch, despite the nearly two-pound weight of the M-15 grenade. Forty feet, give or take, from Bolan's perch to the Simba Social Club's flat roof, tar over plywood waiting to sizzle and blaze when the incendiary blew. He didn't know if the club's occupants would hear his grenade strike the roof, but it hardly mattered. Long before anyone could climb up to check out the noise, its sixty-second burn at five thousand degrees would be well under way.

And the rest, as someone said, would be history.

Bolan made the toss and ducked beneath the parapet of his own roof as the grenade went off, to spare his night vision. By the time he rose and shouldered his weapon, the M-15 fireball was well on its way to burning through the social club's roof and attic, to ignite the second floor.

The panic started seconds later, smoke and gunmen pouring from the double doors in front and spreading out along the sidewalk. Some of the exiting soldiers held guns in plan view, while others kept hands tucked under their jackets or shirts, clutching weapons they chose to conceal.

None of them realized that they were targets in a shooting gallery, until Bolan started dropping them, firing in semiauto mode to make each bullet count. He didn't hurry, worked no special pattern, and had put down half a dozen of the shooters before a couple of survivors spied his muzzle-flash and called a warning to their comrades.

The return fire, spotty and inaccurate at first, changed Bolan's modus operandi. Flicking the Steyr's fire-selector switch to full-auto, he reared up once more and raked the Simba sidewalk gang with the remainder of his 30-round magazine, punching 5.56 mm tumbling projectiles through flesh and bone downrange.

Bolan didn't count the dead and wounded, didn't press his luck by reloading and rattling off a second magazine at the scrambling survivors below. Umaru had the Kia waiting for him one block over, and it was time to go.

Time to select another target from the dwindling hit list and move on.

ONE HUNDRED THOUSAND dollars didn't look like much when it was bundled up and packed into a nylon gym bag. Granted, it possessed a certain weight that lent reality to the idea of parting with substantial funds, but in the scheme of things, it was a trivial amount for any thriving petroleum company.

Uroil had a yearly operating income of nearly eleven *billion* dollars per year, reporting a net income of seven billion. A hundred grand was petty cash. It wouldn't be missed.

Besides, Arkady Eltsin thought, the bastards won't collect it, anyway.

Still, carrying the money made him think of losing it, and that put a knot in his stomach despite Valentin Sidorov's assurances that nothing could go wrong.

Since yesterday, it seemed that nothing had gone right. Eltsin himself had nearly died at the hands of a lunatic sniper, whose poor aim alone had spared him from death.

Eltsin pushed the gym bag across his desk, closer to Sidorov, frowning as he spoke. "You're sure the Chinese will make good on their end of the bargain?"

"I'm as sure as I can be until the moment," Sidorov replied. "They have nothing to gain by backing out on us, and much to lose."

"A risk they may be willing to accept," Eltsin replied. "You know how cheap life is in the People's Republic. They test a nuclear warhead and call it birth control."

Sidorov smiled politely at the ancient joke, then said,

"They're human. I trust them to act in their own best interest. Beyond that, naturally, there are no guarantees."

"And if they try to rob you?"

"I'm taking twelve armed men. At the first hint of any double-cross, we'll turn Lao's men into chop suey."

Eltsin's frown deepened as he replied, "I still can't shake the feeling that Beijing is behind all this trouble, somehow. We know they support MEND's guerrilla war against the government. If they install a new regime in Abuja, it won't be long until Uroil is expelled and our facilities nationalized."

"Which is why we support the Ijaw," Sidorov reminded him, "and why I'll be keeping close watch on the bastards tonight."

"If you suppose that it would help for me to be there—"

"No, no," Sidorov replied almost too hastily. "You're not accustomed to these operations, sir. Why place yourself at risk, unnecessarily?"

"Well—"

Eltsin made an effort to conceal his great relief, but doubted that Sidorov was deceived. The man knew him too well.

Another reason why Eltsin wouldn't mourn if Sidorov suffered an accident.

"Any word yet on the meeting place?" he asked.

"No, sir. They're leaving it as late as possible, I'd guess, to keep us from putting our people in place."

"And it's working," Eltsin said.

"No problem. Between my team and the Chinese, Ajani's men and Afolabi's, we'll have fifty guns at the hand-off, wherever it is."

"And if that's not enough?" Eltsin persisted.

"So far, we've only seen one of two shooters at any engagement in Warri. One white and one black, when they show up together. If our adversaries had an army, we'd have seen more soldiers on the firing line, I promise you."

"I want this money back," Eltsin instructed.

"Understood, sir. Every penny of it."

"And no tricks with the Chinese. The last thing that we need is more bloodshed."

"It ends tonight, sir," Sidorov responded. "Rest assured of that."

"SHOULD YOU BE calling soon?" Umaru asked as they were cruising toward their next target, a numbers bank owned by Idowu Yetunde.

Bolan checked his watch and saw that it was 10:47 p.m.

"Let them sweat," he replied. "I'd prefer them to scramble while we get set up for the show. Twenty minutes is plenty to drive across town, if they're motivated."

"What if they get tired of waiting and give up?"

"We'll know at midnight, when nobody shows."

The Warri numbers racket was a spin-off from Nigeria's National Sports Lottery, with daily winning numbers selected from the final scores of various public sporting events. Whereas the official lottery was created to fund "sports and good causes," however, the outlawed private version was carried out strictly for personal profit. Passage of new laws against black-market lotteries in early 2009, predictably, had done nothing to curb illegal betting.

Experience with battling the Mafia and other gangsters had taught Bolan that the worst pain they could suffer was a hard blow to the pocketbook. Street soldiers were a dime a dozen, especially in Third World slums, but money was the lifeblood of organized crime.

The numbers bank was operated from a small law office on Warri's south side, sandwiched between a barbershop and a boutique that specialized in formal clothes. The flanking shops were closed when Bolan got there, but the bank was running strong behind locked doors.

Not that a lock would stop the Executioner.

Bolan breezed in on a burst of 5.56 mm rounds that sent the back door's dead bolt flying like a piece of shrapnel, ready as he entered for the two heavyweights who came charging to meet him with pistols in hand. Neither was quick enough to beat his Steyr AUG, absorbing three rounds each before they dropped like sacks of dirty laundry to the blood-slick floor.

He found two more men in the counting room, one armed with a shotgun, the other with a calculator. Bolan went in low and firing, cut the shooter's legs from under him, and finished him as he was falling, buckshot wasted on the ceiling overhead.

The accountant thought twice about trying to run or to fight back, then decided against it. At Bolan's direction, he pulled a large satchel from under his desk and stuffed it with cash from the desktop until he could barely close it. That still left several heaps of currency on deck, and Bolan didn't plan on leaving it behind.

He palmed his final Willie Peter canister and held it up for the accountant to inspect. "Get out of here and find a telephone," he ordered. "Call the fire department. Tell them it's white phosphorus. Got that?"

The bean counter nodded, but Bolan still made him repeat it, then gave him a running head start. When he was alone in the bank, Bolan primed the grenade, set it down in the midst of the leftover cash, and then double-timed back to the street.

He could have found a church somewhere and dropped the money in its poor box, he supposed, but Bolan had the sense that he was running out of time. Another strike or two, and he would need to call his pigeons, make sure they knew where to meet him with their money and their soldiers.

If his luck held, all of them would keep the date and make a party of it. And if any of them let him down, he'd have to find them later for a little chat.

Assuming he was still alive.

CHAPTER NINETEEN

Agu Ajani gulped a second shot of whiskey, waiting for its heat to spread from throat and stomach through his limbs, to reach his brain. He thought he would allow himself one more, then stop.

This night of all nights, he couldn't afford to cloud his mind with alcohol. Not when his very life and everything he owned depended on his clarity of thought and the ability to make decisions under fire.

So far, Ajani realized, he'd not been doing well. He had lost count of his murdered soldiers. Any effort to calculate financial losses was hopeless. Ajani could say that he'd suffered a great, perhaps crippling loss, but beyond that...

No! He caught himself. I will not be defeated!

He could battle back, with effort, to regain his former stature and surpass it. With a bit of luck and careful planning, he might even manage to eliminate his leading rival in the process, but he knew that it would be no easy task.

And if he failed, besides his life, he stood to lose another hundred thousand dollars.

Ajani had considered stuffing his satchel with odd bits of paper—or porn magazines, for a joke—but he guessed that the others would insist on confirming that everyone present had come with cash. Afolabi, for one, would be quick to suspect and accuse him of trickery, hoping to shame him in front of the others.

The others.

Ajani was counting on Valentin Sidorov for help against Afolabi at the final showdown. He couldn't predict what the Chinese might do, but he knew that they supported MEND with guns and money. If Sidorov had plans to dispose of them, along with Afolabi and his men, Ajani would cooperate.

But first, the meeting had to be arranged.

Why weren't the damned blackmailers calling?

Twice within the past half hour, Ajani had summoned his personal guard, demanding to know if there'd been any phone calls. Each time, the man answered respectfully, insisting that Ajani would be told the moment any message was received. But there was something in his eyes, a kind of smirk, perhaps, that made Ajani want to rip them from his screaming face.

He wouldn't ask again, not even if the midnight deadline passed without a call. Instead he'd have another double shot of whiskey and attempt, against all odds, to make his racing mind relax.

Taiwo Babatunde had picked eleven of Ajani's best surviving soldiers and would lead them personally to the meeting, if it happened. With Ajani present and armed, that gave him thirteen guns to guard his money bag, the number that Sidorov had negotiated with his master and their Chinese opposition. Assuming that Ekon Afolabi agreed and played by the rules for once in his life, that made fifty-two guns against the unknown extortionists all of them hoped to destroy.

And once that job had been accomplished, it would all

come down to speed and the advantage of surprise. If he and Sidorov could catch Afolabi and the Chinese with their guard down, basking in appreciation of a job well done, a few more seconds of gunfire could decapitate MEND and China National Petroleum in one stroke.

Neither would be so easily eliminated from Delta or from Nigeria, of course. Ajani realized that. But decimation of their leadership would wound both organizations, and might force Beijing to reconsider its future in West Africa. As for MEND, with any luck at all, the power vacuum caused by Afolabi's death might start a fratricidal free-for-all, gutting the group and tearing it apart.

Ajani smiled, enjoying that vision while it lasted, then snapped back to the present.

Scowling at his watch, he muttered to himself, "Goddamn it! Make the call!"

"NICE HOUSE," Bolan said. "Or, it would have been."

The spacious lot on Warri's affluent northeast side had sprouted the skeleton of a potential mansion, beams thrusting skyward while subflooring spread out between them, upright studs sketching the layout of interior walls. The work was fairly well advanced, with part of the roofing completed.

"I understand Yetunde had a hand in drawing up the plans," Umaru said.

"That makes it even worse," Bolan replied. "Seeing the place go up in smoke."

At Bolan's feet, a security guard lay manacled with his own handcuffs, gagged with his own clip-on necktie. Dirt stained his uniform, but that was hardly relevant, since he'd be out of work the following day.

They had skipped down to the bottom of Umaru's list, to take a breather, checking out the gangster's dream house.

Bolan hadn't seen the floor plans, but he could imagine it completed, a three-story monument to Idowu Yetunde's ruthless greed.

"Tough luck," he said, and picked up one of the five-gallon gasoline cans they'd procured en route to the construction site. Tossing the lid away, he spread its contents in a trail along what would have been the mansion's west wall, pausing here and there to splash fuel on the larger upright beams.

Behind him, Umaru was working the far side, laying down his own incendiary trail. It felt like petty vandalism, in comparison to all they'd been through since he launched the Warri blitz, but scorched earth meant exactly that to Bolan. When he chose a target for elimination, no aspect of the enemy's life was secure except wife and children.

Idowu Yetunde had neither.

And what was a half-finished house, beside Yetunde's numbers bank, his gambling dens, the boiler room where lackeys fleeced suckers around the world?

Nothing, perhaps.

But losing it would hurt him in a way that nothing else so far had done.

This wound was personal.

It had been simple, overpowering the single guard on duty at the building site. Umaru had approached him, asking for directions to a neighbor's house, and Bolan had surprised the watchman while he told Umaru that he didn't know the other local residents. They'd left him cuffed and gagged beside a free-standing portable toilet, safely beyond the range of any outward-falling walls.

Ten gallons was enough to get the fire started. They didn't need to saturate the upper floors or to cover the visible construction materials. Days of exposure to the harsh West African sun had made the house-to-be a tinderbox.

When they were done, Bolan and Umaru left their

empty gas cans standing in the foyer of Yetunde's partially built home. Bolan struck a match and lit the trail of gasoline he'd left behind on his brisk circuit of the ground floor, watching as the flame caught and spread. Within a minute they were baking in the heat of dreams consumed by fire, and it was time to go.

"Should we alert the fire department?" Umaru asked as the Kia pulled away.

"I'm guessing one of the neighbors will do it," Bolan replied, "if the city can spare anybody tonight."

He'd been keeping them busy, but someone would answer the call, sooner or later. For Yetunde, it was already too late to salvage his vision. The palace he'd planned for himself had already gone up in smoke.

And Bolan's break was over.

Soon he would have calls to make, a meeting to arrange. But in the meantime, there were more cages to rattle, more soldiers to cull from the herd. He was shaving the odds, bit by bit, and looking forward to the last round of winner-take-all.

IDOWU YETUNDE STARED at the suitcase lying open on the bed in his safehouse, half-filled with clothing he'd packed for the road. He had begun packing in desperation, after hearing that his home-to-be had been incinerated, but he stopped now, feeling anger and a grim resolve replace the early wave of panic and depression.

He had been taking hits all night, suffering one loss after another, while he searched in vain for targets against whom he could retaliate. So far, that effort—like his money and the enterprises he'd built up from scratch in Warri—had been wasted.

But he wasn't beaten yet.

It was a fact that Captain Mashilia had no useful information for him, yet. True, also, that the watchman who'd survived the torching of Yetunde's home could offer only vague descriptions of the same black-and-white team glimpsed at the scenes of his earlier losses.

Yetunde crossed the small bedroom and seized the open suitcase, bellowing with fury as he picked it up and flung it at the nearest wall. His clothing scattered on the floor in rumpled piles, but he ignored it. Fashion sense meant nothing at the moment, with survival riding on the line.

At last, Yetunde realized his grave mistake. While naturally focusing upon his own losses, he had ignored the fact that others had been under fire around him, suffering attacks from the same men who persecuted him. In hindsight, it was clear he should have learned something from that and offered to join forces with the competitors who normally ignored him in pursuit of politics.

They shared a common enemy, and now—if it wasn't too late—Yetunde hoped they could collaborate against the common enemy.

And if it *was* too late? If they rebuffed him?

Well, he'd be no worse off than he was already.

Yetunde removed his cell phone and small black leather address book from his pockets, refreshing his memory of private phone numbers for Agu Ajani and Ekon Afolabi. He had never dialed those numbers, but kept them on file, updated as they changed by spies within each warlord's inner circle.

This night, with their forces dwindling and his contacts out of touch, perhaps dead or dying, Yetunde hoped that the numbers were both still in service.

He dialed Ajani first and listened to a distant ringing.

"Hello?"

The voice that filled Yetunde's ear was apprehensive, hesitant.

"Agu Ajani?" he inquired.

"Is this about the meeting, then?"

Yetunde took a chance and said, "It is."

"One moment."

Thirty seconds later a new voice came on the line. This time, Yetunde recognized it.

"Where are we to meet?" Ajani asked.

"That's up to you," Yetunde said.

There was a brief silence, followed by, "Who *is* this?"

Yetunde identified himself, half expecting Ajani to sever the link. Plainly, he was expecting someone else. But then, the Ijaw leader asked, "What do you want?"

"I hope," Yetunde said, "that we can help each other. If you're willing to discuss it—"

"So they've been in touch with you, as well?" Ajani asked.

"I'm not sure—"

"For the ransom! Are you going to the meeting, too?"

Frowning, Yetunde said, "I haven't been invited yet. But from the sound of it, I wouldn't want to miss it."

"But—"

"If we could start from the beginning…"

"There's no time! Just forty minutes left!"

"Speak quickly, then, and let me help you if I can."

HUANG LI CHAN needed a drink—or, perhaps, several. He denied himself the calm induced by alcohol, however, focusing upon his duty as the midnight hour neared.

He had received no further call from the extortionist who had demanded money in return for the names of those responsible for Chan's humiliating loss of face. A part of him devoutly hoped midnight would pass without another contact, but his common sense rebelled at leaving the grim situation unresolved.

At the same time, Chan questioned Lao Choy Teoh's

plan—concocted with the Russians and a pair of native gangsters—to eliminate the terrorists with swift, decisive action. Chan had no qualms about eliminating those who had offended him so grievously, though he wouldn't be present at their execution, but he wondered if the ambush would, in fact, solve anything.

On one hand, it would silence the demand for cash and might punish the men who had invaded Chan's home, killed his guards and embarrassed him there. Conversely, if the blackmailers weren't the killers, slaying them would simply guarantee that Chan's true enemies remained unknown, unpunished.

Until they struck again.

And if the man who'd held a pistol to his head while Chan faced bloody corpses in his living room wasn't eliminated, Chan had no doubt whatsoever that the bastard would return. The gunman's message on that score was crystal-clear.

That message, so the killer claimed, had come directly from Arkady Eltsin, Uroil's chief of operations in Nigeria. Lao, for his part, had dismissed the name-dropping as classic misdirection, and it did seem odd to Chan that his would-be assassin should name Eltsin, then waltz off and leave Chan still alive.

Peculiar, but impossible?

Chan was confused enough to hedge his bets. Without informing Lao, he had picked four strong, young men from plant security and drafted them as private bodyguards for the duration. All four were former members of the People's Liberation Army Special Operations Forces, and two had served in the elite antiterrorist Snow Wolf Commando Unit before they were discharged. All had killed men in the past, and expressed no regrets.

Would they be good enough?

That question nagged at Chan, making him thirst for liquor, but the answer lay in waiting, not inside a bottle.

And whatever happened, he had done his best.

That wouldn't matter to Beijing or his superiors at CNP, if China lost its foothold in Nigeria, but Chan had made his mind up not to fret about what might happen when he was dead. At fifty-three, he had been raised and educated from his birth as a loyal Communist, who shunned religion and the sort of childish superstitions that depicted ghostly ancestors on high, smiling or weeping tears of shame as they beheld the antics of their spawn on Earth.

Chan gave no thought to what might lie in store for him beyond the grave, but he suspected it was only mold and worms. If so, his troubles ended at the moment when his heart stopped beating and his brain shut down.

Which didn't mean that he was anxious for that final moment to arrive—far from it. But his mind focused on matters of survival and a lifelong fear of painful death, rather than any fantasy of souls in flight.

Lao had pledged that he and his strange bedfellows would solve Chan's problem at their midnight meeting with the blackmailers. Assuming that there was a meeting.

And, if not, Chan reckoned that his four new bodyguards could deal with Lao.

Once and for all.

THE PARADISE CLUB billed itself as a tavern, but Bolan supposed that its neighbors were aware that two-thirds of its floor space comprised an unlicensed casino. They might have known, as well, that MEND controlled the operation, kept the payoffs flowing, while the cream ensured that Ekon Afolabi's troops had guns and ammunition ready when they needed them.

There was a certain irony in bribing the authorities to

keep illicit operations up and running when the profits
from those enterprises served a group of revolutionaries
pledged to overthrow the government, but that summed up
corruption in a nutshell. Once a politician or a cop began
accepting bribes, he sacrificed his oath of office in pursuit
of private gain.

Not that the Paradise was earning much for anyone
tonight. Shock waves from Bolan's blitz had been rever-
berating through Warri for hours now, and everyone
involved in criminal activities had gotten the message. It
was dangerous to work the joints and streets, while
unknown enemies were striking here and there, at random,
claiming lives and trashing property on every side. The operations that couldn't afford to close outright were running
with skeleton crews and beefed-up security, hoping that
luck would protect them.

But it wouldn't spare the Paradise.

Bolan arrived just as two of Afolabi's soldiers were
emerging from the club, grim-faced, clearly unhappy with
whatever task and destination they had been assigned.

And as their luck would have it, they weren't going
anywhere.

He met them with the 93-R, punching a silenced round
through each dour face and stepping around the pair as they
collapsed. The club's front door was still swinging shut as
Bolan reached it, caught it with his free hand and stepped
across the threshold into stale tobacco smoke and muted
voices.

Someone shook a pair of dice and rolled, cursing as he
missed his point. A hollow laugh from someone else
carried no honest humor with it. Ice rattled inside a cocktail
glass, Dutch courage on the rocks.

Bolan had nearly cleared the foyer when a doorman
loomed in front of him, all muscle and surprise. The

lookout's mouth fell open, but whatever he had planned to say never escaped his lips. A muffled bullet severed thought from speech and dropped him in the doorway, where he made a grisly, twitching speed bump.

Bolan stepped across him, half expecting dead fingers to clutch his ankle, and beheld four other soldiers grouped around one craps table. A fifth had gone behind the bar, helping himself to booze.

One of the players glanced up, froze, then barked a warning to his comrades as he fumbled for a weapon underneath his leather jacket. The others were turning to face Bolan when he began firing.

Three rounds gone from the Beretta's 20-round magazine, and that left plenty for the five MEND gunners ranged in front of him. Bolan took the quick-draw artist first, closing his left eye forever with a full-metal jacket 9 mm slug, then shot his way around the craps table, double-tapping the dead man's three companions.

By the time they hit the floor, the guy behind the bar had recognized his danger and was lunging for an SMG he'd left within arm's reach. He nearly reached it, had the fingers of his right hand curled around the weapon's pistol grip, when Bolan drilled him through the ear and sprayed his final thoughts across the back bar mirror.

Silence reigned in Paradise, except for someone's shoes scuffling the floor, briefly, before they came to final rest. Bolan stood waiting in the doorway, ready if the back room yielded any more contenders, but none showed themselves. Content to let it end there, he retreated to the sidewalk, keeping one eye on the club now hazed with cordite.

Outside, Bolan holstered the Beretta, checked his watch and saw that it was close enough. He'd left some nervous adversaries hanging, and he reckoned it was time to tell them where he could be found, if they were still inclined to keep the date.

A trap? No doubt about it.

But he wouldn't be the prey.

He was the trapper, and the men who doubtless planned to kill him didn't know it yet.

CHAPTER TWENTY

Ekon Afolabi was exhausted. He felt as if he hadn't slept for days, although in fact his torment had begun less than twenty-four hours earlier. Afolabi had gone much longer than that without sleep, but this time—

His cell phone made a sound somewhere between a purr and a snarl, vibrating across the coffee table in front of him. Afolabi stared at it for a moment, as if surprised by the sound after all the hours of waiting. Finally, jarred out of his half daze, he lunged to grab the phone and press it to his ear.

"Hello?"

"I hope you haven't been on pins and needles," said the voice he remembered and despised.

"Business as usual," the MEND warlord replied through clenched teeth.

"Really? I'm surprised you ever make a dollar, if your days are all like this. Speaking of money—"

"Yes, I have it," Afolabi interrupted, smothering an urge to spew profanity.

"All of it?" asked his faceless caller.

"Yes. One hundred thousand U.S. dollars."

"Sounds like we're in business."

"Concerning delivery—"

"I'm getting to that," the man said. "You know the Warri Township Stadium?"

"Of course."

"Make that our rendezvous. You bring the money to the center circle, midnight on the dot, and we're in business."

Afolabi glowered at his watch. "That's not much time," he said.

"So don't waste it complaining. Either be there at the witching hour or—"

"I'll be there!" Afolabi snapped, then realized the caller had disconnected.

Seventeen minutes, damn it!

Afolabi vaulted from the couch where he'd been seated, shouting for Taiwo Babatunde and his other soldiers, barking orders even before they responded. His rage and pent-up nervous tension translated to frantic action, Afolabi snatching up the bag of cash and a Spectre M-4 submachine gun from the table where they lay together, waiting for him. Thus prepared, he watched the others shoulder weapons, moving toward the exit where their cars stood waiting, cloaked in darkness.

Stepping from the quasi-safety of his headquarters in hiding, Afolabi felt a sudden stab of paranoia. What if all this business with the money was a ploy to flush him from cover, give his enemies a chance to kill him as he crossed the sidewalk to his vehicle?

But no shots came, and in another moment he was seated in the lead car's backseat, sandwiched between Babatunde and a slightly smaller gunman, their bulk making Afolabi feel like the meat in a sandwich.

Three cars and thirteen men, himself included. Twenty-six guns among them, at least, and some likely carried more than one pistol. Add to that the Chinese, Russians and Ajani's men—the rotten bastards—and they had the making of a small army.

His caller, Afolabi thought, would be surprised.

MEND's warlord hoped that he would have a chance to see the man's face while he was still alive. It would be pleasant to watch as the arrogance drained from his eyes and he gasped out a vain plea for mercy.

For life.

But to kill him, they first had to catch him.

And if they were late…

"Hurry!" he snapped at his driver. "We only have fifteen minutes!"

The others would have to keep up, and if that meant running traffic lights or scattering sluggish pedestrians, so be it. Afolabi wouldn't be late to the meeting.

But what of the others?

His paranoia came back in a rush.

What if the rest were setting him up for a fall, pretending to go along with the plan, then letting Afolabi stand alone?

Worse yet, what if the Russians and his own Chinese were all in it together with Ajani, scheming to dispose of him and shatter MEND?

Seething, his teeth clenched, the warlord told his men, "Tonight, trust no one but your brothers. If the others—any of them—make a false move, shoot to kill."

HUANG LI CHAN felt perfectly relaxed. He'd taken half a Valium to calm his nerves, washed down with twenty-year-old Irish whiskey, and the combination was miraculous. He still remembered his bodyguards, with their leaking skulls, but it was like a memory from childhood, something with no power to affect him now.

By contrast, Lao Choy Teoh seemed more anxious than

usual, his normal stoic demeanor showing signs of strain as he studied the clock on Chan's wall.

"Perhaps it was all just a hoax," Chan suggested.

"A hoax, sir? With two of your bodyguards killed and a gun to your head? With all the rest that has happened?"

"A ploy, then," Chan corrected himself, devoid of rancor. "Suppose our enemy, whoever he may be, had some other design in mind? The blackmail demand may have been a diversion, distracting us from his actual goal."

"Which would be…?"

Chan shrugged and spread his open hands. "Who knows? Some feud against one tribe or the other, perhaps. They kill each other all the time."

"And the attack on you, sir?"

"Misdirection, like the Uroil sniping incident. You'll note that neither Eltsin nor I suffered any personal harm."

"I have considered that," Lao said, "but—"

He was interrupted by the shrilling telephone that sat on a corner of Chan's ornate desk. Lao moved to answer it, but Chan raised a hand to restrain him, then lifted the receiver himself.

"Hello?" he said.

"Tell me you have the money," said a voice that he would recognize in dreams and nightmares. Chan had heard it twice before—once on the telephone, and once while he was standing with a pistol pressed against his skull.

"I have it," he answered, resisting an impulse to smile.

"Great. I'll take it off your hands and give you what you need at midnight. Not a minute later. Meet me at the Warri Township Stadium, at center field."

"I understand," Chan said and listened to the click as he was disconnected.

Cradling the receiver, he asked Lao, "Is everything prepared?"

"Yes, sir. You know it is."

Chan glanced at the wall clock and said, "In that case, you should hurry. You're going to the football stadium, across town. Midnight, as explained."

Now it was Lao's turn to look at the clock.

"Fifteen minutes?"

"Correct. I suggest that you hurry."

Lao bolted from the office without a backward glance, calling the men he had assembled for the final phase of what had been, so far, a hellish day. Chan almost wished him luck, then held his peace.

Whatever happened at the stadium, he was convinced that Lao had outlived his usefulness to CNP, and to the People's Republic of China. Chan didn't appreciate Lao taking the initiative for contact with the Russians, even if it worked out to his ultimate advantage and the company's. There were procedures to be followed in bureaucracies, and those who trampled on the rules for personal advancement should expect no great reward.

At least while Chan still held the reins.

If Lao managed to destroy the scum who had humiliated Chan, more power to him. But it wouldn't save his life. When Chan addressed the mourners at Lao's funeral, he would praise Lao's memory and courage as if they were friends.

But he'd be laughing on the inside, thankful that he'd never have to see Lao's smirking face again.

AGU AJANI CLOSED his cell phone and turned to face Daren Jumoke. "The stadium," he said. "Midnight, precisely."

"Stadium?" Jumoke seemed confused. "What stadium?"

"On Cemetery Road. How many are there, Daren?"

Stung, Jumoke nodded, checked his watch and said, "We haven't got much time."

"The men are ready, and I have the bag. Let's go," Ajani said.

Two cars waited outside, a more or less matched pair of aging Lincoln Continentals capable of seating six people each. One car was black, the other navy blue with rust spots showing near the wheel wells, but Ajani had no time to waste considering appearances.

The men who would accompany him to the Warri Township Stadium were waiting with the cars, each carrying a slung submachine gun or assault rifle, spare magazines and handguns weighing down their belts and pockets. A lone motorcyclist would lead them, his Japanese bike equipped with police lights and siren in case they were slowed by traffic en route to the payoff.

Ajani smiled at the term, and the foolish bravado he'd heard in the caller's voice moments earlier. A payoff was coming, all right, but not the sort his enemy anticipated.

This night, Ajani was settling all manner of scores, cleaning slates as it were. By sunrise, he would stand unopposed in Warri.

If he still stood at all.

There was a chance that he would lose. Nothing in life was guaranteed, especially where enemies with guns stood ranged against him. He had suffered major losses since the plague of violence had descended upon Warri, and eliminating his opponents wouldn't heal those wounds.

But it would help. Oh, yes.

"We were instructed to deliver on the field," he told Jumoke, once the two Lincolns were off and rolling. "On the center line."

"We'll be exposed to any snipers in the stands," Jumoke said, stating the obvious.

"I didn't say we would obey the order," Ajani said. "Only that it was delivered."

"So, you have another plan?" Jumoke asked.

"First, see if any of the rest arrive on time," Ajani said. "If they are late, we must proceed, but not directly to the field. We can divide our force, send six men in on either side, to sweep the stands."

"And if we're seen?" Jumoke asked.

"What can they do about it? If we're quick enough and keep our eyes open, no one inside the stadium can slip away. We'll have them cornered."

"That's if Lao Teoh and the others don't arrive on time. What if we find them waiting for us at the stadium?" Jumoke asked.

"Then we'll have fifty-two men, rather than thirteen. Let them march to the center circle if they like, while we close off the exits and prevent our quarry from escaping."

"There may be some argument against that plan," Jumoke said.

"I don't plan to consult them, any more than Sidorov consulted me when he went running off to the Chinese."

"There's one other possibility we haven't talked about," Jumoke said.

"You mean, what happens if the bastard who's been calling us never shows up himself?"

Jumoke nodded, frowning.

"That's no problem," Ajani said. "With our own men in the stands and everybody else down on the field, we have the high ground, cover, everything we need to finish it."

"Kill all of them, you mean?" Jumoke asked.

"And let God sort them out," Ajani said. "It's really His job, after all."

IDOWU YETUNDE cradled the telephone receiver, frowning thoughtfully while he digested the information he had just received.

The spies he'd hired inside Agu Ajani's gang and MEND were worth their weight in gold. He'd confirmed it: both Ajani and Afolabi were keeping a date with blackmailers at midnight, bearing money and a little something extra to the meeting at the Warri Township Stadium. Beyond that, it appeared that some of their foreign supporters, "security" agents of the Chinese and Russian oil firms, would be going along for the ride.

Carrying money of their own.

Four hundred thousand U.S. dollars in all.

Yetunde understood the premise of the meeting. Someone, seemingly a white man, had offered names and other leads to the persons responsible for Warri's recent spate of violence. Anyone could buy the information, it appeared, for a flat one hundred grand.

Yetunde wondered, briefly, why some of the buyers hadn't pooled resources. Afolabi and the Chinese, say, or Agu and the Russians. But it hardly mattered. If his spies were right—and two of them from separate camps could hardly make the same mistake; in fact, he would have said it was impossible—none of the buyers headed for the meeting planned to pay a cent, in fact.

They wanted satisfaction, without giving up their cash. A pound of flesh, as it were.

Yetunde knew exactly how they felt.

He, too, wanted revenge for all that he had lost. And if he had an opportunity to bank some cash in the process, why not take full advantage of it?

The question was how to achieve his design without being caught up in a slaughter himself.

Yetunde still had soldiers he could call on, but their ranks were dwindling. He'd never had as many guns at his command as either Ajani or MEND. Yetunde provided the Nigerian public with services it desired—sex, drugs, games of chance—while his global fraud network was self-sustaining. He maintained a security force to protect his investments, and to collect from recalcitrant customers, but Yetunde seldom thought in terms of waging war.

For that, he would require an army.

Preferably, someone else's army.

The solution came to him at once, without the blinding light of a divine revelation, but no less inspiring for its lack of celestial fireworks.

Who better to break up the stadium party than someone who was paid to identify and arrest criminals? Someone who also depended upon Yetunde's generosity to support his lifestyle? Who better than Captain Johnson Mashilia of the Delta Police Command?

Mashilia had the men, guns and authority required to deal with lawbreakers. To disarm and arrest them, if he caught them in commission of a crime, and to kill them if they resisted arrest. The captain could perform his legal duty, win official commendation and serve Yetunde's best interest, all at the same time.

And if the criminals resisted, if they forced Captain Mashilia's troops to use deadly force at the crime scene, who was there to say that any money had been found among the corpses? The captain would receive his share, of course, and he'd be free to split that take with his superiors or underlings, as he saw fit. The lion's share, however, should belong to Idowu Yetunde, for the timely tip that made Mashilia's triumph possible.

And there was no time left to waste.

He snatched the telephone and dialed the captain's private number, waiting while it rang twice on the other end. When Mashilia answered with a weary voice, Yetunde gave him no time to protest.

"Listen to me!" he said. "You are about to be a hero, and a wealthy one, at that."

MATT COOPER called the Russians last of all. Umaru sat beside him in the semidarkness, hearing variations of familiar lines for the fourth time in twenty minutes, wondering how Cooper pulled it off.

Not lying on the telephone. He reckoned anyone could handle that, to some extent. But all the rest of it—laying the strategy for a campaign, then carrying it out, surviving one firefight after another on alien ground, somehow tricking gangs that hated one another into a volatile, doomed experiment in collaboration.

It boggled Umaru's mind.

He knew there were standardized tests to quantify genius, questions and exercises that were judged to generate numerical scores and plot them on graphs. But what did it all really prove?

Umaru had seen Cooper in action, both saving and taking lives. And there was genius to it. Cooper managed to accomplish things Umaru would have thought impossible.

At least in part, because he dared to try.

"You have the money, then?" Bolan was asking Eltsin. Pausing, then replying to a question, "Right. The names and everything you need to settle it, however you decide. Midnight exactly, at the Warri football stadium. No late admissions."

Bolan killed the link and closed his phone before the Russian could respond. "All set," he told Umaru as he pocketed the instrument. "They'll be here soon."

"And are we ready?" Umaru inquired. He felt that he should know the answer, but it managed to elude him.

"Once we're in position," Bolan said, "the only thing that's left to do is to get ready for the unexpected."

"Ah, yes. That."

Umaru knew he sounded skeptical.

"It's not so hard," Bolan explained. "Just get inside your adversary's head and calculate what you'd do in his place."

"I've already lost my chance to scout the stadium ahead of time," Umaru said. "And I'm expected with my money on the center spot."

"You are," Bolan agreed.

"That doesn't mean my men must be there with me," Umaru observed.

"Considering they weren't invited in the first place," Bolan added.

"I would have them find the exits, slip inside the stadium as cautiously and quietly as possible. Locate my enemies and stop them from escaping."

"There you go," Bolan said.

"But we have four men—four groups of men—coming to meet us. Arriving together, perhaps."

"All the better," Bolan said. "Any confusion works for us, against the other side. Even if they've made some arrangement to collaborate, you've got the old antagonisms brewing, and they're bound to have a few snafus."

"More targets," Umaru suggested.

"That, too."

"I'll take my place now."

"Good idea."

Umaru rose, holding the Daewoo rifle tucked beneath one arm, descending toward the football pitch. Twin lights mounted on poles illuminated each end of the field but left the center line in darkness as he jogged across it, toward the visitor's side. His comrade in arms occupied the home team's side and had arranged a few surprises for the guests who would begin arriving soon.

Umaru wondered if their preparations would suffice, remembering the placement of the exits, if he needed to escape.

But could he leave the big American behind to save himself?

Scowling at his self-doubt, Umaru reached the viewing stand and started climbing toward his sniper's roost.

THE LAYOUT WASN'T perfect, but it could have been worse. Bolan would've liked more cover than the bleachers offered, but at least he had the high ground, with a sweeping field of fire and ample room to move.

Of course, so would his enemies.

Bolan had walked the stadium before he'd placed his calls, noting the entrances and exits, pegging the various ranges and angles of fire in his mind, leaving a few traps here and there for shooters who would certainly try to sneak up on his blind side. Their handicap lay in not knowing where his blind side *was,* or might be, while the killing ground lay spread before Bolan and Umaru in plain sight.

In short, his adversaries had to come to him. They couldn't camp outside and lay siege to the stadium in hopes of starving Bolan out. An army in the parking lot would draw attention after sunrise, if not sooner, with police patrols scouring Warri for gunmen since sundown.

Time was of the essence, then, a message Bolan's calls had driven home. His targets couldn't know if he would be inside the stadium or watching from a distance as they rolled in with their money and their soldiers for the main event. For all they knew, it might be both. Someone—or several someones—could be waiting inside to greet them, while spotters reported their movements outside.

Any way they sliced it, the way to Bolan lay through the stadium gates, normally chained at night, but currently unlocked, courtesy of a bolt-cutter Bolan had found in the maintenance shed.

Bolan had done what he could to prepare for the battle to come. He didn't know how many guns he'd be facing, or exactly how they'd approach him, but barring an airlift, their options were limited. The field was accessible by vehicle or by foot at either end, and on foot only via two entrances through the stands. Smart planners with men to spare would hit him from all sides at once, but he'd have to wait and see.

Seven minutes and counting.

Patience was among the first things that a sniper learned in training. It might be deemed a virtue of the saints, but it was absolutely critical to long-range killers waiting for a target to reveal himself. Some missions might require a shooter to remain in place, virtually immobile, for days on end, exposed to weather, insects, snuffling scavengers— whatever Mother Nature had to throw at him.

Hours or days of waiting for a man he'd never met to step forward, framed in the crosshairs of a telescopic sight, and meet his death.

One shot, one kill.

And after that, a scramble to escape before the dead man's comrades could retaliate with anything from small arms to artillery and helicopter gunships.

Bolan couldn't see a full-fledged army marching on the Warri Township Stadium to trap him, but he did expect his enemies to pull out every stop at their disposal, fielding their best troops to bring him down. With any luck, their ranks would be depleted and spread thin by Bolan's blitz, some forced to guard facilities their masters left behind while going off to keep the rendezvous. But Bolan harbored no illusion that the firefight he had staged would be a cakewalk.

It was almost killing time.
The Executioner was in his element.
The trick was not to die there.

CHAPTER TWENTY-ONE

Agu Ajani reached the Warri Township Stadium with minutes to spare. His small caravan parked close to the main public entrance, gunmen piling out of the cars with a concerted clicking and clacking of automatic weapons. Anyone close enough to hear or witness the sight would have been alarmed.

But the place seemed deserted.

Lights glowed at each end of the pitch, near the goals, turning the sky above the stadium's facade a washed-out orange. Ajani couldn't see the poles themselves, from where he stood, but knew the layout from attending matches in the past.

All fun and games, then.

Deadly serious this night.

Daren Jumoke nodded as Ajani told him, "Just the way we planned."

No further orders were required. They had planned the maneuver with sketches depicting the stadium, drawing little arrows for team deployment as if plotting a game-winning strategy.

Which, in fact, was the truth.

Ajani carried the satchel of cash in his left hand and a well-worn MAC-10 submachine gun in his right. A pistol and spare magazines for the MAC-10 were tucked into his belt and pockets, causing him to clank a little when he walked.

Ajani liked the sound.

It told him he was dressed to kill.

Jumoke gave the order for Ajani's soldiers to fan out. Eight left the clutch immediately, jogging to different entrances where they would find their way inside the stadium, alert for any sign of lurkers in the shadows. If they met a stranger, armed or otherwise, they had been told to take him down.

Alive, if possible. Dead, just as good.

Ajani checked his watch again, then scanned the faces of the men surrounding him. Jumoke's was deadpan, while the other three wore mixed expressions of anticipation and anxiety. His soldiers loved a good fight—meaning fights that they won, without losing too many of their friends—but they had no great love for mysteries or stalking unknown enemies whose luck had been unbeatable so far.

Ajani knew exactly how they felt.

He was already tired of waiting in the parking lot, wished he could charge inside and get the party started, but he had to give his men sufficient time to reach their posts. And there were still the others to consider—Sidorov and his men, the Chinese, even the bastard Afolabi with his thugs.

"They should be here by now," he told Jumoke.

"We still have three minutes, Agu."

"It will take that long to walk inside."

"We're very close."

"Midnight," he said. "No later."

"If they aren't here within the next two minutes—"

But they were. Some of them, anyway. Ajani saw the

headlights of a three-car caravan approaching, swinging off Cemetery Road into the blacktopped parking lot. And close behind them, more cars, lining up to form a grim, nearly silent parade.

"About time, too," Ajani said.

High beams washed over him as he stood waiting, tightening his grip on the MAC-10.

BOLAN HEARD the cars arriving, didn't need to check his watch to know that it was almost midnight. Truth be told, he would have waited for his adversaries to assemble, but it pleased him that they took his deadline seriously.

When he scanned the bleachers on the far side of the soccer field, Bolan couldn't pick out Umaru. That was good, but someone entering from over there would have a better chance of spotting him. And when they started firing, no one in the stadium would have to guess where either one of them was hiding.

Any minute now.

He saw the creepers first, paired off and entering the stadium by any means available. Two men at each end of the field, for starters, then two more directly opposite, one lurking in each public entrance to the stands. Although they weren't visible from where he crouched in shadow, Bolan took for granted that there had to be two more on his side, standing in darkness, scanning rows of backless plastic seats in search of targets.

But they hadn't spotted Bolan yet.

The major delegates were coming now, not quite marching in lockstep, but close enough. Bolan spotted Ekon Afolabi and Agu Ajani first, trailing point men through the main entrance, flanked by other gunners and lugging their bags.

Filled with what? Would there really be money inside?

The Chinese and Russians were easy to spot, standing out from the Nigerians, but Bolan didn't recognize either one of their bagmen. No problem there. He hadn't expected Huang Li Chan or Arkady Eltsin to brave the dark night and show up in person when others could be sent to do their dirty work.

Whoever they had sent as stand-ins, Bolan took for granted that the men in charge would know their business, and the shooters would be handpicked for their skill.

And it was time to test them.

Bolan let the leading delegation reach the field and start across it, following what would have been the center line if a game had been scheduled and anyone cared to mark it. As it was, approximation would be fine.

He let them come, trusting the group of twenty or so to stop at midfield as instructed. Bolan, meanwhile, scanned the opposite bleachers through his Steyr's scope and picked out the first of his targets.

A spotter stood off to the left, still partially hidden in shadow despite the floodlight at his end of the field. Bolan's mind had marked six others in his final scan, and he was prepared to move on each of them in turn after he fired the first shot, though he couldn't count on any of them standing still.

As for Umaru, well, at this point, it was each man for himself.

Bolan lined up his shot, took a deep breath, released half of it, held the rest—and fired.

EKON AFOLABI recoiled from the first shot as if it was aimed at his face, his knees buckling, his body dropping to a crouch that left him hunched over the satchel filled with cash.

Around him, some of the others were crouching, as

well, a few breaking off from the group, but others still standing upright with weapons in hand, defying the sniper. Among them, Lao Choy Teoh, the head Russian and Agu Ajani, barely disguising his sneer.

"I see him!" someone shouted, but it didn't matter. One shot from the bleachers merged into another, then another, until Afolabi felt that he had to either break and run or soil himself.

And yet none of the bullets whispered past him. None were even close.

"He's found my men!" Ajani bellowed as he raised a stubby machine pistol, blazing away at the home-team bleachers. "It's an ambush!"

Afolabi had already worked that out for himself, without anyone's help. And if Ajani's men were the primary targets, so much the better, in his view. It gave his own soldiers time to return fire, automatic weapons spitting death into the bleachers as they tracked the sniper.

But which one?

Before the echoes of the first shots died away, a second rifle joined the chorus from the other side of the field, redoubling the chaos. And this one *was* firing toward the clutch of men at center field, one of its bullets drilling through the forehead of a Chinese who stood six feet from Afolabi, spraying blood and brains.

And it was time to run—but where? In which direction?

All around him, guns were blazing, making Afolabi's ears ring. He'd drawn his own pistol by now, a Walther P-1 automatic, but he hadn't fired it and had no intention of doing so now, unless he found a clear-cut, stationary target well within his weapon's range.

Another man went down beside him, this one Russian, gasping curses in his brutish language as he clutched his chest and fell, thrashing across the turf, his legs flailing.

Afolabi rolled away from him and came up running, calling for his men to follow him.

"Ambush!" he cried again unnecessarily. "We're getting out of here!"

If only they would follow him.

If only he could find his way.

OBINNA UMARU crawled over concrete, keeping his head down while bullets rattled through the air above him, chipping plastic seats and wooden rails in higher rows. Some of the wild rounds barely whispered, fired so high and wide in haste that they would miss the stadium entirely.

He had shot two men so far, uncertain whether they were dead or only wounded, but there were plenty left to kill him if they found their range and kept their wits about them. So far he'd managed to elude them, but the night was young.

Cooper was concentrating on the flankers, still, taking them down with one or two shots each, shifting each time the ones still standing marked his muzzle-flashes. Umaru had no clear fix on how many gunmen they faced, but he'd counted twenty-one on the field and assumed there'd be at least that many more stationed at other vantage points around the stadium.

All looking for a chance to end his life.

Umaru didn't want to die this way, crawling and hiding from a gang of men whose names he'd never know, but it came down to this at last.

Succeed or fail.

Kill to survive, or spend your final seconds spitting blood onto the pavement where ten thousand sports fans scuffed their shoes on game days.

Umaru found another vantage point while gunmen ranged across the pitch's center circle firing toward the point where they had glimpsed him last, some fifteen yards away. He framed one in the Daewoo's open sights, squeezed off and saw his target stagger, moving on without a confirmation of a drop.

The others were already turning, bringing guns to bear against him, when the sound of an explosion rocked the stadium. All eyes turned toward the sound, including Umaru's, beholding a cloud of smoke rising from one of the exits on his side.

Cooper had warned him of the hand grenades set here and there, with loosened pins and trip-wires. One of them had claimed a victim, visible from where Umaru lay facing his enemies. The shock of the explosion lasted for a heart-beat, maybe two, and then was gone.

Umaru broke eye contact with the mangled body first, returning full attention to his would-be killers on the football field. He saw that their attention was divided— some searching for Cooper, others for himself—and took advantage of it, thumbing the Daewoo's fire-selector switch to full-automatic and spraying the field with the rest of his first magazine.

Soldiers were falling, ducking, running for cover down-range as his slugs flew among them, finding some targets and bypassing others completely. A couple tried returning fire, but couldn't make it count while they sprinted for cover.

Umaru watched them go, replaced his empty magazine and went back on the hunt.

BOLAN HEARD the grenade blast, echoed by gargling screams, and wondered how many shooters had been caught in the blast. It was a simple booby trap, but still ef-fective against adversaries unschooled in guerrilla warfare, who felt overconfident on their home turf.

Still, the explosion would give others cause to watch

their step if they were thinking clearly, and the other two
grenades he'd planted might be wasted.

A second explosion proved him wrong.

More cries of pain, this time across the field, from the
stands where Umaru was ducking, dodging, trading fire
with gunmen on the field. Bolan had gambled on the top
dogs having guts enough to stand and fight when he'd
begun the party by eliminating flankers, but he knew the
crowd at center field could only stand so much before they
broke and ran.

As they were running now.

It was a toss-up whether he should focus on the men
with satchels—two of them familiar from Brognola's
photo files, the others likely security chiefs for CNP and
Uroil—or let them run for now and strip them of their
bodyguards. He didn't care about the money, whether
someone snatched it up and split in the confusion, but if
Bolan saw a chance to save it for a good cause, he wasn't
averse to doing so.

Okay. The bagmen.

Bolan's nearest runner with a satchel was Chinese, a
lithe man sprinting toward the goal on Bolan's right, where
vehicles and foot traffic had access to the field. The Executioner tracked him, framed his man in the scope's crosshairs and squeezed his rifle's trigger.

At the last split second, coming out of nowhere, one of
the runner's bodyguards lunged into Bolan's line of fire and
took the 5.56 mm tumbler that was earmarked for his boss.
It struck him in the chest, a puff of crimson glittering under
the nearest floodlights. As he fell, Bolan's initial target
started zigzagging, shouting at his surviving guards to
cover him.

And one of them had to have seen Bolan's muzzle-flash,
the way they started laying down return fire. The Execu-

tioner ducked his head and rolled away, thankful that shooters firing uphill commonly aimed higher than they should, assuming they took time to aim at all, in a firefight.

He slithered like a reptile, digging in with knees and elbows, feeling every crack and chip in the concrete, while bullets raked the stands behind him. Bolan knew that he could only do so much while he was scrabbling around the bleachers, dueling shooters from a distance. Knew he'd have to get in closer for the wrap-up, if he meant to win it.

Starting now.

IDOWU YETUNDE smiled beneath the fat Zeiss binoculars, enjoying the firefight more than he'd ever enjoyed any sporting event in his life. How fitting that it should be played out on a soccer field, albeit for an audience of one.

Or seven, if Yetunde counted his six bodyguards.

He had remained at a distance, content to observe the action and wait for Captain Mashilia to arrive with his troops, but now Yetunde was rethinking his initial plan. Instead of letting Mashilia seize the money, skim his share and surrender the rest, why shouldn't Yetunde step in and take all the cash for himself?

Of course, the captain would protest, but what could he do? If Yetunde moved quickly enough, the police would find nothing but gunmen and corpses. Yetunde could plead ignorance, suggesting that Ajani, Afolabi and the rest had double-crossed their blackmailers and left the cash at home, preferring bloody vengeance.

By the same token, if he should miss one of the money bags, or even two, Yetunde could argue that some of the players had held out their share of the payoff, cheating all concerned. In that case, he would have whatever cash he seized before police arrived, plus his share of the swag that Captain Mashilia seized.

It was a win-win situation, the kind Yetunde preferred.

And he had helped himself by telling the captain to arrive no earlier than ten minutes past midnight, when they could be sure that everyone who planned to keep the rendezvous was present at the stadium. That gave Yetunde time to make his move before the uniforms showed up to intervene. Initially he'd simply hoped to snare his various competitors and adversaries. Now however…

Lowering his field glasses, Yetunde turned to face his gunmen. "There has been a change of plans," he told them. "We are going in ahead of the police."

A couple of them blinked at that, but no one argued with him. He had chosen well, selecting the most ruthless and courageous of his soldiers, men who flinched from nothing, be it facing hostile guns or slaughtering an infant in its cradle. They would do as he commanded, because none of them feared anything on Earth more than they feared Yetunde's wrath.

"Our task," he said, "is to locate and capture four bags filled with money. Kill whoever stands between us and the bags. Ignore the rest, unless they challenge you. Questions?"

None of his soldiers spoke.

"Right, then. I'll point the targets out as we proceed. Come now, and make me proud!"

Drawing a pistol from his shoulder holster, Idowu Yetunde turned and led his handpicked killers toward the soccer field.

Lao Choy Teoh didn't believe in God, by any name, but he was willing to admit that *something* may have intervened to save his life from the grandstand sniper. Or, then again, it might have been coincidence.

In either case, he was taking no chances.

Running erratically, ducking and weaving as if he were a

football star himself, shouting at his guards to keep pace and serve as human shields, Lao veered off toward the nearest exit he could see. Taking advantage of it would require his entering the stands, climbing a flight of concrete steps where he would be exposed to hostile fire, but staying on the open field was every bit as risky, in the present circumstance.

Outside, his vehicles were waiting. Any of his soldiers who survived the final sprint could drive—or Lao could be his own chauffeur, if that was what it took to liberate him from the trap.

He still had no idea exactly what had gone wrong with the scheme he and the others had concocted. It had sounded good, in theory—adversaries joining forces to defeat a common enemy—but now the line was wavering, about to break, and Lao couldn't have said how many guns were ranged against him in the stadium.

And he no longer cared.

Survival lay in flight. If someone, after all, managed to kill the terrorists who'd laid the trap, so be it. At the moment, though, Lao didn't intend to be a sitting target in a shooting gallery where he had no control over the action.

Gasping with exertion, wincing every time a bullet whispered past him like the voice of death, Lao reached a flight of stairs linking the bleachers to a concrete apron surrounding the main soccer field. He grabbed its rail with his right hand, still clinging to the heavy satchel with his left, and took the steps two at a time, without losing momentum. Lao could hear his guards behind him, firing bursts of automatic fire and cursing as they labored to keep up with him.

He reached the bottom row of bleachers, was about to hit the next long flight of stairs, when another explosion rocked the stands. This time, it was above him, smoke and shrapnel spewing from the very exit Lao had planned to use for his escape.

Gaping, he saw a human form ejected from the roiling smoke cloud in a tumbling somersault, slack fingers losing their grip on an automatic rifle in midair. The acrobat landed on concrete steps, twenty feet above Lao, then bounced into a kind of twirling, twisting dive that brought his body arching down on a collision course.

Lao cursed and tried to dodge the hurtling mass of flesh and bone. Too late. One of the tumbler's feet caught him on his right cheek and pitched him sideways, off into the bleachers, squawking as he fell.

VALENTIN SIDOROV triggered three rounds from his GSh-18 pistol in rapid fire, knowing the bullets were wasted before the first slug left the muzzle. It was a battle reflex, using gunfire to give himself courage, and, with any luck, to spoil his deadly adversary's aim while Sidorov found cover.

The Russian wasted no time wondering how his plan for the payoff rendezvous had gone awry. Any engagement with a well-armed, ruthless enemy amounted to a gamble, even when the odds were stacked in one side's favor. All that mattered to the Russian now was getting out alive.

And with the satchel full of cash.

If he escaped but lost the money, it would be the last straw for Arkady Eltsin and the other Uroil brass. Even if Eltsin took the brunt of blame from headquarters, Sidorov recognized the truism that shit would always roll downhill, and there would be enough to bury him, no matter how much stuck to Eltsin in the process.

With the money *and* his life, he could at least say that the showdown was a wash, with nothing lost or gained. Sidorov didn't count the lives of any soldiers who might fall along the way, since they were paid to take such risks and sacrifice themselves, if need be, for the greater good.

In this case, for Uroil.

Sidorov had taken the same pledge, but his attitude toward sacrifice was flexible. If he could save himself, while others took the fall, so be it. History was written by survivors not just winners, and while life remained to Sidorov, he would find some way to come out on top of any situation.

He was sprinting toward the north end of the pitch, his men around him, laboring to keep up with their leader, when Sidorov heard the wet, ripe-melon sound of an exploding skull. Fragments of bone and brain peppered his cheek, stinging his left eye as he ducked and swerved, too late to miss the worst of it.

The shot that had decapitated one of his subordinates was lost in the general racket of gunfire, but Sidorov understood the skill behind it. If it hadn't been pure luck, it meant that someone with a very steady hand and eye was tracking him, prepared to bring him down and leave him leaking on the field.

Not yet, Sidorov thought, and threw himself into a wobbling shoulder roll as yet another of his men went down, drilled from the stands and dead before he hit the grass facedown.

CHAPTER TWENTY-TWO

Bolan hadn't used all his frag grenades for booby traps. He'd held enough back to be useful in a crunch, and now lobbed one toward three shooters who had charged into the stands, intent on silencing his rifle. They didn't see it coming in the semidarkness of the covered seating area.

It bounced in front of them, then detonated with a thunderclap and riddled them with shrapnel, pitching two back the way they had come, while a third vaulted off to his left, landing hard in the bleachers and staying there, as limp as a dishrag.

The explosion helped distract Bolan's opponents, giving him a chance to shift positions once again. He wasn't trying to evade them any longer, although ducking hostile fire was still a top priority. Instead of rushing to another sniper's nest, Bolan was closing on the adversaries he could see and hoping that he'd overlooked no one in a position to surprise him fatally.

The nearest shooters were a pair of Russians, crouching on the concrete apron of the soccer field, their eyes and folding-stock Kalashnikovs directed toward the spot where Bolan's frag grenade had detonated seconds earlier. It was the reflex Bolan counted on, and now it served him well.

Instead of switching off to the Beretta with its sound suppressor, a waste of time with all the battle noise around him, Bolan shot the taller of the Russians with his Steyr AUG, a single round from twenty feet that drilled his left temple and burst out through the right a microsecond later.

Even as the corpse began to fold, his partner was already turning, his blood-flecked face snarling, his rifle tracking toward the mortal threat. The Russian hedged his bet by squeezing off before he found a target, wasting half a dozen rounds that likely would have made another adversary flinch and spoil his aim.

But not the Executioner.

Bolan's next shot went in somewhere below the gunner's heart and slightly to its left. So much was in there that was essential for survival of the human organism. Impact slammed the shooter backward, swept him off his feet, but he kept firing as he fell, either determined or already dead, unable to release the AK's trigger.

Others had him spotted now, and decent cover on the lower seating levels of the stadium was nonexistent. Bolan's options had been narrowed down to one: attack and give them hell.

No problem.

He had palmed another frag grenade, armed it, and now he pitched it to his left, where Chinese shooters who had climbed the bleachers were returning from their futile quest, angling toward Bolan on an interception course. One of them shouted something to the others, but he had no time to finish as the lethal egg exploded in midair.

Bolan was diving for the deck by that time, kissing concrete as the wicked shrapnel hissed by overhead. A wounded shooter wailed his pain into the night, ignored by

Bolan as he scanned the killing ground for soldiers who were still in fighting shape.

And found a couple of them rushing toward him, firing as they came.

CAPTAIN JOHNSON Mashilia hadn't questioned the order to arrive at Warri Township Stadium at ten minutes past midnight. There had been no need, as Idowu Yetunde had explained the situation to him, gloating all the while.

Four groups of men were converging on the stadium to meet a fifth group, which was trying to extort cash from the rest. According to Yetunde, they were bringing money but didn't plan to deliver it. Instead they meant to solve their problem more efficiently and cheaply, killing off the troublesome extortionists.

Such things weren't unknown in Warri, or across the breadth of Delta State. Gangs commonly "taxed" merchants for "protection," using terror to enforce a code of silence while police were sometimes paid to look the other way. Captain Mashilia knew that for a fact, since he was one of those who took the bribes and saw no evil.

But this night was different.

Mashilia could make himself a hero while taking down two of Delta's worst criminals. Ekon Afolabi alone should be enough to earn him a raise, perhaps a promotion to major, and no one would mourn Agu Ajani's passing, either.

He could kill two greedy vultures with one stone.

The other criminals might pose a problem, since they represented major petroleum firms, but the captain wasn't overly concerned. If they were caught consorting with known felons, armed with illegal weapons while committing a crime, what defense could they raise? Some of them might escape conviction—Delta's courts were as corrupt as its police, if not more so—but he saw no way in which arresting the Chinese and Russians could rebound against him.

And if they resisted, well then, none of them would be alive to testify against him, if a hearing was convened.

Captain Mashilia reached the stadium at 12:11 a.m. He was fashionably late, leading a column of seven military vehicles, including his Jeep and one other, plus five BTR-3 armored personnel carriers. Manufactured in Ukraine, the APCs each mounted multiple weapons—a 30 mm dual-feed cannon with 350 rounds of ammunition, a 7.62 mm machine gun with 2,500 rounds, a 30 mm grenade launcher with 116 high-explosive rounds, and six electrically operated 81 mm launchers for smoke or aerosol grenades—while carrying a three-man crew and six passengers into battle at a top speed of fifty-three miles per hour.

Mashilia heard gunfire when he was still half a mile from the stadium. He frowned at first, but then couldn't suppress a smile.

They had started the party without him, but he was about to crash it. And anyone who tried to stop him would be leaving in a body bag.

AGU AJANI DROPPED the empty magazine from his MAC-10 and pulled a fresh one from his pocket, slapping it into the submachine gun's pistol grip. Reloading forced him to release his grip on the satchel filled with cash, but he still crouched over it, clutching it between his knees, while two of his riflemen flanked him.

"All right," Ajani said. "I'm ready now."

They had stopped near the south end of the football pitch, on Ajani's order, to let him reload the MAC-10. He'd chosen that direction to follow Valentin Sidorov and the other fleeing Russians, but they'd disappeared somehow in the confusion. Ajani supposed his delay in breaking from the center circle was to blame for losing Sidorov, and he would have to do without the Russian now.

Without most of his men, as well.

The eight he'd sent around to flank their faceless enemies were lost, apparently. He'd seen a couple of them fall to a grenade blast early on in the chaotic firefight, but Ajani didn't have a clue about the others. Shot, perhaps, or maybe they had panicked, fled the stadium entirely.

If they were alive, and he survived to track them down, they would regret the day their mothers had delivered them.

Of the four men who had accompanied Ajani to the center circle, only two remained. Daren Jumoke and a young man named Naeto Ejogo had fallen to sniper fire, killed where they stood, within arm's reach of Ajani himself. Jumoke's blood was drying on his shirt collar, adhering to Ajani's skin.

Too bad, old friend, he thought. But death comes to us all.

Ajani, though, didn't intend to die this night.

"Come on!" he snapped at his remaining bodyguards, resuming his jog toward the exit at the south end of the field. From there, he could circle back to their cars and escape, while Sidorov and the rest went to hell, for all he cared.

If he had been a praying man, Ajani would have offered up a prayer for Ekon Afolabi's death. The Russians and Chinese were less important to him, but if they were slain as well, so be it.

Ajani meant to get out with his life, and with his hundred thousand dollars.

And he'd almost reached the far end of the field when he heard the sound of heavy vehicles approaching. As Ajani tried to place the sound, identify it, two armored cars charged onto the field, their big wheels—four on either side, he saw now—churning up the turf.

"Lay down your weapons!" said a ringing, disembodied voice. "Cease firing and surrender now!"

Ajani didn't know which vehicle the voice was coming from, nor did he care. Surrender was the last thing on his mind just then.

Cursing bitterly, he raised the MAC-10 and unleashed a storm of bullets toward the closer of the armored cars.

LAO CHOY TEOH was dazed for several seconds after landing on his head, but rough hands dragged him back to groggy consciousness, hauling him upright. He resisted them at first, grappling to save the satchel he still clutched in spite of the grenade explosion and the impact of the tumbling corpse. Only when someone spoke to him in Cantonese did he cease struggling.

Anxious faces swam into focus, revealing one of Lao's men on each side of him, holding him upright, trying to shield him from incoming fire with their bodies. And there was plenty of gunfire to worry about.

The stands on both sides of the football pitch, hazed with smoke from grenade blasts, still crackled with small-arms fire, but something new had been added. Now, Lao saw armored vehicles entering the stadium from both ends of the wheel—two on the south, three on the north, each unit trailed by open military Jeeps.

An amplified male voice commanded everyone inside the stadium to drop his weapons and surrender, but someone—an African, one of three down near the field's southern goal—sprayed automatic fire at one of the advancing APCs.

And then, all hell broke loose.

While the defiant gunman's bullets rattled off the APC's armored hide, the APC responded with a burst of heavy automatic fire, and the shooter with the submachine gun literally came apart. His two companions bolted, firing as they ran, but both collapsed in clouds of crimson mist before the chopping fire from both APCs.

A moment later Lao made out the legend painted on the side of one armored car. It read Delta Police Command and told Lao that his time was up. Whoever summoned the police now called the shots, and it hadn't been Lao.

Lao snapped a hasty, "Follow me!" at his surviving bodyguards and started once again to climb the concrete steps where he had been knocked sprawling by an airborne corpse. The riflemen were almost on his heels as he ascended toward the exit where at least two soldiers had already died.

But then, the disembodied voice called out to them. "You! On the stairs! Stop where you are! Lay down your weapons!"

Lao hesitated, felt his gunmen turning, was about to shout a warning at them when they opened fire, instinctively. Even before their bullets found their mark, Lao saw the APC's turret rotating to face him, the muzzle of its big gun winking flame.

Thirty millimeter, Lao mused before the thumb-size bullets vaporized his skull and chest.

MACK BOLAN didn't see the Chinese die, but his ears noted the addition of 30 mm weapons to the firefight. A glance showed him police vehicles falling in from both ends of the soccer field and told him he was nearly out of time. He wouldn't fire on cops, and only that would save him from arrest if he remained inside the stadium too long.

But Bolan still had work to do.

And it was possible that officers had ringed the stadium with guns.

What then?

Then, he would die.

Gunned down while fleeing from arrest or murdered later, in a jail cell, it hardly mattered. Bolan wouldn't survive incarceration.

And neither would Obinna Umaru.

Still, Bolan's work remained unfinished.

He would go out fighting, if he made it out at all.

His nearest adversaries were distracted by the amplified calls for surrender, the hammering of heavy guns below them. Bolan took advantage of the moment, stitching three more targets with short bursts from his AUG and brushing past them as they fell, to seek new prey.

But Bolan's enemies were scattering, every man for himself as they bolted for exits, some firing at the APCs and drawing fire in return, others dropping their guns as instructed, then sprinting for cover and safety. The APCs fired on all runners, armed or otherwise, mowing them down with fine impartiality.

Too late for Bolan to get out?

Not quite.

Deciding that he'd have to leave his four main targets to the cops, perhaps remain in Warri until they made bail and he could take them out with sniper rounds or by some other means, Bolan began retreating toward the nearest exit.

Unlike the shooters who were drawing fire, he didn't sprint, or even stand completely upright. He double-timed in a crouch, his retreat less obvious to officers inside the armored cars.

He'd almost reached the exit, almost made it, when two gunmen loomed in front of him. One black, one white. Both holding automatic rifles leveled.

Knowing he was dead before he even tried it, Bolan raised his Steyr AUG to bring them under fire.

OBINNA UMARU was saying a prayer and preparing to flee, ashamed of himself but unwilling to die, when he saw Matt Cooper breaking for an exit on his side of the stadium. He was relieved to see it, hoping one or both of them might have a chance to get away.

Umaru wasn't bound by Cooper's personal aversion to shooting policemen, if it came to that. Most of those he'd personally known were either brutal or corrupt, often both. Ridding the world of one or two, to save himself, meant no more to Umaru than the other killings he'd performed since meeting Cooper.

And if caught, what of it? They could only execute him once.

Umaru was turning away from the field and the opposite stands when he saw two men block Cooper's path. He was too far away to make out faces, but he saw that one was white, one black, and both were armed. In fact, they seemed to have him covered, weapons pointed at his face.

Too fast for conscious thought, Umaru shouldered his Daewoo K-2. It was a long shot for the rifle's open sights, made worse by a sudden near-panic attack, but he aimed for center of mass and squeezed off. One round, and then a jerky sweep to his left for round two, riding the Daewoo's kick against his shoulder.

Umaru blinked once, then again.

Where were the riflemen?

It took another second for Umaru to find them, both sprawled on the deck, one still writhing, the other rock still. Before that fact had time to register, he saw Matt Cooper turning, searching for him in the stands, and raising one hand in salute.

Then he was gone.

Umaru took the hint and bolted, up the stairs and out. Behind him, uniformed police were spilling from the

APCs, through doors on both sides of each vehicle's hull, fanning out on the pitch to confront their opposition. Umaru felt, as much as heard, a lull in firing, turned in time to see a few Chinese and Russians laying down their guns, but then a couple of Nigerians cut loose again, and it all went to hell.

Umaru saw his chance to score a few more hits, and let it pass. The officers were fully occupied below—at least, the ones that he could see from his position in the stands— and he would never have a better chance to exit the stadium.

But if he found more uniforms awaiting him outside, he'd have a choice to make, with life or death at stake.

Cooper, he guessed, wouldn't allow himself to be arrested. Arrest meant worse than trial and prison, in this case. Even if Afolabi and Ajani died in this fight, they would be leaving friends behind to tie up all loose ends. And job one on that list would be elimination of the men who'd put the grim killing machine in motion, for a start. It wouldn't matter if Umaru was condemned to spend his life inside a solitary cell. Someone would reach him, sometime, with a blade or dose of poison, maybe with a can of lighter fluid and a match.

Why wait? he thought, and, smiling grimly, rushed into the waiting night.

VALENTIN SIDOROV came out of his long roll running, dodging toward the nearest bleachers that, with any luck at all, would offer him an exit from the stadium that had become a little slice of hell on Earth.

He had one soldier left, the others dead or missing in the chaos that surrounded him. He would expect those who survived to seek him out, but in the circumstances Sidorov couldn't stand still and wait for them to find him.

Standing still meant death—or at the very least, arrest.

He'd been surprised to see police arrive so soon after the shooting started. Armored vehicles ruled out coincidence. They weren't used for neighborhood patrols, and five of them arriving in a column meant that someone on the inside had betrayed Sidorov and the rest, setting a trap for them while they schemed to surprise the faceless blackmailers.

Or had his enemies arranged for officers to crash the party, as they had manipulated everyone—himself included—to appear in tandem at the stadium?

There was no time to think about that now. Sidorov had the Uroil payoff, still intact, and he was thinking six or seven moves ahead as he proceeded toward the nearest exit.

The police would find his soldiers dead among the rest, but that was no great problem. They had left all their ID behind, as ordered, and if they were later traced to Uroil somehow, well, what of it? None was listed on the company's payroll, and no one would contradict Sidorov's word when he denied that any of them served the company.

As for the cash, it might go missing in the midst of so much violence, and who could say that Sidorov hadn't detailed one of his dead soldiers to guard it? He couldn't be everywhere at once, couldn't do everything himself, watch everyone around him all the time. It wasn't his fault that the payoff meeting had become an ambush, or that the police arrived before he and the rest could finish mopping up their adversaries. Only skill and luck had saved him when—

Half a dozen men appeared in front of Sidorov, filling the exit, blocking his retreat. They were Nigerians, and Sidorov immediately recognized their leader. He had dealt with Idowu Yetunde in the past, using the local gangster as he used Agu Ajani and his other contacts, for Uroil's advancement and his own.

"You are surprised to see me, yes?" Yetunde asked, smiling.

"Nothing would surprise me at this point," Sidorov said.

"You have my money there, I think."

"Your money? No."

The men around Yetunde shifted, not quite leveling their weapons, waiting for the word to take him down.

"Perhaps you are mistaken?" Yetunde asked.

"Not this time," Sidorov said.

He still had nine or ten rounds in his pistol. Not ideal, by any means, but it could have been worse.

Yetunde frowned and shook his head. "Well, if we can't be sociable—"

Sidorov shot him in the face, one round below his left eye, snapping back the gangster's head, then he was rapid-firing down the line of gunmen to Yetunde's left, chosen at random, hoping that audacity and the advantage of surprise might save him yet.

And he had dropped three more before the two survivors opened up with submachine guns at a range of fifteen feet, punching Sidorov backward, down the concrete steps. Before the darkness swallowed him, he saw the bag in his left hand blown open, spewing greenbacks like confetti as he fell.

BOLAN EMERGED from the stadium near its south end. To his left, a small fleet of sedans and SUVs stood empty in the parking lot. A lone police car idled on the far side of the other vehicles, its driver standing at his open door and staring at the stadium, shotgun in hand.

There was enough noise coming from the stadium to keep him occupied, with a variety of weapons hammering the night, from pistols to the 30 mm cannons of the APCs. The cop—a young one, from the look of him in profile—

didn't notice Bolan as he left the stadium and turned back toward the place where he and Umaru had left the Kia parked.

"White man!"

The voice came out of the shadows, challenging. Bolan turned in a half crouch to face it, leveling his auto-rifle in the same motion. He didn't fire at once, because a twinge of curiosity prevented it.

A fatal lapse? It would remain for time to tell.

And if the lone policeman heard the voice? What then?

Bolan couldn't afford a glance back toward the squad car as the man who'd called him stepped into the faint glow of a nearby streetlight.

Make that two men, with the older of them carrying a handgun and a satchel, while the younger held a short-barreled Kalashnikov. Either would kill with ease at twenty feet, the range that separated them from Bolan.

Ekon Afolabi didn't look exactly like the photos in Brognola's file, but Bolan chalked that up to stress he'd suffered since the Executioner's campaign began. Fighting an enemy he couldn't see had aged MEND's warlord visibly.

"I don't know you," Afolabi said.

"No," Bolan replied. "You wouldn't."

"But I think I know your voice, yes?"

Bolan shrugged without losing his target acquisition.

"You tell me."

"I tell you it is so. And now I ask you why you've done this thing to me."

Bolan had no time for debating, and he wasn't in the mood.

"Because I could," he said.

"And now I kill you, for the same reason," Afolabi said, with a crooked, crazy smile. "It will be—"

He was interrupted by a shout of "Hey, there! Put those

guns down!" from the officer who'd been left to watch the parking lot. Bolan ignored it, but the call made Afolabi's face twitch.

"Deal with him!" he snapped at his companion.

Bolan felt it coming, saw the rifleman begin to pivot, firing from the hip before he had his target framed, brass spewing from his AK in a glinting stream. Downrange, a shotgun blast boomed out, wasted.

Bolan shot Afolabi first, a rising burst that sheared through ribs, lungs, heart and spine to kill him where he stood. It was a simple shift from there to drop the younger thug with two rounds through his right-hand profile, blowing out the left side of his face.

A glance back toward the cop showed Bolan he was down, still moving, prognosis unknown. Bolan had neither the equipment nor the skill to save a gut-shot man himself.

As if he'd voiced the thought out loud, he heard a voice say, "We can't help him."

Bolan faced Umaru, read the mixture of emotions on his face and said, "You're right. I know."

"We should be going now."

And just a nod this time, acknowledging the truth.

There was nobody left to watch them as they jogged to their waiting vehicle, sporadic sounds of battle fading as they put more ground between themselves and the arena of the slaughter pen.

CHAPTER TWENTY-THREE

Arkady Eltsin rode the elevator from his basement office to the ground floor of the Uroil building. It was crowded in the eight-by-ten-foot car, with seven bodyguards around him, leaving barely space enough for breathing. But considering his nearest flankers—one of them a garlic addict, while the other seemed to bathe infrequently—Eltsin decided he could hold his breath during the brief ascent.

The elevator door hissed open well before his lungs showed any sign of strain. Two of the bodyguards preceded Eltsin, separating as they left the car to scan the lobby, hard eyes sweeping left and right in search of enemies and finding none. They took their time, hands lingering in front of unbuttoned jackets that concealed their weapons, then relaxed a bit. The one on Eltsin's left turned and nodded to him.

"Clear, sir," he declared.

Eltsin delayed his exit for another two heartbeats, then left the elevator car, the other watchdogs pressing close around him for his transit of the open lobby. Even with the point men satisfied that it was safe, Eltsin still worried.

What if they were wrong?

Worse, what if they were traitors?

And suppose their judgment was correct, no danger lurking in the Uroil lobby. Could the sniper who had menaced Eltsin once before be waiting on the street, somewhere, to cut him down?

Eltsin took a stab at positive thinking. It failed.

He was frightened! And not without reason.

The previous night's meeting, planned by Valentin Sidorov and the others as a trap to slay their common enemies, had failed, to put it mildly. Sidorov was dead, along with all those who had followed him to Warri Township Stadium. Not a survivor in the baker's dozen who had bid Eltsin farewell nine hours ago.

He had been summoned by police to view their corpses at the morgue, lined up on tarps across the concrete floor because the place was overflowing. In addition to the thirteen Russian dead, there was an equal number of Chinese and twice as many Nigerians, with Agu Ajani among them.

The sights and smells were nauseating, but he'd done his duty, answered questions from a stern-faced captain mostly in the negative.

Of course, he hadn't known that Sidorov and some of his other employees had taken guns to fight a battle at the stadium. How could he be aware of such a thing? Uroil was a completely legitimate firm, concerned with nothing but petroleum. If Sidorov had taken on another job, moonlighting somewhere else, Eltsin was unaware of it. Sidorov's benefits and company insurance would be void, in such a case. There was no question of Uroil accepting any liability.

And under questioning, he had known nothing of the CNP's involvement in the previous night's bloody affair. The Chinese were Uroil's competitors, in Delta and elsewhere. Eltsin had met the local CEO, Huang Li Chan, but any cordiality between them stopped far short of criminal conspiracy. If charges were anticipated—

But the captain stopped him there. More time would be required before he knew if anyone besides the men killed at the stadium had been involved in the massacre. Eltsin should be available for further questioning, at need, but in the meantime, he was free to go.

And meet with Huang Chan.

They spoke first on a private line, swept twice a day for taps. All possible security precautions would surround the meeting they arranged, at which they would discuss the late-night slaughter and its ultimate significance to their respective firms.

It worried Eltsin, meeting with the man before he knew what had gone wrong last night. But he might never know, with any certainty, and it was clear that they had much to say between them.

Eltsin's guards surrounded him before they left the Uroil building, one unfurling an umbrella made from Kevlar to conceal him and deflect prospective rifle fire from any rooftops in the neighborhood. They looked ridiculous, emerging in a crush and scuttling toward the waiting limousine, with the umbrella raised against a blue and cloudless sky, but Eltsin had no fear of ridicule.

He was afraid of sudden death.

When they were packed inside the car, with Garlic Breath on Eltsin's left and BO on his right, doors shut and locked, the limousine pulled into traffic, rolling eastbound.

"Watch for Chan's car," Eltsin told the driver. "It's a white Mercedes-Benz."

Eltsin's own limousine was black, a Lincoln Town Car. It could almost symbolize the difference between Uroil and the Chinese, before grim circumstance had forced them to collaborate.

Arkady Eltsin brooded over gray thoughts as the tank rolled on.

HUANG LI CHAN normally enjoyed riding in his white Mercedes-Benz S600 Guard Pullman stretch limousine, hidden behind its deeply tinted windows in air-conditioned comfort. He normally felt safe inside the twenty-four-foot status symbol as he toured Warri's crowded streets.

But not this day.

For openers, the car was crowded. Built to seat ten passengers in decadent luxury patterned on the old Pullman railroad cars—from which the limo took its name—the Mercedes already had eight men aboard, besides Chan, with five more soon expected. Jump seats would handle the overflow.

And then, there was the problem.

It hadn't been solved last night, at Warri Township Stadium. If anything, the move that Lao had planned with Ekon Afolabi and the rest, Russians included, may have made things worse.

For starters, he had lost one hundred thousand dollars, along with Lao and a dozen of CNP's best security men, all but one of them killed in a fight that included police. The thirteenth was unconscious and hospitalized with a head wound. Physicians weren't sure if or when he'd regain consciousness, but Chan was hoping for never.

In fact, he had plans to ensure it.

Meanwhile, this morning's meeting-on-the-move with Arkady Eltsin had been hastily arranged, to discuss their next step in the crisis at hand.

It wouldn't go away on its own, of that he was certain.

A head count from the soccer battleground revealed no corpses that were unaccounted for. The men whom Lao and his companions planned to kill the previous night had managed to escape somehow. Again.

And worse yet, now the Delta Police Command was involved, a nosy captain asking questions that Chan was unprepared to answer. Chan had stalled, so far, pleading ignorance of Lao's actions once he left the office, but that smokescreen was thin and would soon dissipate.

Police admitted capturing three hundred thousand U.S. dollars at the stadium, and Chan assumed they had the other hundred grand, as well. Since no one dared to claim the money, it would be a total loss. Nothing significant in the long view, but still an irritant.

And those who had demanded payment for the information they supposedly possessed were still at large. That was the larger problem, since Chan reckoned they would soon come back for more, perhaps engaging in new acts of reckless violence at the same time.

It had to be stopped, and now, with MEND in disarray and Afolabi's major rival slain, with the Delta police their usual corrupt, incompetent selves, who else would shoulder the burden, if not CNP and Uroil?

It didn't make them friends, comrades or allies. Quite the contrary, in fact. By working together briefly, in this isolated instance, each could demonstrate its strength to the opposition, setting the stage for conquest of Nigeria from its oilfields upward to the National Assembly and the president's mansion.

"Here they are, sir," said Chan's driver, pointing ahead toward a black limousine cruising slowly through mid-morning traffic.

"Keep on to the point arranged," Chan ordered.

"Yes, sir."

Chan and Eltsin had agreed to meet in the parking lot of a nearby shopping center, where Eltsin and four of his bodyguards would transfer to the Mercedes limo as a show of good faith. Or blind faith, take your pick. Eltsin's car would then follow the Pullman around while Chan and Eltsin talked business, however long it might take.

They reached the shopping mall, Chan's driver turning in behind the Russian's black Lincoln.

The cars stopped several yards apart, guards stepping out of both while Eltsin and his party made the transfer. When the Russian had settled in beside Chan, his armed men perched on jump seats, Chan signaled for his driver to proceed.

"And now, my friend," he said to Eltsin, "shall we find the best way to remove these sharp stones from our shoes?"

"I WISH WE KNEW where they were going," Obinna Umaru remarked.

Seated beside him in the stolen Kia, Matt Cooper replied, "They probably won't stop again until they're finished talking."

"That's a problem, eh?" Umaru asked.

"Not really. I don't need a sitting target, just a little lead time."

Glancing at his rearview mirror while he trailed the ebony and ivory limousines, Umaru couldn't see their latest acquisitions lying in the backseat, covered by a threadbare blanket. Cooper had purchased the matched pair of RPG-7s with four armor-piercing grenades from an arms dealer of Umaru's acquaintance on Warri's east side. Two launchers, he had specified, in case there was no time for reloading in an emergency.

"So, I should get ahead of them?" Umaru asked.

"A front tail isn't easy," Bolan answered. "They could turn off anytime, onto a side street, and we'd have to double back. It's time-consuming, and we'd run a risk of losing them entirely."

"What, then?"

"Now that we've got them spotted, shift a block over to left or right and run parallel to the Mercedes. I'll check the map for a good place to swing back and intercept them."

Umaru did as he was told, turning left at the next intersection, then right again to regain his original direction. He accelerated through traffic, sparing the Kia's horn but surging around slower cars when he could. Cooper sat with a street map unfurled on his lap, shooting glances along each cross-street as they passed it, keeping track of their prey on the next street over.

"Okay so far," he said. "Now, if we pick it up a bit, four blocks ahead we've got a roundabout circling the Queen of Sheba's statue."

"Yes, I know it," Umaru said.

"Can you beat the limos there?" Bolan asked.

"Watch me!"

Four blocks. It wasn't much, in terms of time or distance, with the stoplights and the traffic snarled in front of them, but Umaru pulled out the stops, driving like a madman, simultaneously fearing that he would attract police.

They'd had a near-miss at the stadium the previous night, barely escaping as the shootout turned into a massacre by the authorities, and Umaru didn't fancy a replay in broad daylight, with no other targets present to distract police marksmen.

But Cooper relied on him now, and Umaru wouldn't let him down.

He jumped the second traffic light as it was turning red, then raced through another on yellow to reach the fourth intersection downrange. Beside him, Cooper had turned and was leaning into the backseat, checking the rocket-propelled grenade launchers—both already loaded—and clearing the blanket for easy access.

"Almost there," Umaru told him as he swung into a final right-hand turn and gunned the Kia toward the Queen of Sheba's statue, with her sword upraised in her left hand.

A landmark of war, for their new battleground.

ARKADY ELTSIN sipped the Smirnoff vodka Chan had given to him, feeling it light a fire in his gut while the limousine's air-conditioning chilled the sweat on his forehead. Part of it came from Nigeria's unrelenting humidity, the rest from a fear that he might never leave the Mercedes alive.

That would be suicide for Chan, of course, whether Eltsin's men took him out on the spot or CNP's next man in charge had the chore to complete. Seen in that light, a one-way ride didn't seem likely.

But he couldn't rule it out.

Chan broke the ice by asking, "What are we to do about this plague that haunts us both?"

Eltsin allowed himself a shrug. "My next suggestion," he replied, "would normally have been to leave it with the law. Give them additional incentives on the side, perhaps, to be more diligent. But after last night, I believe that avenue is closed to us."

"Agreed," Chan said. "And they have robbed us, as it is. We'll never get our money back."

"Not without claiming and accounting for it," Eltsin granted.

"So, what else is there for us to do?"

"I have requested a new chief of security," Eltsin said, "with ample reinforcements to protect CNP's property statewide. Headquarters has agreed, but I don't expect them for two or three days. By that time there's a chance that I may be replaced."

"You must survive those days, in order to retire," Chan said. "I'm speaking of the present, not tomorrow or the next day."

"First," Eltsin said, "we must defend our respective interests. That is paramount."

"Agreed."

"And second…I may have a useful name."

"One of the enemy?"

"Perhaps. When all of this began, Sidorov told me MEND was looking for a local man who had been passing information to the state police, perhaps to the Americans. They saw him with a white man, possibly a Brit or Yank, who could not be identified."

"What is this name?" Chan asked.

"Umaru," Eltsin said. "Obinna Umaru. They went to his home and found nothing. He's vanished, as far as I know."

"No one just disappears," Chan replied. "If he's dead, there's a corpse we can find. If he lives, there's a trail."

"Well, Afolabi's people couldn't find him. Nor could mine."

"Try harder," Chan suggested. "I will do the same. And if he's still alive, if this Umaru *is* a state police informer, he will be in contact soon. You have ears on the force?"

"There is a man," Eltsin admitted. "He cooperates."

"And I have one, as well. Between us, we should certainly be able to discover if this person gets in touch with his superiors. And when he does…"

"We'll have him," Eltsin said, completing Chan's thought.

"I'm convinced we can persuade him to identify his comrade," Chan observed. "By one means or another."

"Yes."

"And when we have identified him, we eliminate the threat."

Eltsin nodded agreement but didn't reply out loud,

suddenly fearful that Chan might be recording their conversation for later use against him.

"You agree, comrade?" Chan persisted.

Another nod. And then, changing the subject, Eltsin said, "The vodka that you stock is excellent."

Chan frowned at him, as if he doubted Eltsin's sanity. He was about to speak again when the Guard Pullman's driver spoke up, interrupting.

"Sir," he said, "there seems to be some difficulty just ahead. The traffic—"

Eltsin didn't understand the curse in Cantonese, but leaning forward, peering through the limousine's windshield, he saw the cause and mouthed his own profanity.

UMARU STOPPED the Kia at the base of Sheba's looming statue, ignoring the bleats of protest from hands punching horns in his wake. Bolan had to watch the traffic as he stepped out of the car, opened its left-rear door and grabbed the RPGs, then circled around the Kia's tail to take up his position by the statue.

He set one RPG on the trunk lid, trusting its twin pistol grips to keep it from rolling away. The two extra rounds, PG-7V single-stage HEAT projectiles with 93 mm warheads, rested at his feet in a canvas bag. He shouldered the second launcher and waited.

Each high-explosive antitank round was designed to penetrate 19.5 inches of armor plating—far more than was standard on any civilian executive limo, and six times the thickness of normal bulletproof windows. The launcher used a Russian PGO-7 2.7x telescopic site, and its manufacturers claimed a one-hundred-percent probability of striking an auto-size target from fifty yards or less, crossing the shooter's field of vision at speeds up to nine miles per hour.

No problem with a stretch limo approaching on a dead collision course.

Bolan was barely in place when he saw the Mercedes approaching, closing on him like a hungry great white shark. He couldn't see beyond the black windshield, but didn't need to. Chan and Eltsin were inside the car, and that was all he had to know.

The limo driver saw him now, reacting with the brake, then opting for evasive maneuvers. Bolan was ready as the white car swerved, presenting him with an even larger target in profile.

He squeezed off, feeling the rocket's back blast behind him, wondering for a split second if it seared the Queen of Sheba's statue. Thirty yards downrange, the warhead found its mark behind the limo driver's door and punched through the armor, leaving a saucer-size hole in its wake.

The detonation was internal, but the limo's armored hide couldn't contain it. All the tinted windows blew together, Bolan ducking to avoid the jagged shrapnel, while the doors blew open and a portion of the roof peeled back, as if vented by a huge can opener. Flames billowed from the limo, but it kept on rolling with its lifeless cargo, gradually losing speed.

Bolan swapped launchers as the black Lincoln Town Car charged forward, then braked as the driver or someone else inside reconsidered the wisdom of a helpless rescue mission.

Too late.

Bolan had his target sighted by the time the Lincoln started to reverse, bashing the grillework of a small tailgating sedan. More horns were blaring now, and drivers shouting from their open windows, but the noise had no effect on Bolan's aim.

His second HEAT round roared away toward impact, and he crouched to find a reload while he watched it on its way. This one smashed through the Lincoln's dark windshield and disappeared inside, erupting into smoky thunder half a heartbeat later. Since the Lincoln had been creeping in reverse, instead of racing forward like the Mercedes, its engine stalled and died.

With no need for a third shot at the blazing hulks, Bolan retrieved his empty launchers and the two spare rockets, tossed them all into the backseat of the Kia and resumed his place beside Umaru.

"Done," he said. "We're out of here."

They'd covered half a mile before he heard the first faint sirens wailing and began to look for somewhere they could ditch the car.

"What now?" Umaru asked him, his eyes fixed firmly on the road.

"Now, I pack up and catch my ride," Bolan replied. He thought of Jack Grimaldi waiting for his call, and realized that he had nothing much to pack.

As usual.

"And you?" he asked Umaru.

"I've decided that I'll stay," the Nigerian said. "Whatever happens after this—" he shrugged, risking a cautious smile "—I think it may be fate."

"Look, if you need a lift somewhere—"

"No, thank you. I've been fighting for Nigeria, not for a chance to leave."

Bolan could only nod at that and find his peace in silence. He had no idea where fate or luck would take him next, but he could count on trouble.

And the predators could count on scorched earth from the Executioner.